DISCARD

Knit To Kill

Knit To Kill

Anne Canadeo

KENSINGTON BOOKS
http://www.kensingtonbooks.com

KENSINGTON BOOKS are published by

Kensington Publishing Corp.
119 West 40th Street
New York, NY 10018

All Kensington titles, imprints and distributed lines are available at special quantity discounts for bulk purchases for sales promotion, premiums, fund-raising, educational or institutional use. Special book excerpts or customized printings can also be created to fit specific needs. For details, write or phone the office of the Kensington Special Sales Manager: Kensington Publishing Corp., 119 West 40th Street, New York, NY, 10018. Attn. Special Sales Department. Phone: 1-800-221-2647.

Kensington and the K logo Reg. U.S. Pat. & TM Off.

Library of Congress Card Catalogue Number: 2017944858

ISBN-13: 978-1-4967-0861-8
ISBN-10: 1-4967-0861-X
First Kensington Hardcover Edition: November 2017

eISBN-13: 978-1-4967-0862-5
eISBN-10: 1-4967-0862-8
First Kensington Electronic Edition: November 2017

10 9 8 7 6 5 4 3 2 1

Printed in the United States of America

To my editor, Tara Gavin, with sincerest gratitude as she leads the Black Sheep to new adventures!

"A crooked stick will cast a crooked shadow."
—New England Proverb

Chapter 1

"Your last weekend as a free woman, Lucy. How do you feel?" Phoebe stood behind the counter of the Black Sheep Knitting Shop. She stared up at Lucy, her dark eyes shining. "Maybe you should make a bucket list."

Lucy laughed. "Seriously? A bucket list?"

Maggie shook her head. "For goodness sakes, Phoebe. She's walking down the aisle with the man she adores. Not marching to the gallows."

"Sorry. I didn't mean that marrying Matt is some horrible fate. But it is sort of final. Till death do you part and all that? Aren't there a few wild and crazy things you want to do this weekend, that you can't do after you're married?"

Lucy had never considered their prewedding, girls' getaway from a "wild and crazy" angle and didn't know how to answer Maggie's twenty-something assistant.

As usual, Maggie did. "What exactly are you thinking, Phoebe? Are we about to film 'Knitting Group Gone Wild'?"

"That could be an interesting project," Phoebe mused. "But not very likely with this group."

"Thank goodness," Lucy replied. "But I do know what you mean. It is my last weekend of singlehood. And the big day is near. But I don't have anything wilder or crazier in mind than a long bike ride around the island and a few of Suzanne's crazy cocktails."

"That's what you say now. Think about it." Phoebe's tone was quite knowing for her tender age. "We've hit the ten-day countdown, in case you didn't notice. Ten, nine, eight . . ."

"Phoebe, please," Maggie interrupted again. "Let's not make the poor bride any more anxious than she already is."

"I'm not anxious. Not one bit. Not about marrying Matt. Though throwing a big party like this is a bit daunting," Lucy admitted.

"Of course it is. If there's anything we can do to help, please let us know. Let's talk it over this weekend, while we're all relaxing. Did you pack the bridal book we gave you?" Maggie looked up from the carton of yarn she was packing.

"I did . . . something like that." Her friends had thoughtfully given her a bridal book with a white satin cover and pages for to-do lists and reminders. But Lucy preferred yellow legal pads and a bulging, messy folder. It got the job done.

Despite Phoebe's concern, she definitely didn't have cold feet. Not even a cold toe. She and Matt had been living together for over two years, and she had no qualms about joining her life and fate with his. He was definitely "the one." She doubted married life would be much different for them than their life was now.

But Phoebe was right; it was a big step. A till-death-do-you-part deal. Or it should be. She and Matt had both been down this path before, and they knew that married life wasn't always easy. But she felt sure this time would be the charm for both of them.

Maggie glanced at Phoebe. "Suzanne will be here any minute. Why don't we straighten up the shop? I don't want to come back to a mess on Monday. And you are the newly crowned assistant manager."

"That I am." Phoebe snapped her computer shut and set to work.

Phoebe's title had recently been bumped up along with a generous bump in salary. Maggie had also given her a cozy niche to display her original and uniquely designed knitwear. The promotion and perks were well deserved, but Maggie had her own agenda. Phoebe had graduated about a month ago, and Maggie didn't want to lose her.

Armed with a degree in fine art and design, Phoebe had already launched her own business, selling her original creations—socks, bathing suits, hats, head bands, and other hip-looking apparel—online, at street fairs, and at the farmers' market held on the village green every weekend. She'd even had some patterns published in knitting magazines. But she was also Maggie's right hand and seemed happy to continue working and learning from Maggie. The shop just wouldn't be the same without Phoebe.

Lucy didn't notice much amiss, but Phoebe was scurrying about, arranging bins and baskets of colorful yarn and displays of knitting needles and other necessaries.

Maggie was very particular. She loved her shop, which was lovely, inside and out, reflecting her warmth and artistic sensibility.

The Victorian building, once a private home, had been neglected and run-down when Maggie had bought it years ago. But, as usual, Maggie's artistic eye had spotted the possibilities. She left her position as an art teacher at Plum Harbor High School to follow her bliss and turn her passion for needlework into a full-time career. Maggie had recently lost her husband and this radical change helped pull her from a well of grief.

Using her retirement nest egg, she bought the building and set up her business on the first floor: a knitting shop with cubbies of yarn and welcoming couches in the front room, and a large farm table and teaching space in the back. All and all, it was as cozy and inviting as her home.

The storeroom in back had once been a kitchen and was still fully equipped. Lucy and her friends appreciated that, since their group loved to eat almost as much as they loved to knit. Phoebe rented the second-floor apartment, which was a very convenient arrangement.

Maggie was devoted to her business, though she was far less of a workaholic in the last year or so, since her romance with Detective Charles Mossbacher had begun.

Still, she rarely took a day off or closed early, even when she was sick. But when the prewedding girl's weekend was proposed by their knitting group, Maggie didn't make a fuss about closing for four full days. Lucy had felt honored. Even more so now, as she watched her friend arrange a rack of pattern books with a military precision that screamed separation anxiety.

"Hard to leave your cozy nest?" Lucy wasn't one to tease much, but Maggie had fiddled with the rack three times.

Maggie looked as if she wanted to smile, but was holding back. "I love to travel. It broadens the mind and refreshes the spirit. It's the leaving that's the hard part," she admitted. "If Osprey Shores is half as fabulous as Suzanne claims, it will be well worth closing up for a few days. You know me, as long as I have some yarn and needles handy, I'm comfortable anywhere."

There would doubtlessly be plenty of knitting, along with all the other activities they planned to pack in while away. And of course, there would be plenty of downtime to do absolutely nothing. Maybe Phoebe's idea about making a list wasn't such a bad one after all.

A car horn sounded in the drive. Maggie peeked out the front window. "Suzanne's here. Finally."

"I need to run upstairs and grab my stuff. Be down in a jiff." Phoebe set down the basket of yarns she'd been organizing and headed for the staircase in the storeroom, which led to her apartment. "You can lock the front door, Mag. I'll come out the side."

"Good plan." Maggie was behind the counter, tugging out a big duffel and several tote bags filled with needles and yarn. Then, flinging the straps over her shoulders and looking a lot like a curly headed little packhorse, she was ready.

"Let me help you. I left my things on the porch." Lucy unburdened her friend of a few bags, and they headed to the front door.

"I know it looks as if I'm taking half the shop, but Suzanne's friend, Amy, has a knitting group, too. They're meeting tonight, and I thought we could get together, and I can do a little thing on summer yarns and start them off on an easy project."

"That's very nice of you, but this is supposed to be a vacation. For all of us. I don't like to see you working."

"Oh, it's not work. Not really. I wanted to return Amy's favor. Considering how the Cutlers were so generous to loan us the cottage for free. According to Suzanne, the place would be out of our price range otherwise."

From Suzanne's wide-eyed description, the resort community of Osprey Shores did sound luxurious—and out of their league. A quick glance at the website had confirmed it. But it was still generous of Maggie to give her time and energy this way. Lucy could see she wouldn't be talked out of it.

Maggie locked the door and checked it twice. "Besides, you know me. 'Johnny Appleseed with knitting needles,' some wisecracking friend once called me." Maggie caught her glance, then slipped on her sunglasses.

Lucy smiled, the wisecracker in question. "I guess it stuck because it's true."

"Hey guys! Sorry I'm late." Suzanne hopped up the brick path and quickly grabbed a few bags from Lucy and Maggie.

The vivacious brunette was in full vacation mode, wearing a stylish black romper, black wedge sandals, and huge sunglasses. A fresh mani-pedi in scarlet red accented the outfit perfectly.

Lucy glanced down at her own sorry toes, hidden by her leather espadrilles—luckily. She'd been rushing all week to meet a work deadline, and had barely made time to pack and take a shower. But Suzanne had said there was a day spa on the resort grounds. A few hours of beautifying would be the perfect treat on their weekend. Add that to the list.

"Hop in. We'll definitely make up time on the highway," Suzanne promised.

"I had a feeling you'd say that," Maggie mumbled.

Dana sat in the front seat and called out the window. "Don't worry, Mag. I'll keep my eye on the speedometer."

"Ladies, please. I always get you where you need to go in comfort, style, and safety. Don't I?"

Lucy tossed her luggage and knitting bag in the back. "Mostly. I'm still glad Dana's in charge of cruise control."

Peering inside the cargo area, Lucy was not surprised to see two large coolers and several bags of groceries. They were spending the weekend together in a cottage that had a state-of-the-art kitchen, but would surely be out for most of their meals. Still, Suzanne liked to travel with ample provisions and had probably even stowed a few favorite appliances back there.

Lucy had also brought her bicycle, and she clamped it to the bike rack on the back of the SUV once Suzanne closed the hatch.

"I hope you weren't waiting too long. I had a late afternoon closing, and Dana had patients," Suzanne explained.

"I thought Thursday was the new Friday?" Lucy said, slipping on her seat belt.

Suzanne shrugged. "I did, too. But my boss didn't get the memo." She started the engine. "Hey . . . aren't we forgetting something?"

"I think you mean someone." Dana pointed to the shop.

"I'm coming . . . hey, don't leave without me, guys!" Phoebe trotted down the driveway, one hand holding a big sun hat on her head, the other a hot pink rolling bag that bumped along behind like a faithful pet.

In a skimpy yellow sundress and high-wedge sandals, she looked like a long-legged bird—the type they would soon see skittering up the rocky shoreline on Osprey Island. The floppy brim of her hat hid most of her face and all of her dark, color-streaked hair. On the other hand, the sundress hid few of her tattoos.

"We wouldn't dream of leaving you, Phoebe. Don't be silly," Lucy called out.

"I'm holding back on takeoff. Don't worry," Suzanne said.

Phoebe paused in the middle of the driveway, took a deep breath, and adjusted her load. In addition to the suitcase, she also carried a black knapsack, a knitting bag, a pair of binoculars and a camera slung around her neck.

Suzanne got out again and stowed Phoebe's bags in the trunk while Phoebe squeezed into the backseat with the knitting bag, finding her spot between Lucy and Maggie.

Suzanne jumped into the driver's seat again. "Buckle up everyone. Off we go." She hit the gas and zoomed out of the driveway.

"Spoon Harbor Lobster Pound, for the best lobster rolls

in New England," she announced, sounding a lot like a tour bus driver. "Do we need to take a vote?"

"Lobster rolls? That's on my list. Let's check it off right away," Phoebe replied

"I'm all for it. As long we get to the island in time for Amy's knitting group," Maggie said.

"Got it timed perfectly. No worries," Suzanne promised. "We may hit a little traffic on the thruway, but I'll make up time on the local roads."

Dana caught Lucy's gaze and rolled her eyes.

"I've always wanted to try that place in Spoon Harbor. It's written up in all the guidebooks," Maggie said.

"And for good reason," Suzanne promised. "I thought we should kick off our weekend with a treat. We have a lot to celebrate."

"A long list," Dana said. "Phoebe's graduation and promotion . . . and somebody's getting married."

Lucy squirmed under the spotlight. "Yes, poor old somebody. We thought the old spinster would never find anyone who'd have her."

"You know what they say, 'Every pot has a lid. Even the bent one,' " Maggie offered.

"Very true," Dana agreed. "Not that you're a bent pot lid, Lucy," she quickly added.

"Um, gee . . . thanks. I think. Bent or not, I am looking forward to one last fling with my pals. In fact, lobster rolls are on my bucket list, too."

"Your bucket list?" Dana gave her a curious smile.

"Phoebe thinks Lucy should make a list of wild and crazy things she wants to do this weekend, before she gets married. As if she's going to be locked away in a dungeon after she says, 'I do,' " Maggie explained.

"Which I hardly think is necessary," Lucy said. "I am looking forward to relaxing, riding my bike, and having fun with all of you. Maybe a little skydiving or bungee jumping? A hot air balloon ride?"

"You're kidding, right?" Suzanne met Lucy's gaze in the rearview mirror.

"I'm not one to hang on a rope and jump off a cliff, but I've always wanted to try a balloon ride," Dana confessed. "Do you think we can find a place to do that up there?"

"I'll stick to knitting," Maggie said quickly.

"I bet it's awesome. But I'm not big on heights. The ladder in the stockroom is about my limit," Phoebe said. She already had her needles and yarn out to stitch away the long car ride. Lucky girl. Lucy always felt a little motion sick when she tried to knit in a car.

"I'll look into it. But, balloon rides or not, I don't think married life will be any different than just living together. I mean, not much different."

"Probably not. Until you have a baby," Suzanne said in a matter-of-fact tone. "But enough stress for one summer. We'll start working on you about that once you and Matt have settled in."

"Gee . . . thanks for the break." Lucy laughed. But she knew Suzanne, who had needled her to push Matt to pop the question all last summer, and didn't doubt that her dear friend would soon be moving on to the next life goal.

"Amy told me you were going to give a lesson to her knitting group tonight, Maggie." Suzanne glanced over her a shoulder at Maggie. "That's very nice of you. They're all in a tizzy about it."

Amy Cutler, their connection to the deluxe—and free— weekend accommodations, had been Suzanne's college roommate. They'd stayed in touch over the years, though Amy and her husband, Rob, had lived in Southern California for a while. They'd returned to New England almost two years ago, and Suzanne had advised them on finding a new home.

The Cutlers had settled in Osprey Shores, a private resort community on Osprey Island, off the coast of Maine. Amy's husband had done well in the biotech industry, and was working as an independent consultant and inventor. Living in a remote spot, far from a major city, was not an issue for them. He'd apparently done so well that they were able to buy two cottages, one to live in and a second as an investment.

As Suzanne drove steadily toward their destination, Lucy recalled how, at a knitting meeting a few weeks ago, her friends debated where to take her for a bachelorette weekend. Not that she expected them to take her anywhere. The phrase *bachelorette weekend* actually made her a little wary. But they were very insistent. Her wedding was approaching swiftly but they couldn't settle on the right spot for the getaway—the choices ranging from Martha's Vineyard to Mexico.

In the midst of their conversation, Suzanne found a text from Amy, asking if Suzanne could help market the second cottage the Cutlers owned to vacationers. Serendipity, Lucy decided as her friends quickly agreed the island would be the perfect spot for their girls' holiday. When Suzanne asked Amy if the place was available, her old friend had insisted they come and stay for free.

"It's very sweet to hear they're in a tizzy. I'm not such a big deal," Maggie replied.

"Maybe not in Plum Harbor. But on a remote island in Maine, I guess you're hot stuff," Suzanne teased.

"Well, when you put it that way . . ."

"You know I'm only teasing," Suzanne countered.

"You're hot stuff wherever you roam, Maggie," Dana said, smoothing things over. "I can't believe we're finally going away together. How many times did we talk about doing this?"

"There was the house Suzanne found on Plum Island, last summer," Lucy replied. "But that had all been a ruse."

"And even more surprises came out of it," Suzanne reminded her.

"We did go to the Berkshires a few years ago. To that health spa on Crystal Lake, remember? Such a lovely spot," Dana recalled.

"I remember a murderer on the loose the whole weekend," Phoebe reminded them. "It's hard to forget that part."

"Not the best aspect of the trip." Lucy leaned towards the window, to avoid Phoebe's swiftly moving knitting needles. "Despite all the free meals and spa treatments the hotel gave out to distract us."

"This trip will be totally different," Suzanne promised. "The island is small, but very lovely and unspoiled. It was built on the grounds of an old estate, high on a bluff overlooking the ocean. The mansion has been completely restored, every cottage has a water view, and the island's famous cliff walk runs the perimeter of the property. I heard you can walk it in an afternoon. And there's a village nearby, with a lot of nice shops and restaurants."

While her friends chatted about the weekend's agenda, Lucy felt herself begin to doze off. An afternoon nap was a rare treat. A graphic designer who ran her own business from home, she was usually very busy at this time of day, finishing up the last of her work or talking to clients. But pushing to meet a deadline and preparing for this trip had taken its toll. She reminded herself she was on vacation, her bachelorette weekend; a short rest could not hurt.

The next thing Lucy knew, Suzanne was announcing their arrival at the Spoon Harbor Lobster Pound, in a booming, tour-guide voice. They ordered from a counter inside the huge wooden warehouse and ate on picnic tables. The lobster rolls were scrumptious, the best Lucy had ever had, but there was no time to linger for dessert. They quickly piled back into the car and headed farther north.

A short time later, they cruised through a picturesque village, and then crossed a land bridge to Osprey Island. The narrow, two-lane road had a slim guardrail and a shoulder of jagged, grey boulders on either side, where the ocean waves broke and sprayed.

"I'd hate to drive across this bridge in the fog. You could wind up taking a swim pretty quickly." Suzanne was driving much slower now, Lucy noticed.

Dana peered out her window. "Maybe they close the bridge in bad weather. The road is so close to the water, I bet it washes out in a storm."

Lucy didn't doubt it. The island dwellers were probably often trapped there, especially if they didn't have a boat.

Lucy was relieved when they finally reached the end of the bridge. Following a sign that pointed towards Osprey Shores, Suzanne turned right. After a short drive on the island's rustic roads, Lucy saw the entrance and Suzanne steered the SUV through the gates.

"Here we are," Suzanne said. "With time to spare for sunset cocktails and a light supper before Maggie's presentation."

Lucy glanced around as they rolled up to a small, white guardhouse. Suzanne put down her window and spoke to the attendant. "We're guests of the Cutlers. Suzanne Cavanaugh." The guard jotted down Suzanne's name and the license plate number and then waved them through.

They continued down a long tree-lined drive, then followed a deep bend in the road. The view suddenly opened up, and a huge Victorian-era building came into view. It was four stories high, with rows of windows near the roofline and a deep porch with classic columns that wrapped around the entire structure.

"Wow. Is there a hotel here, too? I thought it was all cottages," Phoebe said.

"That's Mermaid Manor. It used to be the summer home of a superrich Gilded Age family," Suzanne explained. "Osprey Shores was built on the family's estate. The mansion was a falling-down wreck when the developer took it over; they've done a great restoration. Now it's used for meetings and receptions. There's a fitness center, a little day spa, and a café on the bottom floor, too. That's where you'll give the class tonight, Maggie," Suzanne noted as they swung by.

"I love those old mansions. This place reminds me a lot of Newport," Dana said.

"It is like Newport. This is the only development on the island so far, but the rest of the shore is lined with estates and huge old mansions like this one. There are still a few fishing shacks clinging to the cliffside, though few working fishermen live here anymore. But, just like in Newport, the cliff walk is accessible to everyone. The monied class didn't want to deny the fishermen easy access to the waterfront."

"Very interesting. You know a lot about this place, Suzanne. Did you study up?" Dana asked.

Suzanne laughed. "A real estate sales trick. It helps to create an interesting ambiance if you know a little history about a place, though I will say that this location needs no help from me to sell it."

A strip of dark blue water was visible behind the mansion, but when they took another turn, they suddenly faced a wide, spectacular view of the ocean. Lush green scenery dipped down a long slope, ending at the legendary cliffs. White cottages were scattered over the hillside, each with a full ocean view; tucked behind shrubbery, an ample distance from their neighbors.

"Wow! What a view! I can see why these cottages are so pricey," Lucy said.

"They've done a fantastic job with the architecture and design. I don't feel as if I'm in a rabbit hutch of condos. Even a super-fancy rabbit hutch," Dana said.

"There are very strict building codes here. It's amazing they were able to build at all. But they did manage to make the cottages look perfectly in keeping with the island."

"They look as if they've been here forever," Lucy agreed.

Maggie nodded. "Very tasteful. Too bad we don't have time to go out on the cliff walk. Is it lit at night?"

"I'm not sure," Suzanne replied. "But I have seen pictures close to the edge. Personally, I'd prefer a stroll in broad daylight."

"I can wait until we can see where we're going," Phoebe said quickly.

Lucy was not surprised at Phoebe's answer. Despite her edgy style and bold talk, she was, deep down, a timid soul. Lucy was surprised at Suzanne's cautious reply; Suzanne was usually the most daring in their group.

"Here we are, number thirty-two," Suzanne announced. She slowly steered the SUV up toward their cottage.

A white gravel walkway led to a covered porch that faced the open water and sky. A perfect summer perch for reading or knitting, or just zoning out. The property was landscaped with a lush green lawn, abundant flower beds, and flowering shrubs. Bathed in late-day summer light, it couldn't have looked more inviting.

They quickly jumped out and grabbed their luggage. Dana led the way to the front door. "I feel like I'm in the English countryside. All we need is cup of tea and some crumpets."

"Forgot the crumpets. But I do have some margarita mix and guacamole," Suzanne offered.

"That will do very nicely," Dana replied.

Suzanne unlocked the front door, and they followed her into a foyer and then, a large main room. Comfortable-looking sofas and armchairs in neutral tones faced a pair of French doors that framed the ocean view. On the opposite wall, a stone hearth was set with wood for a fire and flanked by tall bookcases.

It did look like a cottage on the English countryside, Lucy thought. Inside and out.

As they followed Suzanne upstairs, Lucy caught sight of a gleaming kitchen with white cupboards and marble countertops. On the second floor, they quickly claimed the bedrooms—two large and one small—deciding that Lucy, the bride-to-be, deserved the single.

"To honor your last nights of singlehood," Phoebe said, pairing off with Maggie, while Dana shared with Suzanne.

Lucy peeked into the large bathroom that adjoined her bedroom, complete with a marble sunken tub and noted another weekend goal: a bubble bath with a good book and maybe a glass of wine. When was the last time she'd enjoyed that indulgence? She made a mental note to add it to the list.

The list idea wasn't so bad. She'd have to tell Phoebe she was getting into it.

By the time Lucy had unpacked and freshened up, her friends were gathered on the front porch, sipping cocktails and watching the orange sun slip toward the dark blue sea. The clouds on the horizon were tinged with rose, gold, and even violet. Suzanne's famous margaritas, alongside a platter of guacamole and chips, were set on a side table.

"All the comforts of home," Lucy said as Suzanne handed her a glass.

"Very true. And I already know how strong Suzanne

mixes these drinks," Maggie replied. "I'm not sure I should have one of these. I might flub my presentation."

Phoebe was perched on a porch swing. "You have to toast the bride and kick off the vacation."

"Yes, of course. I didn't mean to be a dud. Who's going to say a few words?" Maggie gazed around at their circle.

"I'll start, even though I'm the bride in question." Lucy raised her glass. "To the best friends a girl ever had, who stick together through thick and thin. Thank you for all the laughs, loyalty, and love we share. And for taking me to this beautiful spot. I know we'll make a lot of happy memories this weekend. Then again, we don't have to travel far to do that. I cherish the time we spend together, near or far. And always will. Married or not," she added.

"Aww, Lucy. That's so sweet." Phoebe seemed genuinely teary eyed as they clinked their glasses together.

"A beautiful toast, Lucy. Thank you," Dana added.

Suzanne nodded as she touched her glass to Lucy's. "Personally, I'd rather you cherish us married. I can't wait to see you and Matt walk down the aisle. Here's to a great weekend with my BFFs. Bottoms up."

"And the dogs," Phoebe added. "You can't forget Tink and Wally, the canine attendants."

Lucy would have like to asked all of her friends to be bridesmaids, but she and Matt had decided to keep the bridal party to minimum. Just her sister as maid of honor and Matt's brother as best man.

But they couldn't leave out their beloved canines, especially since Lucy's dog Tink, a scruffy, mostly Golden Retriever, had introduced them. More or less. Matt's dog Wally, a chocolate Lab, had been a stray, hit by a car and brought to Matt's veterinary clinic by a good Samaritan. When Wally, who had lost a leg, was not claimed, Matt could have turned him over to a shelter, but took him home instead.

The dogs were best friends but not the best trained pets Lucy had ever seen. The rambunctious pair might ruin the ceremony. But even that worry was not reason enough to leave them out.

Suzanne's phone buzzed with a text message. "Amy thinks we should meet at the mansion before the group gets there to make sure Maggie has everything she needs. She says her group is quite excited to have a lesson with you."

Maggie looked surprised and set down her glass. "I'm not really prepared for a big lesson. I hope I don't disappoint them."

"I'm sure you'll be fine. As always." Suzanne tossed back the rest of her cocktail and quickly checked her lipstick in a small purse mirror.

"Come on, Mag. Showtime," Lucy coaxed with a smile.

"Showtime it is." Maggie went inside to collect her knitting bag and other supplies.

Lucy already had her bag. Despite the warm night air, she felt a sudden chill as they climbed back into Suzanne's SUV and headed to the mansion.

Lucy stared out the window at the dark lane. The sky was full of stars, but there was only a sliver of moon. The ocean was no longer in view, but she could still hear the waves rushing in and out, crashing on the rocky shore.

The secluded spot Suzanne had found was unquestionably beautiful. Of that, there could be no doubt. And their brief cocktail hour had definitely started the weekend off on a bright note.

Yet, there was something mysterious and even a bit unsettling about the place. Lucy shook off the feeling and focused instead on her friends' cheerful banter and all the fun they would have in the days ahead.

They approached the mansion, and Suzanne parked in the large drive that circled a stone fountain. The building was even more spectacular and imposing close up, and Lucy hoped to hear some history about it and the family who had lived there.

As they headed to the front steps that led to the porch, Lucy took a moment to study the fountain. A stone mermaid held a large shell. A stream of water gently splashed down into the pool below. Lights from the building and from beneath the water created a lovely sight.

"It's hard to believe that people really lived here," Maggie said quietly. "It was probably just their summer home, besides."

Suzanne led the way. "I could handle it. Honey, I'm home!" She called before opening the heavy, carved wooden door. Then she turned to her friends, grinning.

Lucy followed her friends, glancing up at an intricate stone carving over the doorway—more mermaids, frolicking in sea foam. Or doing whatever it is that mermaids do.

The motif was repeated on the high-domed ceiling of the entryway, painted as carefully as an Italian fresco. The tile floor was black and white, the walls pale blue with gold molding framing the ornate ceiling.

They faced a curved staircase that led up to the next floor. Large rooms with paneled, pocket doors were on either side of the foyer. To the left of the entrance, a young man stood behind a wooden desk. He looked like a cross between a hotel concierge and a security guard, Lucy thought.

A dark blue blazer with an Osprey Shores patch on the chest pocket and an assertive, questioning smile confirmed those dual roles.

"Good evening, ladies. May I help you?"

"We're friends of Mrs. Cutler," Suzanne said. "We're meeting her here."

Before Suzanne could say more, Amy appeared, entering from a passageway just left of the stairway.

As she and Suzanne shared a happy reunion hug, Lucy noticed the two former college roommates were just about opposite in looks. Amy was petite, with pale blond hair, cut in a short, boyish style with a swoop of long bangs. She wore a cotton sundress with a floral pattern, and a pale pink cardigan slung over her shoulders.

"These are my friends from Massachusetts, Justin. I've been expecting them."

"Of course, Mrs. Cutler." Justin's watchdog impulse was quickly curbed. He looked down again at his computer.

Suzanne introduced her friends, and Amy greeted them warmly, looking sincerely happy about their visit.

"I hope you had an easy drive. Did you have a chance to stop for dinner? I can order something for you."

"We had a feast at the Spoon Harbor Lobster Pound," Dana reported. "I won't eat for a week."

Amy smiled. "You can't come all this way and miss that place."

"Not with Suzanne driving," Lucy said.

"We have some coffee and cake set up for the meeting, if you have any room for dessert. Everything is ready for you, Maggie, but we can arrange the room however you're most comfortable. Just follow me."

The knitting friends trailed after Amy, who led them through long hallways lined with antique chests, sculptures, and oil paintings.

"All of the additions and updates to the building are on the lower level—the day spa, café, and fitness center," Amy explained. "I'm going to a yoga class tomorrow morning if anyone wants to join me. It's very laid back and relaxed. You don't need to be a big yoga fan to enjoy it."

"That sounds perfect to me," Dana said. "I'd love to get some kinks out."

"You definitely will. The teacher, Meredith Quinn, is wonderful. She's in the knitting group, too. You'll meet her tonight."

They turned and walked down another lavishly decorated hallway. Lucy gazed around, wishing there was time to stop and appreciate some of the artwork. "The mansion is spectacular. Suzanne said it had to be restored?"

"The family had left it closed and neglected for years. But most of the artwork and sculptures are in storage," Amy said.

Like all grand houses of its era, Mermaid Manor had a history. A few curious questions from Lucy led Amy to tell them a little about the industrialist, Ezra Cooperage, who had made his fortune in brass buttons during the Civil War. He bought the land and built the house in 1882. Ezra had a thing for mermaids. That much was obvious.

Amy told them the tycoon believed he'd actually seen a mermaid one dark night, swimming very close to the shoreline below the cliffs, and had found himself a breath away from giving in to her seduction and plunging into the water after the fishy temptress. According to the story, he built the great house on the very spot of this experience.

Ezra had downed a few too many after-dinner brandies, Lucy suspected. Or perhaps the tale was merely a colorful anecdote people told about the place. He did drown to death while sailing alone on his boat. Who knows? Maybe the mermaid returned and he was ready to take the plunge. Every old house needs a few tall tales, Lucy reflected.

Lucy had always found those siren and mermaid legends extremely misogynistic, suggesting that women—especially beautiful women—had a sneaky, dark side, while men were so forthright and trusting. But she didn't interrupt Amy's guided tour with this comment.

Their journey finally ended in the mansion's library, a large room with floor-to-ceiling bookcases, long windows with cushioned window seats, and even a wooden ladder with wheels, handy for reaching the highest shelves.

Lucy loved books, and the room was her idea of heaven on earth. She stood a few feet from the doorway, closed her eyes, and took a deep breath of its special perfume.

"Are you all right?" Phoebe whispered.

Lucy opened her eyes. "I'm fine. Just soaking up the atmosphere. I love the smell of books. Don't you?"

"More than yarn?" Phoebe looked shocked.

Did yarn even have a smell? Maybe to moths—and Phoebe—but to most people, usually not. Leave it to Phoebe to come up with that question.

Maggie's happy exclamation broke the silence. "Goodness, Amy. I've never given a lesson in such a grand setting." She set her tote bags down on a long oak table and spun in a circle.

"My group usually doesn't meet here, but I thought this room would be big enough. Oh, here they come." Amy glanced at the door as a redheaded woman holding a designer purse and a knitting bag strolled through the doorway.

"This is Helen Shelburn," Amy said, introducing her.

"Am I too early?" Helen asked.

"Right on time," Amy replied. "You get to sit next to our guest of honor."

Helen seemed pleased and did choose the seat next to Maggie. She seemed very friendly and eager for the lesson. More women started walking in. Lucy wasn't that good with names and tried hard to keep track.

An older woman named Betty Rutledge entered next. "I'm so excited for the presentation. Thank you so much for coming to see us." Betty looked as if she was meeting a celebrity and Lucy noticed Maggie blush a bit as Amy introduced them.

"And this is Meredith Quinn," Amy said, as the next woman walked in. "She's the yoga instructor I mentioned. I told them about your class tomorrow," Amy added.

Meredith smiled. "Please join us. All are welcome in my studio."

"I'll be there," Dana replied quickly. Lucy wasn't so sure. She preferred bike riding to yoga, but cast Meredith a welcoming smile.

She definitely looked like a fitness instructor. In her midforties, but petite and slim enough to be a dancer. Her arms—exposed by her sleeveless dress—were lean and toned, and her movements, lithe and graceful.

As Meredith settled in her seat a man entered. Lucy thought for a moment he was in the wrong room, but everyone soon greeted him. Amy introduced him to Maggie and her friends. "This is Dr. Lewis Fielding, our token male member," she teased.

"Nice to meet you. Just call me Lewis," he said, shaking Maggie's hand. "Thank you for taking the time to give us this lesson."

"It's my pleasure," Maggie said graciously.

Lucy knew that many men knit, but, so far, no men in Plum Harbor had ever shown up at their knitting nights. Lewis seemed a serious knitter, though, setting down a bulging knitting bag. He took out a project, a long scarf knit with alternating blocks of dark green and golden yellow, and began working. He had already added the fringe to one side, and it looked as if he was almost finished.

"A present for my granddaughter," he told Maggie. "She was just accepted into college, and these are her school colors."

"Nice idea. I'm sure she'll cherish it," Maggie said.

"I think everyone is here," Amy said.

"Great. Let's begin." Maggie stood to address the group of knitters.

Though Maggie often introduced them to different projects and techniques, Lucy noticed she definitely had more of a theatrical air when teaching a group of strangers, as if she was a guest star on a television craft show. Lucy sat back, enjoying the presentation and her friend's flair.

"Summer isn't a season that most people associate with knitting," Maggie began. "They are mostly non-knitters who are unaware of the joys of summer yarns and summer projects." A basket with several skeins of yarn in Popsicle colors sat on the table in front of her, and Maggie picked one up. "Working with summer yarns is like switching from a cup of hot cocoa to a chocolate ice cream soda. From down coats to tank tops. Summer yarns brighten your knitting spirit."

Maggie pulled a length of yarn from the light green skein. The color reminded Lucy of Key lime pie. "This cotton-silk blend knits as good as it feels, and the airy, light weight makes garments drape perfectly. I'll pass these yarns around so you can get a feel for the choices. No pun intended," she added, handing the yarn to the woman on her left. Betty, Lucy recalled.

"This next skein is pure cotton. The tight twist of the yarn gives a great stitch definition, so keep that mind when you're working with an intricate pattern." Maggie passed a cotton candy-pink skein to Amy, who sat on her right.

"The last yarn I want to show you looks pricey, but it's really quite reasonable. If you look closely, you can see that there's a shiny satin wrap over the matte cotton blend. This yarn has an amazing sheen and drapes beautifully. Projects made with this yarn don't require complex stitchery to look stunning."

Maggie's sample of that yarn was sky blue, and she passed it to Betty again. "Here are three swatches made with the different yarns." She took the three-by-three inch squares from the basket and passed those around, too.

"The project I have in mind for you is a summer shawl. Which might come in very handy up here in Maine, where it cools down at night even on the warmest days." Maggie turned and took a peach-colored shawl out of another tote bag. She spread it on the table as the group "oohed" and "ahhed." She did have a flair for showmanship, that was for sure.

"The eyelet pattern looks complex but is easy to follow. Some of you might even complete it over the weekend," she said with a hint of challenge. "As you can see, the finished product is light, airy, and elegant. I'll be around all weekend to help anyone who hits a few speed bumps."

While Maggie reviewed the pattern instructions, Phoebe flitted around the table, handing out balls of yarn to get the group started. The knitters were eager to choose, and delighted with the bright colors. Lewis was the only one who passed on the shawl project, concentrating instead on the gift for his granddaughter.

Lucy started to read the pattern, but got distracted. Not far from where she sat, a set of glass doors opened to a smaller room, one that looked to Lucy like a private study— a "man cave," circa 1900.

The walls were painted forest green, with dark wainscoting and wooden shutters on the windows. She saw a collection of framed photos hanging there, antique-looking images of rowing teams and groups of men showing off huge fish or other animal prizes. There were lots of bronze plaques and trophies, commemorating past glories of the grand old house and the family that once lived there. A mounted stag's head hung opposite the doorway, its glassy stare taking in the scene with equanimity.

Tonight, the room was fittingly occupied by a group of men playing cards. They were seated around an octagon-shaped table, which was covered in green felt. From where she sat, Lucy had a full view of their game. High-stakes poker, judging from the bets she heard. The men barely spoke, their few words sounding deep and low. Their expressions were intense, yet somehow blank at the same time.

That is, except for the one player who sat at the far side of the table. Older than most of the others, the man's head was bald and shiny, his thin face tapering down to a gray goatee. His dark eyes were bright behind black-framed glasses, and his eyebrows were thick and bushy, rising and falling with his animated expressions and loud conversation.

He tossed down his cards with glee. "Straight flush, my friends. Ace high." Then he swept up his winnings with both hands, taking obvious pleasure in his opponents' defeat. He seemed very unsportsmanlike, even rude.

Lucy wondered if this was just a male thing. It wasn't enough to win. Your friends had to be humiliated? She didn't think so. This player seemed a sore winner, if there was such a thing.

"Caught you again," the bald man added as he scooped up a pile of chips heaped in the center of the table.

A few of the players grumbled. But most did not react.

"Another winning streak for Julian," the player who sat across the table from the bald man announced. "Just like last week. And just as we're about to finish up. I could almost set my watch by the turn in your luck."

The expression on Julian's face flashed from pleasure to anger. "If you've got something to say, Pullman, say it. Unless you don't have the guts."

The other players glanced at each other. One picked up

the deck and began to shuffle. "Come on guys. Let's just finish up. Come on, Derek. Let it go."

Julian's adversary ignored the request.

"Cheater," Derek Pullman said quietly.

"What did you call me?" Julian's tone was sharp and loud. It carried into the library, and a few of the knitters glanced over to the study to see what was going on.

"I said you're a cheater. What part of that sentence don't you understand, old man?" Derek's voice rose, sounding out the words loud and clear. "I don't know how you do it. But I'd bet good money that you do."

Around the table, knitting needles went silent and still. All heads turned toward the argument.

Julian stared at Derek Pullman, then laughed, a grim, cold sound that gave Lucy gooseflesh.

"That's another bet you'd lose. Because that's what you are, Pullman. A loser. Don't blame me for your sorry, pathetic life. You're into me for over ten grand tonight. Probably more once I sort these chips. That's not even counting what you owe from last week's game. Do you think I'll just wipe the slate clean because you call me a few school yard names?"

Pullman stood up from the table. "I'm not giving you a nickel. You're a fraud, Dr. Morton. I wonder if you're even a real doctor. I do know you're a conniving, backstabbing phony who'll do anything to win. Maybe the rest of these guys will pay up like smiling idiots, but you won't get another cent from me."

Julian Morton's thick brows furrowed, and his small, dark eyes glowed with anger. "How dare you. I'll make you pay for your loose tongue. Don't doubt it. I'll sue you for slander."

"You're the one who's going to pay. Watch your back, old man. Your free ride is over. I'll see you rot in hell."

Derek Pullman stepped back from the poker table, slipped his hands under the edge and flipped it up.

The other men called out and jumped from their seats, grumbling and shouting, while cards, chips, and cocktails flew in all directions.

Dr. Morton was trapped in his chair, the edge of the overturned table balancing on his lap. All he could do was toss his hands in the air and yell, as most of the mess—including all of his winnings—slid to the floor.

"You sore-losing bastard! My chips . . . how can I count my chips now?"

Pullman laughed as he headed for the glass doors.

Amy had run up to the doors—intending to shut them on the scene, Lucy thought—but ended up watching the drama unfold. Pullman swept by, nearly knocking her down. His gaze was fixed straight ahead. He stomped out of the library without making eye contact with anyone.

Amy closed the doors quickly, and then pulled down linen shades. The sounds from the room were muffled now, though Lucy could still hear the card players trying to get their bearings.

Amy returned to the table, looking pale and flustered. "I'm sorry for that awful interruption." She spoke mainly to Maggie, then glanced around at the group.

"We never act like that around here, do we?" she asked her neighbors and friends. "What an awful impression our visitors must have of our community."

"No need for you to apologize, Amy." Lewis Fielding shook his head. "It's certainly not your fault."

Meredith picked up her knitting again. She looked unfazed by the outburst. "I can't say I'm surprised. Some people spread joy wherever they go. Julian Morton spreads anger and conflict. No secret about that."

An older woman sitting next to Maggie—Lucy thought

her name was Betty—nodded, her lips tightly pursed. "Not that I wish anyone ill, but Dr. Morton will get a taste of his own medicine someday. Of that I have no doubt."

Amy had not taken her seat again. Lucy thought she looked a little nervous about the gossipy turn the conversation had taken. Though gossip was certainly not uncommon in a knitting circle—about as likely as jelly showing up around peanut butter.

"Why don't we take a break?" Amy said. "There are some delicious desserts tonight. Betty made a beautiful peach tart, and Lewis made some oatmeal and cranberry bars. Coffee or tea, anyone?"

Maggie looked grateful for the suggestion. "Good idea. Let's take a break, and Phoebe and I will come around and answer any questions. Here's how the first few rows should look, if any of you were able to knit during the floor show."

Her quip brought a few smiles and some quiet laughter. Helen showed Maggie her work. "I know it's a lace stitch. But I think I have too many holes."

"No worries. We can fix this." Maggie plucked up the bumpy looking swatch as if it were a prize.

Lucy set her needles aside and strolled over to the display of sweets. It all looked very tasty and tempting. She'd virtuously stuck to a Spartan diet and exercise plan for months, hoping to look super slim in her wedding gown. But she was ready to let her carb-guard down a little this weekend. It's my last fling before the wedding, she reminded herself, as she added a cookie to the slice of tart already on her plate.

She met Dana and Suzanne at the coffee urn. "Sweet tooth?" Dana said, eyeing Lucy's plate. "I thought you were sugar free until the big day?"

Suzanne waved away Dana's remark. "Leave her be. No carb shaming here, please? It's prewedding jitters. Brownies work better than Xanax. Everyone knows that."

Dana laughed and sipped her tea. "That might be true. And no dangerous side effects."

"If you don't count a tighter wedding gown," Lucy said between bites of the tart.

"Live a little, Lucy. Just buy a tighter body smoother." Suzanne took a bite of the oatmeal bar.

"I didn't plan on wearing a body smoother," Lucy replied.

Suzanne shrugged. "There's your problem. You've got to get one. It pushes all your assets into the right place. Those perfect-looking movie stars wouldn't go within ten miles of a red carpet without their body armor."

Dana blinked, looking in awe of the information. "I guess I can't go near a red carpet, either. I don't even know where to find one of those things."

"You're exempt from this conversation, Dana. You won the DNA lottery. Built like a string bean . . . an organic string bean. And I totally mean that as a compliment," Suzanne quickly added.

Dana grinned, choosing the oatmeal bar. "No offense taken. I do like string beans. How about you, Lucy?"

"I like string beans," Lucy insisted around a mouthful of tart.

Dana laughed. "I meant, do you even know where to buy a body shaper? Not that I think you need one."

"I actually don't . . . But I guess I'll look into it." Lucy was trying to be agreeable and get Suzanne off the subject, but she had no intention of being squashed into a tube of suffocating spandex beneath her wedding gown. She could barely abide tummy control panty hose. How would she ever enjoy her big day?

"Don't worry, I'll order one for you," Suzanne said. "A gift for your trousseau. I know what you're thinking, Lucy. You're thinking 'No way in hell will I wear that thing.' But you will wear it, and you'll thank me later when you see how slinky and fabulous you look in the photos."

"In that case, I guess I'll try the cookie, too." Lucy took a small bite, and then tried to change the subject from her wedding day undergarments. Or lack of them. "What about that card game brawl? Quite a scene."

Suzanne moved closer. "An ugly one. I know that Pullman fellow started it, but Dr. Morton looks like a cold customer."

"Gambling, liquor, and testosterone concentrated for a few hours in a small room," Dana said. "A highly combustible combination."

"High-stakes gambling," Lucy added. "That puts the pressure on. Did you hear how much Derek Pullman owes Morton? No wonder he had a meltdown."

"True. But in case you didn't notice, people in this community are pretty well-off," Suzanne whispered, then glanced over her shoulder at a cluster of Amy's friends who stood nearby. "A few thousand bucks might be dinner and a movie. Or a lunch and a quick stop at the mall."

Lucy thought Suzanne had a point. Most of the women in Amy's group did look wealthy. There was a lot of expensive clothes, good jewelry, and fresh, fashionable haircuts on display. The designer handbags and even designer knitting bags were also an obvious sign.

There were a few exceptions, like Meredith. But perhaps she didn't live in the gated community.

And appearances did not always tell the real story. Lucy knew that very well by now. But Osprey Shores was an exclusive and pricy place to live. Maybe the residents here did toss around wads of money for fun.

"Like one of those reality shows about celebrities?" Lucy asked. Lucy was not one to watch TV shows like that, but from what she could gather from channel surfing, it was nonstop massages, personal trainers, and private jets. A few thousand dollars, more or less, would not be missed.

"Exactly," Suzanne said.

"We're definitely not in Kansas anymore," Dana agreed. "But both of those men sounded very serious about the money, lost and won. There were even threats at the end."

Before they could debate the question further, Maggie's voice rose above the chatter.

"If you're done with your break, I thought we could gather around the table again. I'd like to show you how to embellish this pattern if you like."

Lucy headed back to her knitting. Dana was right. It had not been a casual exchange. Anything but. It had been an angry confrontation verging on violence, if you counted the tossed-over table.

The scene had tainted the first night of their getaway, and she hoped her friends wouldn't dwell on it.

But something told Lucy this wasn't the last she'd hear about Dr. Julian Morton.

Chapter 2

Sometime during the night, a thick fog had rolled in over the island. Lucy peered out the bedroom window, surprised to see the dense, cottony weather when all the forecasts had predicted a sunny day.

She'd planned to explore the island on her bike, but decided to join Dana at Amy's yoga class. Lucy had mixed feelings about yoga. The stretches at the start were pleasant enough, and she did enjoy the quiet meditation at the end. It was the middle part that put her off—trying to twist her limbs in various, unnatural poses. Like the balloon animals magicians made at children's parties.

But she did want to kick off the weekend with some exercise. Pedaling around in the damp, misty weather would not be much fun, or even safe, this morning. The island's narrow, curvy roads were dicey enough in broad daylight.

Lucy came down to the kitchen and found Dana and Maggie sipping coffee. She greeted them and walked to the counter to pour herself a cup.

"Who borrowed the sun? Don't they know it's my last fling, anything goes, girls' weekend? The sun should be out nonstop."

"Don't fret, Lucy. The weatherman says the fog will burn off by noon," Maggie replied.

Dana flipped the lid off a cup of Greek yogurt. "In the meantime, want to join me at the yoga class? Amy said it starts at eight."

"I think I will. I still feel squished from the car ride. Where are Suzanne and Phoebe? Still sleeping?"

"Suzanne is out like a light. Snoring up a storm," Maggie added in a quieter voice. "Don't tell her I told you that."

Lucy had shared a room with Suzanne on a previous trip. She knew the ugly truth very well.

"Phoebe went bird watching. She must have gotten up at five. She left a note." Dana already had her knitting out and alternated between the needles and her yogurt cup.

"Bird watching? I doubt if any feathered friends will show themselves this morning," Maggie said. "The birds are probably still tucked in their nests, snoring away, like Suzanne."

Dana smiled. "She's determined to bring back a lot of photos and sketches for Harry. She says the plover or the tern or some local species is nesting. You know how she gets."

Lucy did know. A product of a difficult childhood, adult Phoebe was unflinchingly loyal and went the limit for people she loved, which included traipsing around in the brush and bramble to track down nesting sea birds in this pea-soup fog.

"I hope she's careful," Lucy mused. "Did you see how steep those cliffs are? She could easily lose her balance and take a tumble chasing down birds today."

"I had the same thought," Maggie admitted. "I'll send a text in a little while, just to check on her."

"Good idea." Dana put her knitting away and tossed the yogurt cup. "Looks like it's time for us to go, Lucy. Are you ready?"

Lucy had also quickly eaten a yogurt. As much as they teased Suzanne about her need to travel with a full trunk of groceries, it was nice to find the fridge fully stocked.

"As ready as I'll ever be."

A knock sounded on the door. They looked at each other. "Who could that be at this hour? It's barely eight," Maggie said.

"I'll get it." Lucy was closest to the door. She walked over and pulled it open.

She was greeted by a tall, handsome man. Since she'd been with Matt, she hadn't noticed men much, but this morning's visitor jolted her awake faster than a cup of espresso. He wore khaki shorts and a dark blue polo shirt stretched across broad shoulders and muscular arms. She noticed the mermaid emblem of Osprey Shores on the shirt pocket. He held a metal toolbox in one hand.

"Can I help you?" she asked.

"I'm Sam Briggs, maintenance department. Sorry to bother you so early, but you were first on my list." He made it sound like that was a great compliment. His megawatt smile was the cherry on top, as Suzanne would say. "Mrs. Cutler asked me to check the garbage disposal. She said it's on the blink."

"We just got here last night. I don't think we've used it yet."

"Mind if I take a look?"

"I guess that will be okay. Let me just sound a warning."

While Sam waited at the door, Lucy returned to the kitchen. "Someone's here to fix the garbage disposal. Do you mind, Mag?"

Maggie checked the top buttons on her fuzzy robe. "I'm decent. Let him in."

Lucy returned to Sam and followed him into the kitchen. She couldn't help but notice the wide-eyed expressions on both Dana and Maggie's faces.

"Morning, ladies. How's it going today?"

"No complaints so far," Maggie replied.

Lucy was suddenly sorry Suzanne was in dreamland. She would have enjoyed their surprise guest. She would have been talking about him all day.

"Mind if I check the disposal?"

"Help yourself." Maggie lightly waved her hand.

Sam set his toolbox down and tested the switch. An awful grinding sound emerged from the drain. Suzanne might get to meet him after all. It would be hard to sleep through that racket.

"Sounds like it needs a flush. I'll be out of here in a jiffy." He crouched down, opened the doors under the sink, and used a large flashlight to take a look at the pipes.

Dana turned to Lucy. "This is fascinating, but we'd better go."

Lucy nodded, feeling a little embarrassed that she'd been in a zone watching Sam work. She pulled on a Boston Red Sox cap to protect her hair from the mist, then picked up her small knapsack and slung it over her shoulder.

They left the cottage and headed down the path to the road.

"That guy was hot. He looked like he belonged in front of a camera, not under a sink cleaning out a garbage disposal," Dana said.

"If not Hollywood, then teaching classes at the fitness center."

"Looks like he spends a lot time at a gym," Dana agreed.

"I don't think you get that sort of physique fixing leaky pipes. Or whatever else he does."

"He has just the right amount of muscles. Not all bulked up like a Thanksgiving Day float, but fit looking," Dana said. "Maybe he's a model or an actor part-time."

"Maybe," Lucy agreed. She suddenly felt guilty about making such a big deal over Sam Briggs. Matt wasn't a gym rat, but he loved outdoor sports and was very fit. Since they'd started living together, Lucy's good cooking had gone to his waistline a bit, but he was all hers and very attractive. She thought so anyway. And she loved him to pieces.

"If I wasn't so annoyed about the sun not being out, I'd admit that this fog is stunning," Lucy said, changing the subject.

"It's amazing, like walking through drifts of white smoke, or strolling through the clouds." Dana spread her arms out for a moment as they walked along. "I wonder what it looks like on the cliff walk this morning? Too bad we don't have time to go out there."

"Maybe later, after the class. I hope it clears off by then."

"Me, too. We'd better hoof it." Dana picked up her pace and Lucy took the cue. "Amy said the class fills up fast. Meredith also teaches kickboxing."

"I've always wanted to try kickboxing. I'll put that on my list for the weekend. Surprise Matt with some martial arts moves on our honeymoon?" Lucy paused, bunched her fists, and kicked one long leg out in the air, mocking a martial arts grunt.

Dana rolled her eyes. "Exactly what a guy wants from his new bride on their honeymoon, a martial arts demonstration."

A few minutes later, they arrived at Mermaid Manor. As Amy had instructed, they followed a path and a few flights of marble steps down to the lower level of the building. The additions to the mansion had been done in a tasteful style, the design well in keeping with the mansion's Victorian design. Though, unlike the floors above, everything looked fresh and new.

Something to be said for that, Lucy thought as they entered the fitness center. Her sinuses still hadn't forgiven her for inhaling all those musty books last night.

They quickly found their way to the yoga studio. The door was closed and a group of women clad in workout outfits waited outside, Amy among them.

"Seems to be a little delay," Amy said. "Meredith is usually so punctual. Maybe she missed her alarm this morning."

"It's a perfect morning for sleeping in." Lucy had hit the snooze button a few times.

While they waited, they chatted about the knitting meeting and Maggie's presentation. Amy was very appreciative and said her group had given Maggie rave reviews.

Lucy wasn't surprised. She had a feeling the Osprey Island knitters would be stalking Maggie around the grounds like a celebrity for the next few days, bringing her their botched-up projects.

She expected to see the yoga teacher strolling down the hall from the center's entrance, but a few moments later, she heard the studio door unlock. The door opened, and Meredith stood in the doorway.

She blinked and smiled at them. She looked a bit groggy, Lucy thought. Maybe she had slept late.

"Come in, everyone." She stepped aside and waved her arm in greeting. "Apologies for the delay. I came in early to meditate and lost track of time."

A small brass bowl of incense burned in the corner of the room, surrounded by small candles. Lucy wasn't sure of the scent, but it was sweet and light. A framed picture of an Indian deity leaned against the wall behind the candles. An elephant, with a Buddha-like body. Lucy had done work recently on a project about legends and myths from around the world, and she recognized Ganesh, the Hindu god who removed obstacles. Or so some believed.

The studio walls were painted a warm, burnt sienna, and the floor was a smooth, pale, polished wood. One long wall was mirrored with a dance bar attached, and the opposite wall was glass, framing a wide view of the cliff and ocean, though not much could be seen right now with the fog. One of the sliding doors had been left open a crack, and Lucy was grateful for the fresh, salty air cutting through the incense.

Most of the women had brought their own mats. Lucy and Dana borrowed from a pile in the back of the room and set them down side by side. Amy was in the row just ahead.

Meredith walked among the students as they staked out their places. Not surprisingly, she had a light, graceful step, and a deep, gentle voice. Very soothing, Lucy found. As Meredith passed Lucy's mat, Lucy couldn't help noticing her feet. Lucy's own feet were on the large size and totally flat; she envied anyone with such dainty feet, high arches, and manicured toes.

Meredith's soothing voice was suddenly caught by a cough and a hoarse throat. "My allergies are going wild this time of year. I need to find the neti pot." Her remedy elicited a few chuckles. "Where was I? Oh, right. Please lay back, flat on your mat, arms to your sides, toes pointed toward the ceiling. We'll start with a few gentle stretches . . ."

The sliding door made a swooshing sound as another student slipped inside from the terrace. All eyes turned her way, including Lucy's. She was tall and slim. She slipped down the hood of her pullover and shook out a long, glossy brown ponytail that swung behind her like the tail on a thoroughbred. Her cheekbones were high, her hazel eyes large and wide. Expensive yoga togs—Lululemon, Lucy had no doubt—displayed a perfect figure.

She must be a model or an actress, Lucy thought, then quickly chastised herself for such a sexist assumption. A woman can be beautiful, even as stunning as this one, and choose not to make a living from her looks. Maybe she was a chemical engineer, or a jazz musician or a brain surgeon or . . .

"Oh, it's you. I thought Sabrina was teaching this class," the beauty said.

"Not today, Tanya. Sorry to disappoint." Lucy sensed an edge of disdain under Meredith's measured reply.

"I guess I'll stay anyway." Tanya sighed and unrolled her mat, then looked around for an empty spot to land.

"What an honor," Meredith shot back. "In the future, please arrive on time. And don't use the terrace entrance."

"Honestly, Meredith. Just chill. What happened to *Namaste*?" With that curt rejoinder, Tanya tiptoed to an empty spot beside Lucy, set down her mat, and sat. As Tanya slipped off her flip-flops, Lucy noticed her scratch the top of her long, narrow feet and her ankles with her French-tipped nails. Lucy recognized the telltale red rash.

"Poison ivy? Witch hazel and calamine lotion work well," Lucy whispered.

Tanya gave her a look. Then she yanked down the bottom of her yoga pants and lay back flat on the mat.

Meredith strolled around the room. "Okay, let's begin again, everyone. A deep breath, down into your belly . . ." Meredith closed her eyes and took a deep, centering breath. Reaching to reclaim the inner peace she'd been cultivating all morning, Lucy thought.

Lucy closed her eyes. The interruption had been distracting, breaking the mood. There was clearly tension between the two women, and Meredith's serene vibe had been disturbed by Tanya's arrival.

It must be difficult to be a teacher, Lucy thought. You were bound to have some students that you disliked for one reason or another, but had to put up with anyway.

"Let your spine sink into the floor, let your body go completely limp. Now breathe, a deep breath, into your lower abdomen. Put a hand on your heart and a hand just below your navel. No belly puffing, please. Everything begins and ends with the breath. . . . Your entire life, ladies . . ."

With her eyes closed, Lucy followed the instructions. As her body sunk into the floor, a pleasant, cloud-like lightness filled her chest and limbs. Her mind went blank, and anxious thoughts about wedding plans that spun around her brain all day and night, faded away.

Would Meredith object if she lay like this for the rest of the class?

Before Meredith could give further instructions, the shrill sound of a police siren shattered the silence. First one siren flying by the building and then another. Followed by a different sort of siren—an ambulance or fire truck?

Lucy's eyes opened, and she turned her head to meet Dana's surprised gaze.

"For goodness sakes. What a racket. Will someone please close that back door?" Meredith asked the group.

Dana stood up and walked over to the sliding door. But when more sirens sounded, she stepped outside and walked out onto the stone terrace. She returned moments later, her blue eyes wide.

"There's a parade of police cars coming down the main road. Plus a fire truck and an ambulance." She whispered to Lucy as she took her place again. "Something big is going on out there."

Most of the students in the class sat up, curious and concerned. A few took out cell phones and tapped out text messages, or made hushed calls.

Meredith gazed around the studio, clearly out of sync with her lesson. "If anyone wants to leave, please feel free. But—"

Another siren cut off her words, and she sighed. "I have no idea what's happened. Whatever it is, this racket is too distracting. Let's call off this class, and I'll hold a makeup tomorrow."

Her solution was nearly drowned out by the sound of more sirens. All the women in the room jumped up and quickly rolled their mats. A few were already at the door. Lucy and Dana put their borrowed mats away in the studio cubby. Lucy looked around for Amy and saw her standing at the door. Amy waved, and Lucy waved back.

They stepped out to the hallway together and set off at a brisk pace, with Amy leading the way. "I wonder what happened. I hope everyone is okay."

Lucy hoped so, too. From the number of emergency vehicles that were racing through the gates of Osprey Shores, she doubted it.

As they swept past the reception desk, Amy turned to the young woman seated there. "Do you know what happened? Why are all these police cars here?"

The woman's expression was grim. "I'm not sure. But I heard there was an accident. Someone fell off the cliff walk."

"Fell off the walk? Oh my God. . . . That's awful."

Lucy agreed. A fall from that height, where most of the hillside leading down to the beach was a sheer drop covered with jagged rocks, would likely be fatal.

She looked over at Dana and could tell she had the same thought.

"I'm going to check on Phoebe," Lucy said.

"Good idea," Dana replied quietly. Lucy could tell she was worried but trying not to show it.

They pushed through the glass doors and stepped outside without speaking. Lucy pulled out her phone and sent a quick text to Phoebe. "Are you OK? Back from bird watching yet?"

Then another to Maggie. "Phoebe back yet?"

Maggie answered first. "She's here. Went back to bed."

Lucy showed Dana the text and sighed in unison. But Amy looked upset, Lucy noticed. Of course, she was worried that someone she knew—a friend or neighbor—had taken the tumble.

"It looks like everyone's headed for the walk. The part just around that bend." Amy pointed as they walked down a path from the mansion that led to the famous walkway.

Most of the fog had drifted away. Which was a good thing, Lucy thought, since they were practically jogging along the narrow path as they followed Amy. The very idea of the accident made her nervous about falling herself.

As white gravel crunched under her sneakers, she noticed a few benches to her left, set back from the path and surrounded by huge hydrangeas and rose of Sharon bushes. They appeared pleasant spots for taking in the view. A hip-high white rail fence ran to her right, bordering the path and a fringe of wild-looking, beachy shrubbery.

Not a very high fence, Lucy thought, though it seemed an adequate barrier from the sloping cliff for most people. From what she could see, the cliffside was covered with boulders, and here and there, tufts of greenery. At other points, there was a sheer drop to the beach and crashing surf below.

"Look at the crowd. Just up there. I wonder if it's true." Amy stopped on the path and pointed.

Lucy saw a cluster of people gathered a short distance

away at the rail fence, or at least as close to it as the police and property security guards would allow. Official looking vehicles—police cars and police SUVs—had driven over the lush lawn and parked close to the walk. Two uniformed officers stood on the path next to neon orange traffic cones, obviously stationed there to turn back more onlookers.

"Seems like the police have blocked the path," Amy said.

Dana stood at the fence and turned to face them. "We don't need to join the crowd to see what's happened. Look down at the beach."

Lucy walked over with Amy and peered down at the rocky shoreline. It looked as if the tide was coming in. Lucy saw more police vehicles on the beach, and an ambulance. In the quickly shrinking space between the ocean's foamy edge and the piles of rocks at the bottom of the cliff, an area of the shoreline was cordoned off with tape and more orange cones. A woman and a man dressed in summer clothes kneeled beside a body.

A lifeless body, Lucy realized, noticing how the emergency responders stood at the back of an ambulance, looking on and chatting with each other. If there had been any chance of survival, they would have been working on the fallen victim or loading the person into the ambulance.

It was hard to tell from the top of the cliff, but Lucy thought the corpse looked like a man in jogging shorts, a T-shirt, and sneakers. His limbs were arranged at odd angles, like a starfish that had been dashed against the rocks by the tide.

Lucy caught sight of the body, and quickly stepped back. A bitter feeling rose in the back of her throat. "Oh my gosh . . . what a fate." She turned to Dana and Amy. "I wonder who it is. Someone from this community?"

"Not necessarily . . . a lot of people from town and other parts of the island go out on the walk. It stretches from here all the way to the land bridge, and a few miles past Osprey Shores in the other direction. There's access to the public along the way." Lucy sensed Amy hoped it was someone from outside the community, someone who was not a neighbor.

Dana gave a final glance and looked over at Lucy. "A tragic accident. His poor family."

"Yes . . . what a way to go," Lucy agreed.

"Lucy! Dana!"

Lucy looked up the path. Suzanne and Maggie walked toward them. Had they been first to the scene?

"Someone fell off the cliff. A jogger. It's so awful," Suzanne said.

"Do the police know who it is?" Amy asked.

"I think so," Maggie replied. "Though nobody in the crowd seems to know yet."

"Did Phoebe sleep through that racket?" Lucy asked.

"She woke up. Quite grumpy, I might add. She didn't want to go back outside with us, either."

"But of course, we had to be lookie-lous. Even on vacation," Suzanne admitted.

A white pickup truck displaying the Osprey Shores logo bumped across the lawn and pulled to a stop near the walkway. Sam Briggs emerged from the driver's side, and a woman came out of the passenger door. Two uniformed policemen walked up to her.

Lucy recognized Sam's passenger immediately. The underwear model . . . who could easily be a brain surgeon, Lucy corrected herself again.

"That woman was in our yoga class. I think her name is Tanya," Lucy said.

"Tanya Morton. Julian Morton's wife," Amy replied quietly.

"You mean she's married to that awful man at the poker game last night? The one who caused the uproar?" Maggie asked.

Amy nodded. "Yes. Though I wonder why Sam drove her here. Maybe he was at her cottage, and she got a call from the police."

"Not a good sign," Dana said quietly.

"It can only mean one thing," Suzanne said. "That must be her husband's body down on the beach."

Lucy knew that, too, but hadn't wanted to be the one to say it aloud.

She watched Tanya Morton wait by the police car, her head bowed, her hands covering her face. Sam stood next to her. He reached out and touched her shoulder, then crossed his arms over his chest.

The officers soon walked Tanya over to a vehicle that looked like a big dune buggy, its large, high wheels suitable for off-road or driving on the beach. Tanya took a seat and a police officer got in the driver's side. Lucy had often been on the beach in her hometown after dark and seen this sort of police department jeep patrolling the shore.

The jeep turned in a tight circle on the grass and then roared down the road to the entrance gate. Sam watched a moment, then got back in his truck and drove away.

"Where are they going?" Lucy asked.

"There are a few foot paths that lead down to the beach, and a long flight of stairs. But there's only one road, about a mile down the shoreline," Amy said. "I guess he's taking her that way."

To identify the body, Lucy guessed.

"Wow . . . I can't believe it." Suzanne pushed her sunglasses up onto her head. "Talk about here today, gone tomorrow. We just saw the guy last night, alive and kickin'—and giving everybody hell. I don't even know the man, and I'm in shock."

"It is a shock. One that will have your neighbors reeling," Maggie said to Amy.

Amy sighed and nodded. She zipped up her nylon hoodie, and rubbed her arms as if she felt a sudden chill, even though the fog had burned away to reveal a blue sky and high, puffy white clouds. "I'm sure the whole development is buzzing by now," she said. "Julian Morton was very well known. Though I can't say very well liked."

If last night was any indication of Dr. Morton's social skills, Lucy had no doubt that Amy's words were true.

Amy pulled out her phone and tapped a text message. "I want to tell Rob. He went surf casting this morning. He's probably not back yet."

She sounded a little worried about her husband, Lucy thought. Or maybe she's just set off balance by this horrific news. After all, she knew the man personally. Whether or not she liked him, it was still a shock to hear that Dr. Morton had died so suddenly and in such an awful way.

"Rob must be wild about fishing if he went out in that fog," Suzanne said. "How can the fish even see the hook?"

Maggie looked puzzled. "I don't think you want the fish to see the hook, Suzanne. Only the bait. Maybe they sense that."

"I have no clue." Amy shrugged and tucked the phone back in her pocket. "He's tried every sport and outdoor pastime—tennis, golf, kayaking, and even model trains. This is the only one that stuck. He's really gotten into it since we moved here. He's got all the gear and clothing, and every once in a while, he even brings home a fish."

Everyone laughed. Lucy secretly identified. Matt often teased her about the same thing, saying she seemed to like the outfits and gadgets for her hobbies as much as the actual activity.

"He enjoys it. That's the main thing," Dana said. "Fishing is a very meditative pursuit. Maybe he needs the alone time to mull over his ideas for new inventions."

"That's just the way I feel about knitting," Maggie said. "It calms the mind and soul."

"Me, too. And I've encouraged him to knit. Even though our group is mostly women, there's Lewis Fielding. He's not afraid to seem feminine, and he turns out some beautiful work. Maybe in the winter," Amy added, "when it's too cold for Rob to stand out on the beach."

"The weather has certainly taken a turn this morning. For the better," Maggie said. She glanced over at the crowd still stationed by the police vehicles and yellow tape that marked off the area of the accident. "I don't know about all of you, but I think we've learned everything there is to know so far about poor Dr. Morton's passing. I'm going to head back to the cottage."

Lucy and her other friends had also seen enough and agreed to join her. Amy's cottage was not far from theirs, and she decided to walk back with them. A few minutes later they reached a turn in the path that led to Amy's place.

"I'll check in with you later," Amy said to Suzanne. "Maybe we can meet up at the pool? I don't think it's a good day for the beach, not with all the police down there. It will probably go on for hours."

"Yes, let's meet at the pool. Don't forget to bring your knitting," Suzanne replied.

"I rarely leave the house without it. See you later."

Despite Amy's cheery wave, Lucy still sensed some anxiety, like static on a smiley face screen saver. It's the bad news we just heard. It upset her, Lucy told herself.

As they turned up the path toward their cottage, Lucy spotted Phoebe. She was knitting, of course, seated on the porch swing, the needle clicks coordinated with the back-and-forth motion. Lucy was sure she could never manage that feat.

"Hey, everybody. Glad you finally came back. I was getting lonesome." She finished a row and looked up at her friends. "Especially after the creepy news I just heard. That awful old guy at the poker game—the one with the goatee?—he fell off the cliff."

"Yes, we know," Maggie said. "How did you hear?"

"I was on the beach, sketching birds and taking photos. The plover are nesting now. They're adorable, all cuddled up in their nests in the dunes."

"I bet they are, if you like birds. But how did you hear about Morton? You didn't see him take the swan dive, did you?" Leave it to Suzanne to find a brash pun in the question.

"Suzanne. Some respect for the deceased, please," Maggie said.

Suzanne shrugged, not looking very contrite.

"No, I didn't see him fall. Thank goodness." Phoebe put her knitting aside. "The shoreline is very curvy. I walked pretty far down the beach and around a bend to see the birds. I did hear . . . a scream. Then some fishermen who were down there shouting to each other. A little while later, I heard all the sirens, so I walked back up the shoreline to see what was going on."

"Goodness. That must have been a ghastly sight." Maggie stared at Phoebe with a grave expression.

"Once I found out what happened, I didn't go closer. But I did see his body, from a distance. It had landed on a big pile of rocks." She sighed and let out a long breath. "I knew there was no hope for the poor man. There were lots of police officers there. They took down everyone's name and asked us some questions. I didn't really understand why. I mean, the guy must have tripped or slipped or something. It was just a horrible accident."

"You know the police. They need to be very thorough in a case like this." Dana took a seat in a wicker chair, and Lucy did the same. "The next of kin need to know how an accident like that could have happened. They need a sense of closure."

"Not to mention a detailed report for the lawsuit they'll probably file," Suzanne added. "I bet the Morton family can get millions out of this developer. Maybe that fence isn't high enough or strong enough for joggers. Maybe the gravel on the path is too slippery."

"Maybe he got disoriented in the fog," Lucy offered. "And took a step in the wrong direction."

"That's all it would take," Dana agreed.

"But could not have happened if there was better lighting on the walk." Suzanne sat on the wicker couch and slipped off her sunglasses.

Phoebe had brought out a pitcher of lemonade, a bowl of corn chips, and salsa. That had probably been her breakfast, Lucy realized. Phoebe picked up a chip and crunched noisily.

"Suzanne, you missed your calling. You should have been a lawyer," Maggie said.

"Thanks, but I'll pass. That line is even more stressful than real estate. I might have been hugely successful . . . but I would have also been plain huge." She held out a chip clutched between her thumb and index finger. "See this? Stress eating. I don't know why, but hearing that someone died always makes me hungry. Even though I don't even know the guy."

"Oh, the poets knew all about that reaction. It's perfectly natural. Eat, drink, and be merry," Maggie offered. "For tomorrow yea may—"

"Don't even say it," Phoebe interrupted. "We all know the punch line. And that one about gathering rose buds, too."

"I'm hungry. I hardly had any breakfast," Lucy said. "Let's have an early lunch and head to the pool."

"Good plan. Lead the way." Suzanne rose from her seat on the wicker couch and popped a last chip in her mouth.

Just as Lucy was about to go inside, she spotted a police officer walking up the path. She turned and glanced at her friends. They all looked interested to see the reason for this visit, and waited silently as the blue uniform came closer. Dana and Maggie came to their feet.

"Good afternoon, ladies. I'm Officer Hobart, Eaton's Landing police department." He was in uniform but still flashed his ID. "As you may already know, a resident fell to his death from the cliff walk this morning. We're meeting with everyone in the community to find eyewitnesses, or to see if anyone has information that can help us put the pieces together."

Dana stood nearest to the officer. She glanced at him, her head tilted to one side. "To understand how the accident happened, you mean?"

Officer Hobart took a pad and pen from his back pocket. "We can't say for sure that it was an accident yet."

"You mean someone may have pushed him? Or he jumped off intentionally?" Lucy didn't mean to just blurt out her questions but she could tell from her friends' faces that they wondered the same thing.

"We're still investigating how and why it happened." The officer's expression remained serious and unreadable. "I only have a few questions. This won't take long."

After taking down their names and contact information, he asked what had brought them to Osprey Shores.

"A girls' getaway," Suzanne explained. "Lucy is getting married next weekend. We wanted to take her away for some fun."

"Not that much fun so far, with all that fog and someone falling off a cliff," Phoebe mumbled.

The officer glanced at Phoebe and then back at his pad. "Did anyone know the deceased, Dr. Julian Morton?"

"We never met him. But we all saw him last night at the mansion," Maggie explained. "We were in a knitting club meeting in the library, and he was in the adjacent room, playing poker."

"And got in a big row with another player," Suzanne cut in. "The other player's last name is Pullman. I don't remember his first name, but I'm pretty sure he lives here. Maybe you've already heard this story?"

Officer Hobart looked interested. "You're my first stop. What was the argument about? Did you overhear that, too?"

"Everybody did," Lucy said. "Dr. Morton was gloating about taking another winning hand. It sounded like he'd been on a lucky streak. The other player, Pullman, accused him of cheating. Which Morton denied."

"But it came out that Pullman had lost a ton of money and was pretty deep in debt to Morton. Over ten thousand dollars," Suzanne said. "When Morton goaded him about that, calling him a loser and other names, Pullman lost his temper. He stood up, shouted something, and flipped the poker table over. He said he wasn't going to pay Morton a nickel of the debt because he believed Morton had cheated to win the money."

Officer Hobart busily took down the story. "What else did Pullman say? Do you remember?"

Dana had not said anything so far but now spoke up. "Morton accused him of slander and said he was going to sue. Then Pullman laughed and said something like, 'You're the one who's going to pay' and 'Watch your back, old man.' "

" And 'I'll see you rot in hell,' " Suzanne added. "I remember that because I thought it was getting pretty nasty."

Officer Hobart was taking down the story in a quick, efficient hand. "Anything else you'd like to add?" He looked around at the group.

"That's it, I think." Lucy glanced at her friends to see if anyone remembered an important detail she, Dana, or Suzanne had left out. "After all the shouting and table turning, Pullman stomped out of the room. We shut the door between our meeting and the card players' room, so we didn't hear anything more."

The officer made a few more notes and turned the page of his pad. "I just need to ask you all what you were doing this morning, between seven-thirty and eight-thirty."

Dana answered first. "Lucy and I went to a yoga class at the fitness center. It was supposed to start at eight but there was a delay. When it finally started, all the sirens were too disrupting, so it was cancelled. We came out and followed the crowd to see what was going on."

"I stayed here in the cottage, knitting," Maggie said. "Suzanne was with me. She was sleeping in a bit this morning."

"Hey, I work full-time and have three kids. A few extra hours of sleep is an annual event. You have no idea."

"Don't worry, Suzanne. I don't think Officer Hobart will give you a ticket for sleeping late," Lucy quietly teased.

The police officer finally cracked a smile. "You're in luck. We just took that one off the books." He turned to Phoebe. "And where were you, Ms. Meyers?"

"I went down to the beach pretty early, around five

thirty. I wanted to take photos and do some sketches of the piping plover."

The police officer looked surprised and curious. "How did that go? Find any in the fog?"

"Quite a few, all cuddled in their nests. I think the fog added a lot to the photos. I'm going to print some in black and white."

Lucy had to smile at her reply. It didn't take much to get Phoebe musing over creative projects, even when being questioned by a police officer.

"How long were you on the beach?" the police officer asked in a more serious tone.

"About two hours, I guess. Until I heard the sirens. I did hear sort of a shout before that, but I didn't pay it any mind. I thought maybe one of the fishermen had gotten a big catch. The surf was very rough and loud. It was hard to hear anything clearly. But when I heard the sirens, I walked back up the shoreline and saw some fishermen and a few other people who'd been out on the beach, all huddled together, talking. They told me what happened. And I saw Dr. Morton's body, where it had landed on the rocks . . . from a distance."

Lucy saw Phoebe's involuntary shudder.

"Did you see him fall?" he asked quickly.

Phoebe shook her head. "I wasn't looking in that direction. I was looking mostly down, at the birds. Even if I had looked up at the cliffs, I'm not sure I would have seen anything from that part of the beach."

"All right." He paused and checked his notes, then glanced back up at Phoebe. "Don't delete any of your photographs, or edit them in any way. Detective Dunbar will probably want to see them."

"Sure . . . that would be okay," Phoebe replied, though Lucy sensed she didn't like the idea of giving her new camera to the police, even for a short time, or getting any more involved than this brief question and answer session.

"I think that's all we need right now. We'll be in touch," he added, looking directly at Phoebe.

Phoebe seemed nervous and didn't answer.

"Thank you, Officer. Of course we'll try to help as much as we can," Maggie said smoothly.

"How long are you staying?"

"We leave on Monday," Suzanne said.

He nodded. "Enjoy your weekend."

"Thanks, I'm sure we will." Suzanne sounded a lot more confident of that fact than Lucy felt at the moment.

When Officer Hobart was finally out of earshot, Maggie said, "Sounds like they're not certain it was an accident."

"Maybe they already know that it wasn't," Dana said. "I don't think the police department would be going door-to-door like this if they thought he'd just slipped."

"Good point. Even considering my liability lawsuit theory," Suzanne said. "Foul play. Or suicide. For goodness' sake, it's so stressful to consider the possibilities. I'm hungry again."

"Let's make lunch, and then head to the pool, as we planned," Maggie said. "Dr. Morton's death is awfully upsetting, but we can't let it ruin our weekend."

"Good point," Suzanne agreed. "Let's stick with our plan—hang out at the pool and work on our tans and our knitting. Then figure out what we want to do for dinner. I feel sorry for Dr. Morton and his family, but there's nothing we can do to help the situation."

With murmurs of agreement, Lucy's friends followed her inside to change into swimsuits for an afternoon at the pool.

But Lucy could tell, despite their resolve, it was difficult to ignore the cold shadow that had drifted over their revelry. And, impossible to shield themselves from the disturbing details that would surely come.

Lucy knew her beloved BFFs. News of Julian Morton's death was akin to a brush with poison ivy. No matter what they said about ignoring the event, puzzling over how and why he took a deadly tumble would vex them, like an itch aching to be scratched.

Myself included, she silently admitted.

Chapter 3

Lucy and Maggie were the first to arrive at the Osprey Shores Pool Club; they stood at the entrance a moment, taking in the scene.

Turquoise water sparkled in a large, kidney-shaped pool where a waterfall glided down artfully placed stones and splashed at the deep end. The stone terrace and landscaping were seamlessly in tune with Osprey Shores's tasteful elegance. White canvas canopies flapped in the breeze, providing deep shade for the cushioned lounge chairs, arranged in neat rows on both sides of the pool. There were also several umbrella-covered tables.

Attendants, wearing polo shirts and shorts in the Osprey Shores colors, circled the pool, delivering fresh towels, or taking orders for food and drink.

Lucy led Maggie to a group of five empty chairs, one for herself, three for the rest of her group, and one for Amy, who had sent a text to say she was running late, but would meet up with them soon.

She felt awkward as a visitor, claiming so many seats. She hoped the attendants didn't ask what she was doing as she dropped items from her tote bag onto each saved chair—a paperback novel, a magazine, a napkin-wrapped peach in a sandwich bag, a tube of sunscreen, and a water bottle along with a pack of gum. Luckily, she had over-packed for the simple outing, as usual.

A fresh beach towel, with white and blue stripes and a small mermaid emblem, sat neatly folded on each empty chair. Lucy chose her own seat and spread out the towel. Of course, Osprey Shores provided towels, to keep everything matched and classy.

She had one in her bag, covered with pink and orange flowers, but she didn't dare take it out since it would clash horribly. There was probably a rule about that.

The terrace was surprisingly empty, with only a few residents sunbathing or swimming, despite the perfect weather. The day had evolved from dense fog to a crystal blue sky and bright sunshine. A cool breeze blew in off the ocean below.

"If you don't like the weather in New England, just wait twenty minutes," her mother always said. Today that old motto rang true.

Lucy sat back and gazed out at the view, a wide blue ribbon of water and whitecaps beating against the rocky shore. She could also see a long, curving section of the cliff walk. She much preferred a beach to a pool, but the terrace was the better choice today, all things considered.

A few police vehicles remained parked in the area of Morton's fall, and yellow crime scene tape blocked part of the walkway, then trailed down the cliff. Lucy assumed that it outlined a large swath of shoreline and rocks, where the police were searching for evidence.

She spotted at least two investigators in hazmat suits working their way through the dense brush on the hillside. One wore a belt and harness with a safety line connected to the top of the cliff, like the kind she'd seen rock climbers wear to halt a fall.

It was difficult terrain to investigate in order to ferret

out clues, not to mention the wind that was blowing the evidence in all directions.

Lucy glanced at Maggie and decided not to share this observation. Her friend was right. They were here to relax and enjoy themselves. They shouldn't let Dr. Morton's death take center stage, however tempting it was to discuss.

Maggie didn't seem to notice the police activity. She had quickly claimed a nearby umbrella table and pulled out her knitting. Lucy didn't have much left in her knapsack to distract herself, and she didn't feel like knitting yet. She took out a Maine guidebook and a tube of sunblock.

Sam Briggs strolled through a gate at the far end of the pool. He carried a long pole with a big net on the end, designed to skim off leaves from the top of the water. His eyes were covered by sunglasses—wayfarer style, of course. A dark blue baseball cap covered most of his thick blond hair.

Lucy sat back and gazed down at her book. A few minutes later, the well-built handyman had worked his way around the pool to their side, and soon, he was working near their chairs.

"I knew the sun would come out for you. Catching some rays?" Sam said.

Lucy looked up from her book. Oh, brother. Did those lines really work for him? "We are. Thanks."

"They keep you busy around here, don't they?" Maggie asked.

He reached out and swooped up a few leaves, then pulled back the net. "They do indeed. I don't mind. Keeps me out of trouble. My middle name."

He looked straight at Lucy and smiled. Lucy thought she may have even spied a wink under his sunglasses. She didn't feel flattered by the attention. Just the opposite, a bit repulsed.

He was obviously the type of guy who thought he was irresistible to women. Not her type at all. She was glad she still wore her cover-up over her suit and gently tugged it further down her legs. She flashed her engagement ring as she opened her book again.

Sam waved good-bye, mostly to Maggie. Lucy acted as if she didn't notice. He returned to his work and had soon moved down the poolside, chatting with other groups of women on his way.

"You seem to have caught the eye of Mr. Maintenance," Maggie said after a while.

"He's just likes attention. I'm sure he flirts with all the women sitting out here."

Maggie laughed. "Yes, probably. He could certainly have his pick."

Lucy wasn't sure about that, but Sam would have definitely agreed with Maggie. She looked up from the guidebook and saw another man who looked familiar. He had staked out a lounge directly across the pool. He pulled off a T-shirt and shorts to reveal a tiny Speedo bathing suit. Lucy was not a fan of that look. When he slipped off his wraparound sunglasses, she was certain of his identity.

"Look, on the other side of the pool," Lucy said. "It's Derek Pullman."

Maggie looked up from her knitting. "So it is. Good job. I didn't recognize him without his clothes on."

"I'm going to pretend you didn't say that," Lucy replied. "Don't you think it's interesting that he's out here? After the scene he made last night, most people probably think he carried through on his threat. I'd be hiding out in my apartment."

"Maybe he's being bold. Trying to show everyone he has nothing to hide."

"Hence the choice of swimwear," Lucy mumbled. "He does seem the brazen type. Maybe he did push Morton over the edge and figures it's best to carry on as if he had nothing to do with it."

"Hiding in plain sight and all that? If he's the one, the police will figure it out, either way." Maggie examined her stitches then turned her work over and continued knitting.

Lucy sensed Maggie didn't want to speculate any further about Derek Pullman, or Morton's death for that matter. Which was just as well she decided, and returned to her book.

"There's Betty from Amy's knitting group." Maggie waved to Betty Rutledge who was walking their way.

Betty waved back and soon stood before them. "I thought I might find you here today. It's perfect weather for a dip in the pool. The ocean is lovely but so rough and cold, even this time of year."

Lucy was smearing lotion on her legs and looked up to greet Betty with a smile. The woman wore a large floral print dress, what Lucy's mother used to call a muumuu. A Tilley sunhat, white canvas with a floppy brim, was tied under her chin. Below the hat brim, gigantic black sunglasses covered most of her face. They were the kind that prevented cataracts, but could also serve double duty as safety glasses during welding projects. A beach tote with a mermaid emblem was hooked over one arm and a Vera Bradley knitting bag over the other.

"Hello, Betty. Nice to see you again." Maggie put her knitting on the table and took a sip from her water bottle. "Would you like to join me under the umbrella? I avoid the sun this time of day. It's nice and cool under here."

"I'd love to. Thanks. It's easier for me to knit in the shade, too. I can't fit my reading glasses under these infernal glasses. But doctor's orders. That's what it comes down to when you get older—'Don't do this, don't do that.'" She shook her head and laughed. "Live it up while you're still young. You have plenty of time to be cautious and careful later. And we never know when our time is up, do we?"

"Very true." Maggie's tone was pleasant enough, but Lucy could tell she wasn't pleased with the dark pivot of the conversation.

But Betty's advice rang true to Lucy. A person should value and enjoy each day, especially on vacation. She wasn't going to make a real bucket list, as Phoebe had urged her, but maybe she should check the guidebook for some activities a bit more daring than collecting sea shells or drinking iced tea with real sugar.

Betty settled into her shady seat and opened her knitting bag. "I'm sure when Julian Morton got up this morning, he didn't expect it would be his last. You heard what happened, didn't you?"

Maggie nodded. "Poor man. What a tragedy."

Betty shrugged and made a little grunting sound. "A gruesome way to go. But I don't think there are too many around here shedding tears." Betty leaned closer to Maggie. "I don't even think his widow is ruining her mascara over it. If you know what I mean."

Lucy had finished applying the sunblock and wiped her hands on a towel. "We saw Tanya arrive at the cliff walk, then the police drove her down to the beach. She seemed to be crying."

Had Tanya been crying? Lucy saw her cover her face with her hands and assumed as much.

"She looked quite shocked," Maggie added.

"Shocked by her turn of good luck, maybe. Everyone knew she wanted out of the marriage, but Morton had made her sign an airtight prenup, and he wasn't parting with a nickel. It's the same way he dealt with his first wife, Meredith."

"Meredith Quinn, the yoga teacher?" Lucy asked.

"That's right. Their son, Cory, is grown and out on his

own, but she still needs a few jobs to keep a roof over her head. While her ex is living in luxury with his trophy wife, a former model," Betty added. "Mostly for catalogs— bathing suits and lingerie. That sort of thing."

Really? Lucy was not surprised, but somehow, disappointed. Did the world have to be so obvious?

"Now Tanya stands to inherit the lot. I suppose Cory might get something, but he and his father never got along. So that's questionable. Morton had a fortune, people say."

"Interesting," Maggie murmured, her gaze focused on her knitting. "How are you coming along with the lace shawl project? Have you gotten the hang of that open stitch?"

Lucy guessed that Maggie was trying to shift the conversation away from Dr. Morton, even though back home, she and her pals often engaged in this sort of gossip while they were knitting or hanging out together. Especially if someone they knew had died under such suspicious circumstances. They had helped in a few investigations in their hometown and discovered the murderers before the police could puzzle it out. Maggie took pride in that fact, though Lucy guessed her friend just wanted to be on vacation this weekend and keep her nose out of this local, nasty business.

"I put that project aside," Betty replied. "I need to finish this baby blanket. I'm going to be a grandma again."

"Congratulations," Maggie said sincerely. "A boy or a girl?

"My daughter and son-in-law didn't want to know. That's why I'm starting with a blanket and a little hat. White with a yellow ribbon along the border." She held the blanket up and showed Maggie the open work edge where the yellow ribbon would be threaded through later.

"Very nice. That's lovely yarn you're working with, too."

"Organic merino. Cost a fortune, but I only needed a little."

Lucy knew she shouldn't steer the conversation back to Morton after Maggie had so artfully gotten Betty onto another track. But she couldn't help it. She was curious. "What did Dr. Morton do for a living? I mean, how did he get so rich? Was he a famous surgeon or something?"

Betty laughed. "Nothing like that. I think he was trained as a cardiologist, but most of his work was in medical technology. His inventions were used during surgery. Special, tiny cameras and things like that. I'm not sure of the details, but he had been telling everyone that he'd come up with something new and was about to make a fortune with it. I suppose at his memorial—if there is one—someone in the family will tout his successes. They say he was a real genius. Maybe that's why he didn't get along with people. He felt superior," she speculated.

Maggie cast a questioning glance at Lucy, but Lucy ignored it. She wanted to hear more. "Did you know him?"

"Depends what you mean. Were we friends or even friendly acquaintances? No. I don't believe I'd exchanged two words with him since he and Tanya moved in about a year ago. But I knew him long before that."

"Really? How's that?" Lucy set aside the guidebook and waited for Betty to answer. Maggie shot her a more meaningful "why are you encouraging her?" look, but Lucy ignored her and turned back to Betty.

Betty looked down at her knitting, smoothing the strand of yarn. She seemed to be conflicted about disclosing more details.

"You don't need to tell us if you don't want to," Maggie said.

Betty shrugged and started knitting again. "I told the police this morning, so I might as well tell you. With the gossip mill kicking into high gear right now, I'm sure it will get around in no time."

Probably true, Lucy thought. Though she didn't interrupt Betty.

"It's a small world, up here in New England especially. It so happens that Julian Morton went to the same summer camp as my younger brother and I. A very pretty spot on a lake in Vermont. I was a junior counselor there at the time, and my brother, Ted, still a camper. Ted had a rivalry with Julian all summer. Some of the boys called him Julie, a girly nickname. It drove him crazy." Betty smiled, remembering. "You know how boys are. They love a competition, especially at that age. He and my brother were always going toe-to-toe, at sports and with the girls, too. Ted was good-looking and very popular, but not stuck on himself. Not one bit. He was just the type of boy other kids gravitated toward. A great personality, and such a sunny smile."

Betty paused, straightening a length of the white yarn. Lucy wondered where this story was going. Some sort of mean prank would be the punch line she guessed.

"The last week of camp, there was a big field day," Betty continued. "Teddy beat Julian in a swimming race, a one-on-one matchup. The whole camp was there, and most of them cheering Ted on. Morton couldn't stand to be shamed. That night, when everyone was celebrating on the beach, and the trophies were given out, Morton pushed my brother into the bonfire."

"Oh my goodness, how horrible." Lucy sat stunned and took a deep breath.

"It was. I'd give a million dollars to erase that sight from my memory. To forget the sound of my brother . . . well, you understand." Betty put her knitting down and adjusted her reading glasses. Lucy could see that it still pained her to tell the story, and she was suddenly sorry that she'd pressed to hear more.

"That is cruel. Boys at that age don't have sound judgment. Something to do with brain development, I've read," Maggie added. "But that's just heartless. A total lack of human empathy."

"Julian Morton wasn't that young. He was a teenager at the time, and any child over the age of three knows better than that. It wasn't an accident. I was sitting right there. I saw the whole thing."

"How awful for you." Lucy could barely imagine the scene—the panic and helplessness Betty must have felt. And she was so young at the time, too.

"My brother had burns on more than half his body. He survived, thank God. But he was never the same. His whole personality changed. He's done all right for himself, but he's damaged. Outside, and in. I've carried it with me, too," she added. "I know it's irrational, but he was my little brother, and I've always felt it was my fault somehow. I was there. I should have protected him."

It was a sad story. Sad and frightening. How could someone be that vindictive?

"Was Morton punished? Did your family take any legal action?" Maggie asked.

"He was a minor at the time, pretty much immune to legal consequences. My parents took on the camp and settled out of court. I don't think they even got enough to cover the medical bills. Morton insisted it was an accident. He claimed he saw my brother slip and fall into the fire. It all happened in the blink of an eye, and nobody could say for sure if they saw Morton push Ted. But my brother knew." She picked up her knitting again. "I never doubted Teddy's story. I already knew what sort of boy Morton was, and I knew the sort of man he would become."

Betty's words chilled Lucy to the bone, despite the bright sunlight beating down on them. Last night, she'd heard Betty say that Dr. Morton *"would get a taste of his own medicine someday."*

Now she knew what Betty meant. The incident between Julian Morton and Betty's brother was a boatload of foul medicine—a dose large enough to do in anyone.

"Where's your brother now? Do you see him much?" Lucy was curious about the way Ted's life had turned out.

"Yes, I do. He and his wife live in Moody Beach, not far from here. He raised a lovely family, a girl and a boy. Grown now, and out on their own. Teddy's in insurance. He works from home mostly, which suits him," she added.

"I'm just curious, Betty. Didn't Dr. Morton recognize you when he moved here?" Maggie asked. Lucy had wondered about that. And she also noticed that Maggie was asking questions now, too.

Betty shook her head. "Not that I ever knew. My maiden name is Oliver, and I look a heck of lot different than I did at seventeen," she added with a rough laugh. "Frankly, if the last time I'd seen myself was back then, I wouldn't recognize me either."

Lucy didn't doubt it. She was only thirty-six and could hardly recognize people she knew from high school when they popped up on Facebook, or in real life.

"I wouldn't have known him by sight, either But, of course, his name got my attention." Betty checked the stitches on a row and turned her work around.

The white baby blanket looked so soft and pure. A flag of innocence, heralding new life. A strange counterpoint to their conversation, Lucy thought.

"I wondered if it could be the same Julian Morton. My family had no idea what had become of him. We didn't want to know," Betty continued. "I nosed around a little and found out for sure that it was him. His personality hadn't changed, I'll tell you that much. It had only gotten worse."

Pushing a teenage rival into a bonfire was a low point in anybody's book. What could be worse?

Lucy was relieved to see the rest of their friends enter the pool club and head in their direction. Suzanne's black and white print patio dress fluttered in the breeze. Her dark hair was pushed back with a thick white band—the outfit suitable for a cocktail party or an art gallery opening, Lucy thought. Clomping along on high cork sandals, Suzanne waved brightly, as if she hadn't seen Lucy or Maggie for days.

Dana and Phoebe followed. Dana in a large, loose pastel shirt a lot like Lucy's cover-up, and Phoebe wearing a huge straw hat and a white sundress with embroidered flowers around the bodice. She looked like a tourist on a tropical island except for her feet, which were covered with white ankle socks and shoved into low-heeled sandals. A very retro touch, Lucy thought.

"You made it. What took you guys so long?" Maggie put her knitting down and turned to face them as they chose lounge chairs.

"A little medical emergency," Dana replied. She glanced at Phoebe who was unpacking her tote bag.

"I must have stepped in poison ivy this morning when I was bird watching. My feet are driving me crazy. I just want to scratch them into next week."

"Poor Phoebe." Lucy deeply sympathized. "Did you bring any calamine lotion? Maybe we should go into town and get you something from the drugstore."

"We got her covered, literally," Dana replied. Lucy noticed a pink rim around the ankle socks. "We also brought some ice packs. That can cool the itching down fast."

"Definitely," Lucy agreed. Phoebe had already removed two plastic ziplock bags filled with ice and laid them on her feet with a sigh.

"Here, turn your chair so your feet are in the shade." Lucy got up and helped Phoebe rearrange her seat.

"Thanks, guys. I'll be okay. It's just annoying."

"I'll say. I hope you can rally and go dancing with us tonight." Suzanne dropped her canvas tote on a lounge chair next to Lucy and pulled out a tube of sunscreen.

Maggie's head popped up from her knitting. She peered at Suzanne over her glasses. "Dancing? Is that the plan?"

"It is now. I hope you'll agree." Suzanne smoothed a handful of lotion over her arms. An expensive brand only found in department stores, Lucy noticed. "I caught up on a few client calls while Phoebe was examined by Doctor Dana. Looks like I finally found a buyer for a big old colonial that's been on the market for ages. I could get a nice offer by the end of the day, and I want to take everyone out for dinner to celebrate," she added brightly.

"That's too generous of you," Maggie said. "But good luck. I hope you get the call."

"I had some messages to answer, too," Dana said. "Nothing urgent. I think my patients can sense when I put a toe over the Plum Harbor town line. Even for a weekend." She sat at the table with Maggie and took out her knitting.

"They say moths can smell a mate from over a thousand miles away. Maybe it works the same for therapists," Phoebe offered. She'd landed on a lounge chair next to Suzanne.

"Possibly. They do seem to pick up on some vibe. . . . Oh, hello, Betty. Nice to see you," Dana greeted Amy's friend.

"Nice to see you, too, dear." Betty nodded in Dana's direction.

"Betty was just telling us a story about Julian Morton. An incident that involved her brother when they were young," Maggie said.

"Really?" Lucy could tell from Dana's tone that her interest was piqued. "So you knew Dr. Morton?" Dana asked.

"Not really. Not in a friendly way. But we do have history. Maggie can tell you about it later. I don't mind. But I'd rather focus on more pleasant thoughts right now. I'm glad to see the fog burned off, and you have some nice weather for your visit."

When in doubt, talk about the weather, Lucy noted. She actually didn't want to hear Betty's sad story again, though she was sure the rest of her friends were very curious. Maggie would surely catch them up later, once Betty left.

There was a lot to consider in her unnerving tale. Betty had good reason to want to see Dr. Morton fly off a cliff. For that matter, so did her brother, who didn't live that far from here, Betty had said.

"Hey, everyone!" Amy waved and walked toward them from the opposite side of the pool. Lucy had not noticed her enter. She was carrying a tray with several tall, icy-looking drinks in plastic glasses. "Sorry to keep you waiting. I brought you all some iced tea. You must be feeling toasty out here by now."

She set the glasses of iced tea on the umbrella table, and everyone thanked her and took a cup.

"Did police officers come to your cottage? They came to ask us questions just as I was about to leave to meet you," Amy said, and took an empty lounge chair on the opposite side of the table.

"Yes, a police officer stopped by and asked us questions, too." Maggie paused and sipped her tea. "It sounds like they're interviewing everyone in the development, which makes me think they suspect foul play."

"They do, definitely." Amy spread out her towel and settled on her chair. "A friend of mine works in the management office. A security guard told her that the police believe someone struck Morton on the head first, then pushed him over. They could tell by the position his body was in when he landed, and from his injuries. She wasn't certain of all the details."

Lucy didn't need to hear the details. She felt a lump in her throat and didn't reply. She'd had a feeling that Morton's fall was not an accident, but hearing this tidbit confirmed it. Morton's death had been a cold-blooded, premeditated act. Nothing less.

"Wow. That's big." Dana squeezed a lemon wedge into her tea. She was a big fan of lemons and always said the juice detoxified your body.

"Did you tell the police about the argument at the card game?" Suzanne stirred her tea with a straw, the ice cubes rattling. "They must be hearing about it from everyone who was at the knitting meeting. And the card players, too, come to think of it."

"I did tell them. What I could remember. It happened so fast. I guess the police will talk to Derek Pullman. He made real threats to Dr. Morton. My friend also told me that Morton called security very early in the morning, before he went out jogging, because someone had vandalized his car. A brand-new BMW, parked in his driveway."

Lucy glanced across the pool. The lounge chair where Derek Pullman had been sitting was empty, his belongings gone, too. He must have left without her noticing.

"Vandalized it? What did they do?" Lucy sat up, curious now.

"Someone wrote CHEATER in red spray paint on one side of the car. The security guards said Morton was livid and shouted so loud, they thought he would wake up the whole community."

"I guess Morton accused Pullman of the graffiti." Dana paused her stitching and turned her work over. She was working on the lace shawl pattern, in a pale yellow yarn, and making good progress. "That's exactly what Pullman called him last night at the card game."

"I thought so, too." Amy looked nervous and shaken, fishing out some knitting from her tote bag. Morton's death had rattled her. But most people who lived here probably felt the same. This morning, everyone thought it was a tragic accident. Now it appeared to be murder.

"It sounds like something Derek Pullman might have done, considering how angry he was with Dr. Morton last night," Betty said in her matter-of-fact manner. "Derek does have a temper."

"And Pullman owed Morton a ton of money in gambling debts. Definitely a motive to do him harm," Lucy said. "But if you plan on pushing a person off a cliff, would you really bother vandalizing their car right before the dark deed? That part doesn't make sense to me."

"Good point. I was thinking the same thing myself." Suzanne nodded, swirling her tea. "It does seem like overkill. If you'll excuse the pun."

Lucy gave Suzanne a look. That was a bad pun. Even for the real estate sales diva.

Dana put her work down in her lap. "Maybe Pullman never planned on killing Morton, but the two met on the walk and had a confrontation. They nearly came to blows last night at the poker game."

Maggie had set her knitting aside, too, but now took it up again. "That's possible. But, from what Amy heard, Morton was struck on the head before he fell."

"Maybe Pullman was defending himself," Suzanne said.

Lucy thought that was possible. Though it would be interesting to know where Morton was struck. On the front of the head? That would be the likely spot someone would hit in a self-defense situation. But if the blow was on the back of Morton's head, that would probably mean someone had snuck up on him.

Before Lucy could share this insight with her friends, she noticed a woman walking toward them. Something told Lucy she wasn't another resident, or even a visitor. She wore a black T-shirt, tan Bermuda shorts, and running shoes that squeaked in the wet spots near the pool edge. A thick, curly ponytail stuck out the back of a baseball cap, and her eyes were covered by dark, aviator-style sunglasses.

She stopped at their group and smiled briefly. "Afternoon, ladies. I'm Detective Rose Dunbar. I'm investigating the Morton incident." A laminated ID tag hung from a cord around her neck. "I'm looking for Phoebe Meyer. Anyone here know where I can find her?"

All eyes turned toward Phoebe.

"That would be me. I'm Phoebe." Phoebe sat up in her chair and adjusted her hat, which had flopped over her face.

"I understand you were out early this morning and took some photographs?"

The detective walked over to Phoebe's chair and slipped off her glasses. Her face was bare of makeup, her skin lightly tanned. She had large blue eyes, and thick lashes and brows. A sprinkle of freckles gave her a youthful edge, though Lucy guessed the detective to be in her late thirties or early forties.

Whatever the number, she was quite fit; she probably worked out with weights or practiced martial arts. Lucy could see Rose Dunbar dealing out a roundhouse punch or a swift, swinging kick.

"Yes, I did. Officer Hobart said you might want to see them. I have the camera right here. I can send you all the files."

"We'd like to borrow your camera and check the files in our lab."

"Oh . . . all right. That makes sense, I guess." Phoebe picked up her big straw bag and started wading through it, tossing random items on the lounge chair until she found the camera.

"Here it is." Phoebe handed over a black camera case. "Do I get a receipt or something?"

"Sure, I'm writing it for you right now." The detective had taken out a pad and scribbled on it.

"When will I get it back? We're only here until Monday morning. I can always take pictures with my phone, I guess, but the camera is a lot better."

"I'm sure. Tough break on your vacation. But there could be something in the photos that will help us. There are no security cameras out there. Not like the rest of this place," she explained. "A few folks were on the beach and the walk this morning, despite the fog. But no one saw Dr. Morton fall. At least that's what they say."

Someone might have seen him go over the edge, but they didn't want to get involved, Lucy knew the detective meant to say. But she was too professional and discreet to put it that way. Though she did sound frustrated.

"I was down on the beach when he fell. I didn't see anything. I mean, until it was too late," Phoebe added.

Detective Dunbar nodded and handed Phoebe the receipt. Then she took the camera carefully in hand.

"I'll get this back to you as soon as I can. Officer Hobart has your contact info?"

"Yes, he does. My cell phone and all that."

"We won't keep it long. I want to examine these photos

today." She put her sunglasses back on and tugged down her baseball cap. She seemed about to leave, then turned back to Phoebe.

"So you were out in the fog this morning, taking pictures of the plover? The nesting area is restricted to foot traffic."

Did she doubt Phoebe's story? But what connection could Phoebe possibly have to Dr. Morton? Lucy wondered why Detective Dunbar would bother questioning her again.

Phoebe looked as if she wondered, too. "I know. I saw the signs. I'd never disturb the birds. I stood outside the boundary and used a telephoto lens. My boyfriend, Harry, is a sculptor and works in ceramics. He's really into aviary forms. I promised I'd bring back some photographs and sketches for him."

"Sure, that's cool," the detective said. "But if you want my advice, let Harry get up at the crack of dawn and take his own bird photos. He'll respect your boundaries, believe me."

Phoebe seemed surprised by the advice. And that it came from such an unlikely, unsolicited source. Lucy was, too. She thought she might laugh, but didn't dare. She could see her other friends had had the same reaction.

Detective Dunbar may have spoken out of turn, but pinned Phoebe in record time. When it came to relationships with the opposite sex, Phoebe did have a problem with boundaries. She was the good-hearted, ever-forgiving, totally giving type. Some young men in her past had definitely taken advantage.

Phoebe began collecting her belongings and dropping them back in her bag. She looked a bit miffed and maybe even insulted.

"Thanks . . . I think," she said quietly.

Detective Dunbar pulled a card from her pocket and

gazed around at the group. She dropped it on the umbrella-covered table.

"Here's my number, just in case you remember anything you forgot to tell Officer Hobart. Thanks for your time."

They sat silently as the police officer left the terrace, the rubbery squeak of her shoes on the damp stone fading in the distance.

Lucy looked over at Phoebe. She was packing her tote bag and wouldn't meet Lucy's gaze. A bit embarrassed, Lucy guessed.

"I know it's annoying, but it sounds like you'll get your camera back quickly."

Phoebe still didn't look up at her. "I hope so. The thing is ... right before I came down here, I looked over the photos I took. To see if I got any decent shots."

Phoebe paused and looked up at her friends, her voice nearly a whisper. "I saw something in one of the pictures I took on the cliff walk, before I went down to the beach. There was something in the background ... or someone. There was like a shadow, in the bushes near the walkway. Right where Dr. Morton fell."

Chapter 4

"A shadow? What sort of shadow?" Suzanne was the first to pounce, her voice low but insistent. "A man's shadow, or a woman's shadow?"

Phoebe shrugged; her hat flopped to one side and she pushed it up with her hand. "I don't know. Just a shadow . . . in the bushes, near a bench. Right near the spot where Dr. Morton went over. I wasn't very close, and Officer Hobart said not to edit the files, so I didn't enlarge the image. It might just be the fog. Or a reflection on the lens? The light was eerie."

"Sounds to me like you think it was a person," Suzanne persisted. "Not the fog or an optical illusion."

Before Phoebe could reply, Dana cut in. "Suzanne, please. Let's not interrogate poor Phoebe. She's already answered enough questions for one day. Let the investigators figure out if it's more than a shadow. That's what those fancy crime labs are for."

Phoebe cast Dana a grateful look. Then she made a face and gently scratched her poison ivy through her socks. "Good idea, Dana. I'm sorry I told you guys anything. Some people get carried away."

Suzanne tilted her head to one side, with an apologetic look. "I didn't mean to interrogate you, but one of your photos could break this case wide open. You may have taken a picture of the killer, and it could be the lead Detective Dunbar is looking for. Smile, you're on Phoebe's bird camera."

Amy looked alarmed. She put her knitting down and sipped her tea. "It was so foggy this morning. And Phoebe said the shadow was in the distance. I doubt they could make out details that clearly."

"I disagree. Don't you watch those crime lab shows?" Betty put her knitting aside and stood up. She stretched a moment, her hands at the small of her back. "They have all kinds of computer programs that put a face together from the tiniest bits of information. My kids had a puzzle where you made different faces, switching the eyes, nose, and mouth. It's like that, only computerized."

"I've seen those shows. And I remember those puzzles," Maggie said. "Once they come up with a possible face, they run it through computer programs to find a match. It's not just people who have been arrested and have a record; they have a huge database to draw from. It's quite amazing," Maggie added. "We'll just have to wait and see if there was anything significant on your camera, Phoebe. I guess the police will tell you when they return it."

"Maybe," Betty agreed. "But we've got a very active grapevine here in Osprey Shores. I have no doubt we'll be up to date with any progress the police make. Right, Amy?"

Amy was knitting again, her fingers working quickly, her gaze fixed on her clicking needles. "Yes, we do. Though you can't always believe what you hear. There will be plenty of plain old gossip and wild rumors flying around."

"Very true. Some of us call this place Hearsay Shores." Betty laughed quietly at her joke, then slipped her tote bag over her arm and adjusted her sunglasses. "Nice to chat and knit with you, ladies. Enjoy your stay."

"Nice to see you, too, Betty," Maggie said politely. "I'm sure we'll see you again before we go."

"I hope so." Betty smiled at everyone, and then headed out from the umbrella shade into the bold sunlight.

"I'm going for a swim. Anyone want to cool off with me?" Dana slipped her cover-up over her head. She wore a turquoise blue one-piece with a T-style back, designed for serious swimming.

"I'll take a dip with you." Lucy stood and pinned her hair up with a large clip.

"You two go ahead. I'll be in soon. I'm sure you want to do laps. I'm more of a floater." Suzanne's phone sounded, and she quickly answered. Lucy could tell from her suddenly serious expression and tone that the call was important.

The conversation was a quick one and obviously positive news. Suzanne said good-bye, dropped the phone, and jumped up from her seat, fists pumping in the air.

"Yes! The offer was accepted! They're going to contract on Monday. I never thought that old barn would go, but it just goes to show, there's a buyer out there for anything."

"Congratulations, Suzanne. It's amazing how you just sit here, sip iced tea, and make money." Maggie sounded envious.

"I'm sure it wasn't that easy." Lucy knew how hard Suzanne worked, driving her clients around endlessly, and working with property sellers, lawyers, and bankers. There were all the "lookers" who never bought, and all the people who almost bought, but then backed out at the last minute. Suzanne earned her money, that was for sure. She just made it look easy.

"Not exactly, Maggie. But it is a sweet moment when your chickens come home to roost. Or whatever the expression is." Suzanne sat back on her chair and put her feet up. "By the way, tonight's dinner is on me. Let's pick out a fun spot. With good food and a water view."

"Suzanne, that's too generous. You don't need to treat us," Maggie said.

"I want to. It's also in honor of Lucy's big last-fling weekend. Let's find a place with music and dancing."

Music and dancing? Lucy suddenly pictured a big disco ball with a lot of sunburned bodies squirming and writhing beneath it. She was just looking forward to a cup of chowder and a fisherman's platter, broiled, with salad on the side. Okay, maybe fries. But that was as far out of her comfort zone as her imagination wandered.

In fact, a rustic, homey eatery with window service and wooden picnic tables would have been fine, too. She didn't need a fancy restaurant with a hot night spot. She'd never been a fan of that sort of place, even when she'd been single. It was sort of intimidating.

"That sounds perfect and fun." Dana seconded the motion before Lucy could raise an objection. "Let's check the guidebook and look online for possibilities."

Amy looked up from her knitting. "I know a place you might like. It's in town, on a dock, with a great water view. Very stylish and popular, and the food is good, too. It's called The Warehouse. I think there's a DJ and dancing on the weekends."

Suzanne waved her hands, as if directing traffic. "Stop right there. That's perfect. Are you and Rob free? Can you join us?"

Amy didn't reply for a moment. "It's sweet of you to include us. But maybe you and your friends want to spend the night together on your own. I won't be insulted."

Lucy found Amy's response quite considerate. But their circle was hardly that exclusive. "Please come, Amy. We'd love for you to join us, and we'd love to meet Rob. This group definitely spends enough time alone together," she added with a laugh.

"More than enough," Maggie said, staring down at her knitting. "I mean that in a good way."

"In that case, we'd be happy to come." Amy rose and carefully gathered up her belongings. "I have to run. Send a text when you know what time to meet and all that."

"I will," Suzanne promised. "This is going to be fun. Dig out your dancing shoes, everyone. And psyche yourself up for some tequila shots."

"Oh dear. I can't meet either of those prerequisites, but I'll come anyway." Maggie glanced at Lucy and winked.

Dana laughed but Phoebe looked uneasy with the plan. She met Lucy's gaze with an eye roll.

Lucy smiled. "You told me to do something wild and crazy this weekend, Phoebe. Don't dancing and tequila shots count?"

"Not quite what I had in mind," Phoebe said quietly.

Phoebe was the youngest in their circle by far, and Lucy wondered if she dreaded being embarrassed by the sight of her older friends dancing and letting it all hang out. Like the way Lucy had felt when she was younger, watching her parents on the dance floor at a wedding doing the twist and the swim.

"Don't worry, we won't embarrass you," Lucy whispered. "If Suzanne goes off the rails, I'll rein her in."

"Good luck with that. You may as well stand in front of a speeding train," Phoebe whispered back. "It's cool. You guys do what you have to do. I know how to call a taxi if I need to slink away early."

"Good plan. I might join you."

Lucy had brought one long patio dress with a flower pattern and one pair of good earrings. The combination seemed to suit their evening plans, and the dress would hide most sins while dancing, she decided. She added a few touches of makeup, twisted her long hair into a big, low knot at the back of her head, then went downstairs to meet her friends.

As she walked out to the porch, she heard Maggie talking, relating the story Betty Rutledge had told them at the pool, about her brother and Julian Morton.

The horrid tale had lingered in Lucy's thoughts. The more she considered it, the more it seemed a good motive for murder. Betty Rutledge did not seem the type to push someone off a cliff; she didn't even seem physically capable of the feat. Lucy wondered what her friends thought.

"What about the brother? Is he still alive?" Suzanne asked Maggie as Lucy walked out onto the porch.

"Yes, he lives nearby in a town called Moody Beach. Betty said he works in insurance and raised a family. But he's never been quite the same."

Lucy took a seat on the porch swing next to Phoebe. "Even though it's decades later, it's the 'never been quite the same' that makes you wonder if he's still simmering with anger and would have taken revenge."

Everyone was sipping white wine and Suzanne had made them crostini—goat cheese mixed with basil and a touch of garlic, spread on lightly toasted rounds of French bread. Lucy picked one up and took a bite.

"Anything is possible. Maybe some incident in his current life made the past more acute and pushed him to finally act," Dana said. "It can happen like that. Even decades later. It is a shocking tale, and interesting that Betty would be so forthcoming. It's not the sort of personal story most people would disclose to strangers. And we really are strangers to her."

"I thought about that, too," Lucy managed around a mouthful of crostini. "Betty said she'd just told the police the whole story and expected it would get around the development quickly. Maybe she wants to convince everyone that Morton was a cruel man and doesn't deserve any pity."

"Maybe." Maggie took a sip of her wine. "She may also think that by being so forthcoming about this bad history, she won't look like a possible suspect." Lucy had finished the appetizer and was considering another. Their dinner reservation was for nine o'clock, much later than she and Matt ate dinner. Her stomach was grumbling.

"I thought of that, too." Suzanne nodded. "Hiding in plain sight. Though she would have to be hiding some muscles under that muumuu. She doesn't look capable of swinging a cat off of a cliff, never mind a six-foot man who was in fairly good shape for his age."

"Do you really have to use that analogy?" Phoebe complained. "Poor cat . . ."

Suzanne rolled her big eyes. "Sorry . . . you know what I mean."

"I do," Maggie replied. "She would have needed help. Which brings us back to her brother, I suppose. Though there seems no lack of neighbors who may have teamed up with her."

Before anyone could speculate who those candidates might be, Maggie glanced at her watch. "I think we should leave this puzzle to the police and head to the restaurant. We don't want to miss our reservation."

Dana set her wineglass down, too. "Good point. They barely fit us in. It must be the local hot spot."

"That's what I'm hoping." Suzanne placed the glasses on a tray along with the leftover appetizers. "I'll just dump this stuff in the kitchen, and we'll head out."

* * *

The nearby village of Eaton's Landing was small, but charming, filled with shops, galleries, coffeehouses, and restaurants.

"This place is adorable." Dana was watching out her window as they cruised down Main Street. "We'll have to come back and go shopping."

Suzanne nodded. "Agreed. Maybe tomorrow? Amy said the waterfront is at the end of Main Street. She said to look for signs for the Old Dock. I think we're headed straight for it."

Suzanne's calculations were correct. Main Street ended in another lively area, with more restaurants, bars, and even a theater, all set along a large waterfront park. They followed the signs and soon found their destination.

The eatery still looked like a warehouse, except for a large black and gold sign and a scarlet awning above the entrance. Valets in scarlet windbreakers jumped forward to open the vehicle's doors. As Lucy's group emerged, Suzanne tossed a young man her keys.

"Having dinner, ma'am?" the valet asked.

"We'll be here for a while. Park it wherever you like, fellas."

Lucy glanced at Dana, who was biting back a smile. "I've never gone out partying with Suzanne before. She's very . . . committed," Dana whispered.

Lucy thought that was a diplomatic way of putting it. "I think we need a designated driver," she whispered back.

The restaurant was on the first floor, below the dance club. The dining room was cavernous and lively. Not exactly Lucy's favorite sort of place, but fun for a night out with the girls. Exposed brick, worn wooden beams and pipes, and industrial chic touches created an edgy mix. Steel and wood tables were offset with plush leather seats in the bold scarlet signature color. A huge glass wall framed a view of the harbor and twinkling lights along the waterfront.

"Our table isn't ready," Suzanne announced after chatting with a hostess. "Let's wait at the bar. I don't think Amy and Rob are here yet, either."

The bar area was also stylish and edgy looking, and very crowded. The friends huddled together, waiting to order drinks.

A bartender stood nearby, pouring from different bottles into a blender, her hands moving as swiftly as a juggler's. Lucy tried to catch her eye, but she was clearly concentrating on her recipe.

Lucy suddenly recognized her. It was Meredith Quinn, the yoga teacher, though she looked much different tonight in a tailored scarlet blouse and sleek black pants, her hair pulled back in a tight ballerina bun. Her appearance seemed surprising and totally out of sync with her surroundings.

Maybe because she identified Meredith with Amy's knitting group and the yoga studio? This place was a different planet from those worlds.

Meredith was somewhat older than most of the staff, but there probably wasn't much money in yoga instruction, even at the Osprey Shores Fitness Center, and a bartender at The Warehouse would definitely earn good tips.

Lucy had often heard it was hard to make a living in a resort town, and people who lived there year-round had to string together two, or even three jobs to make ends meet. That was the downside of living in such beautiful surroundings.

After Meredith had poured and served the blender drink, she walked over to Lucy's group, greeting them with a smile.

"Nice to see you, ladies. Here for dinner, or just drinks and dancing?"

"We'll start with dinner and see how that goes," Lucy replied. "It's wild in here."

"Just the usual Friday night. And it isn't even the height of the season. Are you out on the town?"

"We're kickin' up our heels a bit," Suzanne replied. "Is the music good? What time does it start?"

"Around ten. It's definitely loud. I'm not sure if that's good or bad." Meredith winced with a playful grin as she wiped the bar with a fresh towel. "Can I get you anything to drink?"

Everyone gave their orders, mostly white wine, though Suzanne read the special cocktail menu with care and eventually ordered something called a Bikini-tini. Lucy asked for sparkling water with lime. She'd never driven Suzanne's truck-like SUV, but this could be the night. Somebody had to stay sober, she decided.

Amy and Rob found them in the crowd, and Amy introduced her husband. He shook hands all around, looking genuinely pleased to meet Amy's friends.

He wasn't a tall man, probably about her own height, Lucy guessed, five foot nine or ten, but he looked very fit and had an air of success about him. Dressed in a navy linen blazer and grey pants with a stark white shirt that contrasted with his tanned face and dark hair, he seemed quiet and serious, listening thoughtfully to their chatter. Maybe he was a little shy or self-conscious, the only man among the gaggle of women. He did have a bright, warm smile.

Lucy couldn't picture him as a fisherman. Maybe because all the die-hard fishermen she knew back in Plum Harbor were a bit grubby looking. Rob Cutler looked too neat and clean shaven, often smoothing back his dark hair with his hand, too particular to handle squirming bait or fish guts. He seemed more like a golfing type.

He looked amused as Suzanne taste tested her drink. "What exactly is in a Bikini-tini?"

Suzanne shrugged. "I'm not sure. It's sort of a martini mixed with pineapple juice. I've always wanted to wear a teeny bikini. At least I can drink one." She lifted her glass and toasted her companions as they laughed.

Lucy was the last to be served. "Here you go. I didn't forget you." Meredith set down a tall, fizzling glass on a cocktail napkin.

Lucy thanked her and took a sip. "Don't mind Suzanne. She's acting out a little tonight. I'm sure you've had an unsettling day. I mean, after hearing about Dr. Morton." *Your ex-husband, who was pushed off a cliff.* The words ran through Lucy's head, but, of course, she didn't say them aloud.

Meredith's expression turned grim, and she rubbed a spot on the bar with extra vigor, but Lucy couldn't tell if she was sad or angry.

"I won't be a hypocrite and say I'll mourn the man's passing, but I didn't wish him ill. Heaven knows I'd have every right. It may sound coldhearted, but I honestly don't feel anything. Despite all the years we were married, he was always a stranger."

She looked up at Lucy, seeming surprised at her own admission. Lucy didn't know what to say.

Meredith returned to tidying the bar. She straightened a pile of napkins and filled a glass of stirrers. "I was young when we married. Twenty-two. Julian was almost twenty years older, accomplished, successful. He'd published books and taught a class or two at the college I attended. That's how we met, in a coffeehouse on campus. I couldn't believe he was attracted to me. I felt honored. He dazzled me. Swept me off my feet. He had a forceful personality and could be charming when he wanted something. Or someone."

She seemed wistful and lost in her memories. Then she looked back at Lucy. "I didn't know that what I felt wasn't love, not real love. I know now, thank goodness, what it means to feel that another person can see your true self and love you completely. No false flattery or emotional manipulation. With Julian, I was always on my toes, afraid of his judgment and rejection. And his anger. Real love is a great gift, Lucy. If you ever find it, hang on with both hands."

Lucy smiled, feeling suddenly shy. "I will. I mean, I am. I'm getting married next weekend," she confided. "I do know what you mean."

Meredith gave Lucy a wide, warm smile. "Good for you. I wish you every happiness." She drew out two tall tap beers and placed them before her customers without spilling a drop of foam. "Do you have any children?"

Lucy shook her head. "My fiancé has a daughter from his first marriage. She's sweetheart."

"That's great. But don't deny yourself the wonder of having a child. My son Cory was the best thing to come out of my marriage, by far. I'd do it all over again, to know I'd have him."

"How old is he?"

"Twenty-five. Julian gave me a lot of grief, but I stayed in the marriage until Cory was ready for college. So I guess we were divorced about seven or eight years ago. Cory didn't inherit his father's scientific talents, but he has a good mind for business. He's in grad school, in Boston, finishing an MBA."

"How did he take the news? Is he okay?" Lucy wondered if she was getting too personal, but Meredith had been so open about her feelings and her past.

"He was shocked, especially when he heard the way it happened. But Julian was an awful father. They were never close, even though I know Cory wished it could have been different. But a person can't give what they don't have. I always told my son that, though I don't know if it made him feel any better." Meredith had been mixing a drink in a shaker with chopped ice, and shook it forcefully. "I have a feeling he still held out hope that someday the relationship would change. And now it's too late."

She poured the pale pink liquid through a strainer into three martini glasses, then garnished the edges with juicy slices of orange and sprigs of mint. "Cory is on his way up to Maine now. Last I heard, Julian didn't leave him anything in his will. Even though Cory is his only child, that didn't mean much to Julian."

It sounded to Lucy as if Meredith and her ex-husband had discussed Cory and Julian's will recently. But she felt it would sound too nosey to ask.

"Julian probably left it all to some strange scientific foundation," Meredith added. "He once told me that when he died, he planned to have his head frozen at some weird laboratory, so someday, he could come back from the dead. When they figured out how to clone him a new body, I mean."

It was a ghastly thought, though Lucy had read about that theoretical technology somewhere. "I think I've heard of that. Cryonics?"

"That's it. Must have cost him a fortune to sign up." Meredith set the martini glasses on a tray at the end of the bar, and a waitress whisked them away. Then Meredith began to laugh so hard that she started to cough. She covered her mouth with a wad of napkins and turned away from Lucy.

"Excuse me." She finally caught her breath and shook

her head. "It just strikes me as funny. Julian was one of the most despised people I've ever known. Who would want him to get a do-over?"

Lucy offered a small smile at the dark humor. The manner in which Julian had died, bouncing down a rocky cliff, probably nixed the head-freezing plan. No danger of a do-over now.

Even though she claimed not to feel anything about his death one way or the other, Meredith had spoken some harsh words against her ex-husband. She clearly did feel something. And it wasn't sorrow.

A hostess came to the bar and called Suzanne's name. "Here we are!" Suzanne waved to her, and then herded the group, drink in hand. "Come along, everyone. Our table is ready. Finally."

Lucy said goodnight to Meredith and followed her friends through the softly lit dining room. They were led to a large table by the window. Outside, the harbor looked dark and smooth, and the curving coastline was dotted with golden lights. Out on a rocky peninsula, a lighthouse blinked against the inky blue sky.

"Isn't this lovely," Dana said as everyone found a seat. "Thanks for steering us here, Amy. It has such a great atmosphere."

"And the food is good. I'll vouch for that." Rob smiled and patted his stomach, which was perfectly flat. He looked like the type of guy who watched his waistline and was careful about his appearance. Not vain, exactly, but someone who liked to stay young and fit looking.

Lucy found herself seated next to him with Amy on his other side. She slipped her napkin on her lap and opened her menu. "What do you recommend, Rob?" she asked, browsing the selections.

"Everything's good. The catch of the day is always very fresh and tasty," he added.

"We should be eating more 'catch of the day,' but Rob never seems to catch anything when he goes out fishing." Amy's face was half-hidden by her menu as she delivered the remark.

Rob's cheeks flushed, and his mouth got tight. Lucy could see the reaction even in the low light. Perhaps the time he spent out on the beach, surf casting, was a sore point for them.

"Not for lack of trying, honey. As I often tell you, those striped bass are too smart for me. I'll bring home a nice dinner for us one of these days."

"I think it must be hard to fish with a rod and reel. Most fishermen use radar to find fish these days," Suzanne said. "Which doesn't seem fair to me at all."

"My husband is all for giving the fish a fighting chance." Amy reached over and patted his hand. "As long as he enjoys it. That's what counts."

"That I do." Rob looked back at his menu.

"How long have you been surf casting?" Maggie asked.

"I took it up this past spring, but it takes a while to get the knack. I might invest in a lesson or two."

"Have you lived in Osprey Shores long?" Lucy asked.

"Almost two years," Amy replied. "We raised our girls in California. Rob had a job at a biotech firm lab there. But once our daughters left for college, we decided to come back to New England."

"I also had a small side business in medical technology. I still do some consulting."

Dana closed her menu and placed it on the table. "Amy says you're a famous inventor, Rob. She said you have a few patents and have invented some amazing gadgets. One for cardiac patients?"

Rob looked embarrassed again, but this time, not in an angry way. Pleased by the attention, he seemed a modest man. "Amy brags about me too much, but, yes, I've come up with some gadgets. I've been very lucky. We're comfortable, and we've been able to retire earlier than most people." He smiled at Amy and put his arm around the back of her chair.

"It think that's so cool. So impressive, I mean," Suzanne said. "What sort of things have you invented?"

"Let's see . . . my most recent idea was a microchip that's inserted in the heart muscle of patients with chronic heart failure. The chip transmits their vital signs—pulse, blood pressure, and blood flow through the major arteries—through the internet. Right now many of these patients need to hook themselves up at night to devices that record and transmit the information overnight, but the chip streamlines that process, and the information output is ongoing. They just wave a reader over their chest, press a button, and the report goes directly to their doctor, who can even read it on a smartphone."

"That's amazing. And so helpful," Lucy said.

"It's much more accurate and up-to-date info as well. A doctor can respond immediately and adjust medication or let the patient know they need to come into the hospital."

"It's very . . . futuristic," Dana said. "Like the scanner that Bones used on *Star Trek*."

"It reminds me of putting a chip in your cat or dog," Phoebe said, "so if they get lost, you can find them."

Rob laughed. "It's not quite same technology. But in the ball park."

"His most amazing invention is a teeny, tiny camera used in heart surgery, for doing a bypass or valve replacement," Amy said. "Rob figured out how to shape the lens so that it could take in views from all different angles. Sort of like . . . well, a disco ball." She laughed and shrugged. "Unfortunately, he didn't get much credit for that breakthrough."

Rob gave her a look. Lucy wondered if he was annoyed at the analogy, or her admission of him missing out.

"That was very early in my career. We all have to pay our dues."

He shrugged. "Though I would describe the device more like the eye structure of a fly. That's where I got my idea. They can see what's coming from all directions."

"That must be why they're so hard to swat. I thought I just had bad reflexes. They always outsmart me." Phoebe seemed pleased to learn this fun fact.

"Flies aren't smart, Phoebe. They just have amazing eyesight. 'Look deep into nature, and then you will understand everything better.' Albert Einstein said that. I look to nature for models of engineering and technology. The simplicity and beauty of natural forms and organisms seem to hold the secret to so many questions we ask in the lab."

Amy smiled and gazed around the table, proud of her husband's thoughtful reply. Robert Cutler was an intelligent and deep-thinking person, there was no doubt. And a bit more poetic than Lucy expected.

A waitress arrived and took their order. Sorting through the many complicated-sounding gourmet offerings, Lucy finally settled on a dish called GRILLED BOUNTY FROM THE SEA—a fancy name for a fisherman's platter, she decided. Suzanne had teased her mercilessly, egging her on to order the most expensive dish, ASIAN FUSION LOBSTER TAILS WITH GINGER-MANGO CHUTNEY.

"I'm not big on foods that are . . . fused," Lucy replied simply. "To each her own."

"Here, here," Maggie raised her glass and nodded at Lucy. "You order the lobster if you like, Suzanne. It's your party."

"I think I will. Another Teeny Bikini . . . I mean Bikini-tini would be nice, too," Suzanne told their waitress.

"I'll have another sparkling water, please," Lucy added.

She was definitely driving that SUV tonight. Now there was no question.

The appetizer course soon arrived, and the rest of the meal passed with pleasant conversation about local sights to visit and knitting projects. As dessert and coffee were served, Lucy heard pounding music coming from the floor above. It seemed to be shaking the light fixtures.

"Sounds like the dance club is open. I'm not sure I have enough energy for that segment of the evening," Maggie said. "It's been quite a day."

"First the fog, and then the news about Dr. Morton," Suzanne said. "That was a downer. No pun intended. That's why I think we need a little lift. We need to shake out the toxins."

Rob laughed. "Interesting theory. In the olden days, people did try to dance out toxins, especially bites from poisonous insects," he said. "The Italian Tarantella for instance."

"I know it well. Though it's not danced much at Italian weddings anymore," Maggie remarked.

"I love a circle dance at a wedding. Or a conga line. It really gets the party going. Are you jotting this down, Lucy?" Suzanne glanced across the table. She was smiling, but Lucy wasn't sure if she was serious or not.

"Even though we didn't know Dr. Morton, it was upsetting to hear about his death. Did you you know him?" Dana asked the Cutlers.

Amy shook her head, spooning up a last bite of crème brûlée. Rob stirred a sugar cube into his cappuccino and set the cup aside. He answered for both of them. "Only from a distance. We may have exchanged a few words, but he wasn't the friendliest guy around."

"I understand that Dr. Morton also invented medical devices. In fact, he worked in the same area as you. Cardiology," Maggie said. She didn't usually order dessert, but

Lucy knew that she could never resist Key lime pie. Lucy watched her turn her dish to regard the slice from a different angle of attack.

"Who told you that?" Rob sounded curious.

"Betty Rutledge," Lucy replied. "She seems to know a lot about Dr. Morton. She knew him when he was a boy." Lucy decided to stop there, unsure if Betty's story was hers to tell.

"Morton and I were in the same area of research, but it's a big field. I've probably read a study he published or attended the same conference. It's hard to say. But I didn't know him professionally." Rob blew on the foamy top of his coffee and took a sip.

Maggie seemed to be enjoying her pie, but did pause to reply. "The police definitely suspect foul play. They took Phoebe's camera. They wanted to look at the photographs she took this morning on the cliff walk and beach while she was out bird watching."

"They did?" Rob set his coffee down and glanced at Amy. Lucy could tell that Amy had not told him about Phoebe's camera. "What were they looking for exactly?"

Phoebe shrugged. "I hardly saw a soul out there. Just the birds and a few fishermen on the beach. Maybe some people out walking who stopped to see the body. I didn't see Dr. Morton when I was on the cliff walk, but I did find a shadow in the background of one shot. It was in the shrubbery near the spot where he fell. I couldn't tell if it was a person or not."

Rob nodded. "Interesting."

"It is all very interesting," Amy said, setting the empty dessert ramekin aside. "But I think we should get upstairs to the music. Before we lose the inspiration."

"My thoughts exactly." Suzanne signaled for the check and despite everyone's protest, wouldn't let her friends contribute. "It's my party. For Lucy," she added. "Now go upstairs and shake that little booty, girlfriend," she ordered Lucy. "It will be good practice for your wedding. You are going to dance then, aren't you?"

Lucy felt embarrassed with everyone laughing and staring at her. "Of course I am. But for goodness sakes, Suzanne . . . get a grip."

Suzanne looked suddenly contrite. "I'm sorry. You know my intentions are good. It is time to break out of your little Lucy shell. We don't want you to have any regrets when you look back on your last-fling weekend."

Why did everyone keep calling it that? As if she had a terminal disease?

"All right. Let's dance. On one condition, Party-Hardy Sue. You give me the car keys."

Suzanne laughed. Her lobster-tail dinner and molten fudge cake had absorbed most of the Bikini-tini effect, but Lucy didn't want to take any chances. The night was young, and the bar was still open.

"Deal. Love the nickname. I might put it on my business cards. Or maybe get a personalized license plate."

Dana rose from her seat and placed her dinner napkin on the table. "Onward and upward."

"Indeed." Maggie stood up and grabbed her purse. She did not look very happy about the plan but didn't want to ruin anyone else's fun, Lucy suspected. "I need the ladies' room. I'll meet you upstairs."

"I'll come with you, Mag." Lucy quickly followed, buying time before her dance floor debut. She would wait until the floor was so crowded, no one would notice her out there. And after a few earsplitting songs, they could surely persuade Suzanne that it was time to go.

Maggie set off for the restroom at a brisk pace, dodging waiters and waitresses. Lucy couldn't keep up. She recalled seeing a sign near the bar and found her way.

As she walked past the long row of stools, Meredith

waved. Lucy noticed her speaking to a man who sat at the end of the bar, but Meredith left him when another customer summoned her.

Lucy only saw him from the back. He wore a tweed sports coat and tailored shirt. Something about him seemed vaguely familiar. When he turned, her guess was confirmed. It was Lewis Fielding from Amy's knitting group.

He greeted her with a smile. "Hi Lucy. Here with your friends?"

"We just had dinner. We're going upstairs for the music . . . if you can call it that."

"I wouldn't myself. More like a heavy, amplified back beat. It does bring in the crowds on the weekends."

"I can see that." She wondered what had brought him to The Warehouse on a Saturday night. He didn't seem the type for a heavy, amplified beat. More the type for baroque harmonies. He was also older than most of the customers. But, perhaps, Lewis was out hoping to meet someone. He did seem the picture of a lonely, single guy, eating his dinner alone at the bar.

"Enjoying your stay so far?"

"Mostly. We were lucky the weather cleared up today. We spent the afternoon at the pool. Though the bad news about Dr. Morton did cast a shadow."

Lewis nodded with an empathetic expression. "It's shaken the whole community. How did you hear about it?"

"Dana and I were in Meredith's yoga studio. So many police cars were flying by, Meredith decided to cancel class. We went out and followed the crowd, and soon heard Morton had fallen—or been pushed—off the cliff."

"I was just getting back from the hospital. One of my patients had a late-night emergency. I had no idea what was going on, but I heard pretty quickly. Not many secrets around here," he added.

There were some secrets, Lucy wanted to say. Like who pushed Dr. Morton. But she didn't want to contradict him.

"I visited Tanya this afternoon, to offer my condolences and support," he added. "I don't know if she'll hold a memorial service. She doesn't think her husband would have wanted one. I was thinking of organizing a support circle at the mansion. Maybe tomorrow night. People may want to share their feelings."

"That sounds . . . helpful," Lucy replied carefully. From what Lucy had heard, the predominant feeling about Morton's passing seemed to be relief and good riddance.

Lewis laughed. He had a nice smile and warm, dark eyes. An attractive man for his age, she thought.

"I know what you're thinking. Most people disliked the man. That's true. But it can be even harder to find closure when a mourner is left with anger and negative feelings."

"In that case, from what I've heard today, I'm sure the support circle would be very helpful. And popular."

"Maybe I should combine the gathering with some knitting. Knitting is great relaxation therapy. As effective as meditation. Gets the good brain chemicals going."

"I can't argue with that. How will we know if you're holding the group?"

"I'll post some flyers in the mansion. Word will get around."

"I'll keep a look out." Lucy said goodnight and headed on her way.

She was almost certain her friends wouldn't be interested in taking part in Lewis's support circle, even if knitting was involved. But she was curious. Curious to see who would turn up.

Once upstairs, Lucy searched the dark, crowded scene. She quickly spotted Suzanne in the middle of the dance floor, showing off her moves. Dana may have been dancing with her. It was hard to tell if Dana wanted to own up to the connection.

Amy and Rob danced nearby, too, in a much more sedate style, but they seemed to be enjoying themselves. Maggie and Phoebe stood off in a corner, near the bar. Lucy walked up to them.

"I won't dance, don't ask me," Maggie greeted her.

"I wasn't going to. Isn't that an old song?" Lucy nearly had to shout to be heard over the music.

"It is. Even outdates my era," Maggie remarked.

"I'll dance with you," Phoebe shouted eagerly.

"What about your poison ivy?" Lucy asked, fishing for an excuse.

"I hardly notice it now. I took an antihistamine."

"Oh . . . great." Lucy tried to sound happy about that news, but she had hoped to avoid dancing.

Her friend saw right through her. "Come on, Lucy. Tonight's the night. You know what Suzanne said," Phoebe reminded her.

"I remember. It doesn't bear repeating."

" 'Non, je ne regrette rien'," Maggie replied in a lilting tone. "That's an old one too. Édith Piaf?"

"I know it well, Mag."

The DJ had switched to a pop tune from a few summers back, one Lucy did know—"All the Single Ladies."

"Okay, Phoebe. Sounds like they're playing our song. Let's just do it."

Pleased by the invitation, Phoebe grabbed Lucy's hand and tugged her out to the middle of the floor, her flouncy skirt swaying to the rhythm.

Maggie toasted them from the sideline. "Dance out the toxins, Lucy, as Suzanne says. You have less than a week before Matt 'puts a ring on it.' "

*   *   *

Contrary to her prediction—or was just a naïve hope?—Lucy's friends insisted on staying at the dance club for more than just a few songs. After a while, she enjoyed the dancing, too, and with Phoebe and Suzanne egging her on, they even sent a selfie to Matt. They all looked sweaty and looped. Lucy especially, though she hadn't taken a sip of alcohol all night. She hoped he'd get a laugh out of it.

Amy and Rob left a little before midnight. But not before Amy insisted that they come to her house for brunch the next day. Lucy and her friends happily accepted. Lucy hoped her group would soon follow the Cutlers, but Suzanne had to be dragged off the dance floor closer to 2:00 AM, insisting that she dance out a medley of ABBA's greatest hits.

Lucy and Maggie, the most sober in the group, herded the others down to the exit and into Suzanne's SUV. Lucy strapped herself into the driver's seat.

She'd never driven a truck, but the Sequoia was close enough. She shook off a bit of drowsiness from the late hour and turned to her friends. "Here we go, headed home everyone. I'm going to take it slow, but make sure you're wearing seat belts."

Suzanne was already asleep, lightly snoring, her head leaning on the window. Phoebe reached over and checked her belt.

Maggie sat at the other window and Phoebe, in the middle. They both looked as if they would drift off as soon as the Sequoia got rolling. Dana sat in the passenger seat, looking a bit more awake and alert than the others. Lucy was thankful for that. She knew the directions—it was almost a straight shot from the village to Osprey Shores—but it was nice to have someone to chat with. So I can stay awake, too, she thought.

As Lucy expected, her friends in the backseat were all

fast asleep before they'd even driven through the village. Dana did stay awake for a while, but once they came to the long, dark stretch of road that led to the land bridge, Dana's head tilted toward the window, and soon her eyes closed, too.

Lucy turned onto the land bridge, steering carefully down the narrow, two-lane road and feeling even more grateful that she had skipped the cocktails all night. There was a guardrail, but it wasn't very reassuring. Lucy guessed it was high tide by the waves crashing against the huge rocks on either side of the bridge. The moon was almost full and cast a silver light over the rippling waves—a lovely sight, but distracting, Lucy thought. Finally, she reached the other side of the bridge.

It was a short ride from the land bridge to Osprey Shores, and Lucy felt relieved as she turned the big vehicle into the gate. She thought for sure that talking to the security guard would wake her friends, but they slept soundly as she gave her name and the address of the cottage.

The pretty, curving lanes were silent and empty. Lucy drove slowly, looking for the street that led to their cottage. Somehow, she took a wrong turn and ended up on a street called Hurricane Hill. Once she realized she was in the wrong place, she pulled into the first driveway to turn around.

Lucy was surprised to see a man at the front door of the cottage on the property. He didn't seem to notice the SUV in the driveway, maybe because he was too busy knocking very loudly, almost pounding, on the door.

Lights came on in the house. Lucy was already backing the Sequoia out onto the street, but the vehicle was big and the driveway narrow. There was a mailbox on a post at the curb and she didn't want to mow it down.

She didn't know what was going on at this cottage, but

it seemed an emergency. As she slowly backed the vehicle toward the street, the man turned to look at them.

Lucy saw his face clearly. It was Sam Briggs. He stared at the vehicle a moment. She wondered if he would recognize her and her friends.

The front door flew open. Tanya Morton stood in the doorway wearing a pale pink robe and a very angry expression. She peered out at the driveway for a moment, then opened the door wide enough for Sam to go inside. The door quickly slammed shut.

Lucy finally reached the end of the driveway and turned the vehicle around on the street. She was still not sure of the way back to the cottage and decided to head in the direction of the gatehouse and look for the turn again. As she rounded the next corner, she noticed a white pickup truck parked on the otherwise empty street. Lucy recognized the mermaid symbol on the truck's door as she drove by. It was Sam Briggs's truck, she guessed, parked a discreet distance from Tanya Morton's cottage to avoid gossip.

She wondered what she'd just witnessed. Why would Sam Briggs be banging on Tanya Morton's door in the very small hours of the morning? Were they having an affair? It certainly seemed possible, though there could be some other reason for the nocturnal visit.

Maybe tomorrow, when her friends were awake and alert again, she would tell them about this strange sight and they could spin out some theories.

Chapter 5

Lucy was the first one up the next morning. She took her mug of coffee out to the front porch and gazed at the clear blue sky and softly rolling whitecaps. The sun still hugged the horizon, and it seemed perfect weather for a bike ride.

Just as she was deciding, Dana came outside with a mug of tea, still in her pajamas, too. "Beautiful day. I'm so glad there's no fog this morning."

"There was a little last night, when we were on the way back from the club. The rest of you were too sleepy to notice."

"Sorry. One minute we were talking, and the next thing I knew we were at the cottage, and you were waking me up." Dana sipped from her mug. "By the way, it was nice of you to be the designated driver. Especially since this is supposed to be your wild weekend."

Lucy shrugged. "I didn't mind. I don't need all the extra calories in those fancy club drinks right now."

"Very true," Dana nodded.

Lucy considered telling Dana about the wrong turn, and how she'd ended up in front of Dr. Morton's cottage and seen Sam Briggs visiting Tanya at two in the morning, or maybe even later.

But before she could mention it, Dana said, "I was thinking of exploring the cliff walk. Want to join me?"

"I was thinking of the same thing. But on my bike. What time are we due at Amy's? Do you know?"

"Not until eleven-thirty. We have plenty of time. Mind if I join you?"

"That would be fun . . . but you didn't bring your bike."

"I spotted a few loaners outside the fitness center. It looks like anyone can use them. They probably weigh a ton and have no gears left, but I'll try my best to keep up with you," Dana offered with an appealing grin.

For a long time, Dana was the rider with the sleek, imported cycle, and Lucy had been pedaling around on a yard-sale clunker, enduring Dana's teasing. Last summer, Matt had given her a sleek, state-of-the-art bike for her birthday. Along with an engagement ring, hidden in a state-of-the-art water bottle.

"That's okay. I don't mind a slower pace today. After clubbing with you guys, I hope my legs can push the pedals."

"I actually had a leg cramp last night from all that dancing," Dana confided with a laugh. "Don't tell anyone. It made me feel old."

"No worries. I definitely used some muscles that have not seen action in a while. Bananas are the cure," Lucy promised. "And some yogurt. Let's have a quick bite and head out."

A short time later, Lucy and Dana were pedaling on the cliff path. Though she preferred biking on pavement, the tires on her fitness-style cycle handled the rough gravel easily. Dana's borrowed bike had thick mountain bike tires, which gripped the gravel, but slowed her down even more.

They kept to the middle and the right side of the path,

though Lucy knew that wasn't the correct lane to ride in. The view off the cliff, to the left and just beyond the fence rail, made them both nervous and even gave Lucy a touch of vertigo.

The path opened up at one point, with a viewing spot. Lucy peeked over the edge where the ocean crashed on a rocky shoreline, and sea birds were circling, fighting each other for bits of a fish that one had caught and held clamped in its beak.

"We're up so high, the birds are flying below us. Did you notice that?" Lucy asked.

"I did. I think it's more than a hundred and fifty feet down to the beach from here. Wait. . . . Let me take a photo for Phoebe. She'd like to see this."

Lucy stepped back from the edge and even grabbed the back of Dana's nylon biking shirt as Dana tried to catch a good shot of the circling sea birds.

"It's nice of you to think of Phoebe. But let's not get carried away. Or blown away."

Dana laughed and stepped back. "Thanks, pal. I nearly lost track of my footing. Maybe the same thing happened to Morton. Maybe he just got carried away, taking a selfie."

"I doubt it, but I can see the headline if that turns out to be what really happened—SELFIE OF DEATH." Dana laughed as Lucy took a sip from her water bottle. "I wonder if he heard a mermaid singing in the fog, and she cast a spell on him. You know, like Ezra Cooperage, the tycoon who built Mermaid Manor?"

" 'I have heard the mermaids singing, each to each. I do not think they will sing to me,' " Dana replied.

"T.S. Eliot. One of my favorite poems." Lucy turned and looked out at the view again. "Aside from those far-fetched theories, I can easily see how someone who wanted Morton out of the way could cause a tumble from this spot."

"Me, too." Dana got back on her bike. "It doesn't take too much imagination, either."

They rode on for a while, until the walk curved around a bench and a clump of shrubbery. Then the path was blocked by yellow crime scene tape. Lucy and Dana hopped off their bikes and looked over the area within the tape.

Lucy pointed at the path. "Look at those greyish-white bits. That's not gravel. It looks like plaster. I bet the investigators took a few shoe impressions. Those tracks look large, like they were made by a man's shoe."

Dana peered at the spaces where the plaster casts had been made. "Either that, or a woman with exceptionally large feet." She glanced at Lucy. "You're tall. What size shoe do you take?"

"Oh, usually a nine. Or a nine and a half. Depends on the shoe . . . sometimes a ten," she admitted.

"Don't be embarrassed, Lucy. You can't help your shoe size. You're pretty tall. You might tip over if your feet were any smaller."

"Good point. I never thought of that," Lucy said drily. "What else do you think they found?"

"There were probably some bloodstains on the rocks. I bet they were looking for clues all along the cliffside, trying to determine the path of Morton's fall. That's why they had people in hazmat suits suspended from the cliff yesterday."

"I bet they were looking for anything," Lucy agreed. "The brush just behind the fence looks smashed down, too. I wonder if the police did that, searching the area. Or if this was the place where Morton fell. Maybe the killer had to give an extra push to get him over the edge."

"Or drag the body, if he was hit on the head with a stone, as Amy said." Dana's expression was grim as she stared at the spot Lucy had noticed. The image gave Lucy chills. "Whoever killed Morton must have known his habits and waited for him."

"Probably. We'd better be careful around here. Don't step off the path. It's loaded with poison ivy." Lucy had learned to spot the pesky weed quickly—the distinctive formation of three green leaves and red stems—which grew in abundance on either side of the path.

"Goodness. Look at that." Dana stood very still for a moment. "I can catch it just by looking at it."

"Me, too. Let's get out of here."

They carefully walked their bikes around the shrubbery and viewing bench, and the circle of crime scene tape. Then they got back on the path and began riding again.

"There must have been some clear physical evidence at the scene for the police to suspect foul play," Lucy said after a while.

"There must have been something in addition to the blow to Morton's head. It sounds like they have no eye-witnesses and no security cameras along the walk. There's Phoebe's shadow photo, but I don't think that will amount to much."

Lucy agreed, despite all the fancy face-recognition technology out there. "There doesn't seem much evidence for them to go on at all."

"Except for a long list of people who despised the man," Dana replied. "I'm sure they'll start with that."

They pedaled along in silence a few moments, then Lucy said, "When I was driving last night, and you were all asleep, I saw something very interesting."

Dana turned to her. "Really? What was that?"

"I made a wrong turn after I came into the development and ended up in front of Dr. Morton's cottage. I saw Sam Briggs at Tanya Morton's front door, knocking really hard with his fist. Like he was very angry. Or maybe he had been knocking a long time and she hadn't heard him."

"Really? Did she open the door?"

"Yes, she did. She looked annoyed, as if she'd been sleeping, but she let him in."

"That is interesting."

"When I finally found my way out of the cul-de-sac, I spotted his truck parked a street or two away. I guess he didn't want to park in front of her cottage for some reason."

"I can think of a few."

"I was thinking about it and remembered that he was the one who brought her down to the cliff walk and the police needed her to identify Dr. Morton's body."

"Come to think of it, I recall her coming in a white pickup truck, too. I thought it was just a neighbor or friend driving her over because she was shaken up."

"No, it was him. He got out of the truck and waited a while, until the police drove her away in that dune buggy."

"I didn't notice that either," Dana said. "But in light of what you saw last night, it would be interesting to know why Sam ended up driving her. He must have been with her when she got the news. Usually, the police will visit personally, and then bring the next of kin to identify a body. But maybe Tayna heard it from a neighbor, and Sam was with her."

"Yes, that's what I thought, too." They hit a hill and Lucy shifted gears, bearing down on the pedals. "Maybe they're having an affair. We know she wanted a divorce from Morton."

Dana was behind her, her bike taking the hill at a slower pace. "That's the first thing that comes to mind, but it would be tricky in this community to dally with the local handyman. I wonder if Amy has heard any gossip. We should ask her."

"Good idea," Lucy agreed. "I'm sure Dr. Morton will come up in the conversation at brunch sooner or later."

"No doubt," Dana said between huffing breaths. Finally, they reached the top of the hill and stopped for a moment. Lucy took a swig from her water bottle. It had been worth it to push up the hill. The view was stunning.

"I know it doesn't seem like much. But I think you should tell the police what you saw, Lucy."

"Do you really?" Maybe Dana was right. But Lucy was on vacation and didn't want to get involved. "Can't the police solve this without my gossipy tidbit?"

"Maybe . . . maybe not. They probably already have Tanya on their list of suspects, due to the divorce and money issues. Spouses are often the culprits in cases like this one. What you saw would give them more to go on, in that direction."

"I guess so, but . . . ugh. I hope I don't have to give a statement or testify in court or anything like that. I'm on vacation. My last fling. I really don't want to get involved."

"I'm sure you don't. Just think about it," Dana suggested. "I know you'll do the right thing."

"Thanks . . . that makes me feel guilty already."

Dana laughed. "I didn't mean it that way."

"I know. The funny thing is, I never saw Sam Briggs as Tanya's type. But opposites do attract."

"Even if they are having a dalliance, I agree. I don't see Tanya sticking with a blue collar guy like Briggs for long," Dana said between gulps of cold water. "I think he'd just be a transitional relationship."

Lucy laughed. "You would come up with something like that."

When they returned to the cottage, everyone was up and getting ready to meet Amy for brunch at her cottage.

Suzanne emerged from the bathroom, a towel wrapped around her wet hair. She looked groggy and even a bit grumpy. Definitely a one hundred and eighty degree turn in her mood since last night.

She poured herself a cup of coffee and swallowed some ibuprofen. Dana glanced at Lucy. Lucy could tell that they were both dying to tease Party-Hardy Sue about too many Bikini-tinis. But Lucy didn't want to rub it in. Suzanne looked like she already regretted her indulgence.

"Look at you two. Out exercising already? How disgustingly virtuous." Suzanne flopped on the couch with her coffee mug dangling from one hand.

"We went for a bike ride," Lucy said. "A short one, but I'm feeling it. Must be all the dancing last night."

"Tell me about it." Suzanne rolled her eyes and pressed a hand to her forehead. "But it was so much fun. What doesn't kill you makes you stronger. Right?"

Lucy had never been quite sure that famous line was true, but she agreed anyway. "Yes, definitely. Want an ice pack? Or some ice water? It's good for a hangover, and a banana wouldn't hurt either," Lucy said, offering her universal cure.

"The water sounds good. But I can't even look at food." Suzanne stuck her tongue out. "Did you ever hear me say that before?"

Dana and Lucy looked at each other. "Maybe you should skip the brunch and go back to bed," Dana suggested. "Join us on the beach later?"

"Don't worry. I'll rally." Suzanne took the tall glass of water Lucy offered. "A few pineapple martinis aren't going to ruin my day."

Lucy admired her determination, though Suzanne still looked pale, and she had to turn away as Lucy peeled a banana to help soothe her own aches.

"That's the spirit, Dancing Queen. And remember, what happens on Osprey Island, stays on Osprey Island," Dana told her.

"I hope so," Suzanne agreed heartily. She picked up a pair of sunglasses from the coffee table and slipped them on, even though they were indoors. She laid back again and sighed.

At precisely half past eleven, the group arrived at Amy's cottage, a short distance down the lane from their own. Suzanne had rallied enough to dress.

As soon as Amy opened the door, Lucy was greeted by tantalizing, buttery breakfast smells.

Their hostess greeted them cheerfully. "How is everyone faring after our wild night?"

Maggie laughed. "One of us is feeling the effects. But she's marching on bravely."

Suzanne wandered in at the back of the group, still wearing her sunglasses. Her face was bare of makeup, except for a dash of lipstick, and her long hair was pulled back into a ponytail. "I know I overdid it. But that's what vacations are for, right?"

"So true. And I have the perfect elixir for you. It's basically tomato juice and horseradish, but I mix in some other secret ingredients. Come on back to the sunroom. This will cure what ails you," Amy promised.

Lucy followed her friends through the living room to an adjoining dining room. The cottage was lovely, decorated in muted, neutral colors. She noticed linen-covered chairs and pale yellow couches with colorful pillows, interesting area rugs on a polished wood floor, and original art on the walls.

Amy led them into a large, sunny room next to the kitchen. There were more couches, a huge flat-screen TV hanging over a fireplace, and another dining area. Most of the walls were glass, framing a beautiful view of the grounds and the ocean. Lucy and her friends took seats at a long, farm-style table neatly set with floral cloth napkins and white plates. There were two baskets of warm muffins and croissants.

Lucy helped herself to a carrot muffin and passed the basket to Phoebe, who studied it carefully.

"These look yummy," Phoebe said. "I'm glad I don't have a hangover. Looks like Amy's a great cook."

"I think so," Lucy agreed.

Amy slipped into the kitchen and appeared a few moments later with a tray of cold drinks—iced tea, lemonade, sparkling water, and the tomato juice hangover elixir. "I made mimosas too. With fresh orange juice. Anyone interested?"

"I'd like one," Dana said. "I can never resist a good mimosa."

Suzanne pressed her hand to her head and closed her eyes a moment. "I'll have to pass on that treat today. But I will try your potion." She took a glass from the tray. "Any port in a storm."

"I think you'll be pleasantly surprised. And back on dry land very soon." Amy headed back to the kitchen. "Help yourself to the muffins. I'm just going to grab the food."

"Need any help?" Lucy was sitting closest to the kitchen. She rose and followed Amy, who was removing a large casserole from the oven.

"I made some baked French toast with blueberries, and two different omelets. And there's a fruit salad in the fridge. Could you bring that out, Lucy?"

"No problem. Happy to help. The menu sounds wonderful." Lucy pulled open the state-of-the-art chrome fridge and quickly found the salad. As she carried it into the sunroom, she saw Rob saying hello to her friends. He had on shorts and a polo shirt, a wad of newspaper under one arm.

"Hi honey. Want to sit with us?" Amy set down the pan of French toast in the middle of the table, along with a pitcher of syrup. "There's plenty of room. Just pull up a chair."

"That's all right. You ladies will have more fun without me." He grinned. "I'm going outside to read the newspaper." With a little wave, Rob headed out the French doors to their patio.

Amy brought in two large omelets, one with cheddar and mushrooms inside and tomato bits on top. The other held a creamy combination of roasted asparagus and goat cheese, with dill mixed into the eggs and more sprinkled on the platter.

"Everything looks delicious," Maggie said. "I don't know where to start."

Amy looked pleased by the compliment. "Start any-where. I'll pass the omelets around," she added, picking up a platter.

Lucy eagerly took portions from every dish. The bike ride had whet her appetite. She felt bad for Suzanne, who loved good food but only took small spoonfuls due to her queasy stomach.

Still, Suzanne had lavish praise for the cook. "You shouldn't have gone to all this trouble, Amy. You must have gotten up at the crack of dawn to cook all this deli-cious stuff."

"It didn't take long. I fixed the French toast last night and left it in the fridge. It comes out even better if it soaks a while. I'm sort of an early bird by nature anyway."

"We have some early birds among us as well." Suzanne glanced at Lucy and Dana. "Those two were out on a bike ride while the rest of us were still in dreamland."

Amy smiled at Lucy. "That is ambitious after last night's partying. Where did you ride?"

"On the cliff walk mainly," Dana said. "We didn't go far."

"We stopped at the crime scene. We were speculating on

how Dr. Morton fell, and if someone had helped him," Lucy admitted.

"Do the police know anything more?" Maggie asked Amy. "I was wondering if there was any inside gossip."

Amy shrugged and pushed a bit of omelet around her plate. "Not too much. But I did hear something about Derek Pullman."

Before she could go into the details, the doorbell rang. Amy wiped her mouth on a napkin. "Excuse me while I get the door. We're not expecting anyone."

Amy rose and headed for the foyer. Lucy and her friends began to eat. With no one talking, it was easy to overhear Amy and her unexpected guest.

"Hello. Can I help you?" Amy said.

"Detective Rose Dunbar. We met yesterday, at the pool?"

"Yes. I remember." Amy's tone was lower, a little shaky.

"Is your husband in, Mrs. Cutler? I'd like to speak to him."

"He's out on the patio. Reading the newspaper. What is this about?"

"It's about Dr. Morton."

"But we told you everything we know yesterday. There's really nothing more to say."

"We have more questions for your husband. May I come in?" Detective Dunbar's tone was firm.

"Yes . . . yes, of course," Lucy heard Amy say.

Lucy and her friends had all put their forks down. They glanced at each other, exchanging worried looks. Detective Dunbar's visit didn't bode well. It seemed more than routine.

Amy hurried through the sunroom. She glanced at her guests and gave a careless shrug, though her expression was grim. She looked upset. Anybody would be. She stepped outside to the patio and a few moments later, she followed Rob into the house.

Rob seemed nervous, his mouth set in a tight line. He didn't glance at anyone as he headed to see Detective Dunbar in the living room. Amy followed, then suddenly looked back at Lucy and her friends.

"Sorry for the interruption. We have no idea what this is about."

"That's all right, Amy. You do what you need to do," Suzanne said.

"I'll be right back," she promised.

Lucy and her friends sat in silence again, picking at their food.

"Why do the police need to talk to Rob again?" Suzanne asked in a hushed tone. "Amy and Rob hardly knew Morton."

"There must be some reason," Phoebe whispered back.

"There must. Let's listen," Maggie said.

"At the station? Why can't we just talk here?" Lucy heard Rob say.

"I'd like to do a more formal interview. You intentionally misled us yesterday, Mr. Cutler, when we asked if you had any relationship with Dr. Morton," Detective Dunbar said.

"I had nothing to do with him. We didn't speak. Didn't even say hello. Ask anyone around here."

"But you and Dr. Morton had a prior relationship. You both worked at Newquest Labs, in Burlington, at the same time. Why weren't you forthcoming with that information?"

"I don't know. It didn't seem important, I guess. I thought you wanted to know if we were friendly with him now. Besides, I had little to do with Morton at Newquest. I was very low on the food chain back then, and he was a big fish. I'm sure he didn't even know I existed."

"I'm not so sure," the detective replied. "We have more questions. It will be easier if you come now. Willingly."

Willingly? That word set off Lucy's silent alarms. Did that mean that, otherwise, they would bring him in with a warrant?

"Of course, I'll come, Detective. I have nothing to hide. But I want my attorney present. I have a right to that, don't I?"

"You do," Detective Dunbar said.

"Oh, Rob . . . what's going on? I don't understand." Amy sounded upset.

"Call Walter Addison. Tell him to meet me at the police station. Don't worry. It will be fine."

"I'll call him right away." Amy sounded like she was trying her best not to panic. "I'll follow you in my car and wait at the station until you're finished."

"If you like, Mrs. Cutler. But this may take a while," Detective Dunbar said.

"You wait here, honey. I'll call when I'm done. I'm sure Addison will drive me back."

Before Amy could reply, Lucy heard Rob and Detective Dunbar go out the door. Lucy and her friends couldn't sit still any longer. They trailed into the living room, and stood by as Amy watched Rob walk down the path to the waiting police car.

Amy took out her cell phone and quickly dialed. Calling their attorney, as Rob had requested, Lucy assumed. Lucy could tell from Amy's side of the conversation that the lawyer was surprised by this news, but he would head to the police station immediately. That was some relief, Lucy thought.

Through the big bay window in the living room, Lucy saw a uniformed officer help Rob into the backseat of the cruiser. Detective Dunbar sat up front in the passenger seat and the uniformed officer sat behind the wheel. The cruiser started up and drove away.

They didn't have the lights or sirens going, but it was

bad enough. Several neighbors had come out and stood on their lawns to watch. Others peeked behind curtains and shades, or stood in their doorways.

Amy turned to Lucy and her friends, looking pale and bereft.

Her eyes filled with tears. "I'm so afraid. What's going to happen? What are they going to do to Rob?"

"He'll be fine, Amy," Suzanne promised. "The police will question him about his prior connection to Morton, and then they'll let him go. It sounds as if there's not much to tell, but they have to investigate every lead. His lawyer will make sure he's not in there a minute more than he has to be," she insisted, sounding like her usual brassy self again.

Amy nodded, but didn't look assured by Suzanne's prediction. "He did lie to them about working with Morton. He only told them he had nothing to do with Morton, as a neighbor. Which was true. The Mortons moved in about six months after we did. It was such a strange coincidence, and we even considered moving. But Rob vowed he would keep his distance and act as if Morton didn't exist," Amy continued.

"Really? Why was that?" Dana asked.

"Because Rob did know him years ago at Newquest Labs. They were very distant on the corporate ladder, like Rob said, but Rob worked on a project for Morton—an invention that was really Rob's idea. But he didn't have the stature to get funds to develop it.

"He showed the design to Morton, believing he would help. Instead, Morton stole his idea and claimed it was his own. He cut Rob out of all the credit, and the profits. Which were considerable."

Dana gasped. "That's awful. When did this happen?"

"Let's see . . . Rob had just finished his doctorate. I guess it was over twenty years ago."

"Didn't Rob call him on it? Didn't he complain to someone higher up in the company?" Suzanne asked.

"He tried. But Morton knew all the angles. And he had the power on his side. Rob was just a bench scientist, easy to brush off or replace. Rob hadn't patented his idea before bringing it to Morton, so it was hard to make a case in court. Morton claimed he'd had the same idea and had been working it, too. He said he had perfected it faster."

"What was the invention?" Lucy asked.

"A super-miniaturized camera for non-invasive surgery. Rob mentioned it last night, the camera able to view in all directions, like a fly's eye, so the surgeon can get a complete view within a blocked artery. Or inside the heart's different chambers."

"Yes, I remember Rob talking about it at dinner," Lucy recalled. "Very ingenious. Having that idea stolen was a deep betrayal and must have been very upsetting."

"Upsetting isn't the word for it. Traumatic would be closer. We were so young, and this was Rob's first breakthrough. He didn't realize there were many more great ideas to come," Amy said. "He'd trusted Morton. He respected him. Morton's lies and deception were a shock. It cut very deep."

"It sounds shattering," Dana said. "How did Rob cope at work after that?"

"Not well. He couldn't hide his anger or contempt for Morton. He had several blowups with him and wouldn't give up, trying to get Morton to make things right. Morton had him fired. That was the last straw. Rob couldn't eat, couldn't sleep, couldn't believe he'd been so naïve and trusting. And he couldn't believe that Morton could lie to so many people with such a straight face. Morton was a horrible man without any conscience or morals."

"So it seems," Dana said. "And Rob never got any justice or satisfaction? From the laboratory or the court?"

"None at all. We pursued it in court for over two years, but Morton had bigger lawyers and much more money. And there was no patent. We finally gave up." Amy sighed. She looked pale, Lucy noticed. Watching Rob taken away by the police had been distressing enough. Recalling this sad history had added to that distress.

"Rob was so upset at one point," she continued, "he went to Morton's house to confront him. When Morton wouldn't come out, Rob threw a rock through his front window. Morton finally did come out, and Rob said some awful things. I knew he was just blowing off steam. After all he'd been through, it wasn't surprising. I knew he'd never hurt anyone, not even Morton. But Morton went to court and got an order of protection. The police must have found a record of that."

"That must be how they made the connection. And why they suspect Rob now," Maggie agreed. "But it's still not enough for the police to detain Rob for very long. Especially with his attorney there. It all happened long ago and there's no evidence to tie Rob to Morton's death."

"And he has a good alibi for the time of Morton's death, right?" Suzanne asked.

"He was on the beach, fishing. I'm sure other fishermen saw him there. And Rob had no intention of digging up the past. He may not have forgiven Julian Morton, but he would never seek revenge. He'd certainly never kill him."

Lucy hoped not. To be on the beach at that hour placed Rob at the crime scene from Detective Dunbar's perspective, but Lucy didn't want to point that out and upset Amy further. "I know it seems like Rob's incident with Dr. Morton is a strong motive. But it was a long time ago, and Rob never had any contact with Morton in all those years,"

Lucy reminded Amy. "Meanwhile, there's a long list of people who have good reason to want Dr. Morton out of the way. With more immediate concerns, you might say."

Amy nodded, still looking shaky and worried. "That's true, I suppose."

Suzanne stepped close to her old college friend and rubbed her shoulder. "Oh, Amy. What can we do to help?"

Amy forced a smile. "Just having you here is a help," she said. "Let's finish our meal. You must be starving by now."

"I know this is all very upsetting. But I'd hate to see all that lovely food go to waste," Maggie admitted.

"Maybe by the time we're done, Rob will call and tell me he's on his way home."

"Maybe," Maggie replied optimistically.

Lucy doubted that. She knew Maggie probably did, too, but was trying to be supportive. Detective Dunbar seemed geared up for a long chat. Rob might make it home around dinnertime, she thought.

Amy popped the platters of baked French Toast and the omelets into the microwave. The interruption had caused all the food to go cold, as well as the good spirits of their get-together.

After they'd finished the delicious entreés, Amy brought out dessert. She'd made a lemon cream pie, its tart flavor the perfect complement to her menu.

They tried not to talk about Morton's murder, but it was almost impossible to avoid the subject.

"So what did you hear about Derek Pullman?" Suzanne asked. "You were going to tell us just before Detective Dunbar came. Did they find out he was the one who vandalized Morton's car?"

"My friend in the security office said that it was definitely him. They caught him on a security camera," Amy replied. "So the police questioned him again, but he has a good alibi. He left the grounds for his tennis club in town very early, and said he was there all morning."

"Sounds solid. But he could have gone there and then left for a while, at least for long enough to push his poker-playing nemesis over the edge. I'm still betting on Pullman, good alibi or not." Suzanne licked a bit of lemon cream from her spoon. "With all those gambling debts, and then stating publicly that he thought Morton had been cheating at the poker games? That's a strong motive to want to see the guy dead."

"I suppose so," Amy agreed. "I don't know Derek, and I certainly don't wish anyone ill, but I did hear that his life isn't very rosy right now. He recently lost his job as an investment banker, and his wife left him soon after. The money he owed Morton wouldn't have been a burden for him at one time. But it probably is now. He obviously resented having to pay Morton back once he'd decided that Morton had beaten him by cheating at the card game."

"Good point," Lucy said. "The police might be digging into Rob's past relationship to Morton right now, but Pullman has a much stronger motive to want Morton out of the way. They've got to like him better for the crime. Maybe they can't find anything to tie him to the scene. Or maybe his alibi is holding up."

"Maybe," Maggie said. "But that can change quickly."

"There are others the police might have on their list," Dana said. "Lucy saw something very interesting last night. I think she should go to the police with it."

"Really? What was that?" Amy lifted her head, wanting to hear more.

"I was driving everyone back last night. It was a little after two, I guess. I made a wrong turn and ended up right in front of Dr. Morton's cottage. I saw Sam Briggs banging on the front door, and then Tanya let him in. She didn't look happy to see him. I mean, it wasn't like some big lovey-dovey reunion. She actually looked angry. He did, too. But she let him in, and later I noticed his truck parked a few blocks away. I suppose so the neighbors wouldn't see it in her driveway."

"Oldest trick in the book." Suzanne released a long sigh. "There are plenty of people besides Rob who wanted Morton out of their life. Tanya should be suspect number one, being the disgruntled wife, itching to get divorced from her tightwad husband, who was going to send her off with bubkes from his fortune."

A thought suddenly came to Lucy. "Speaking of itching . . . Tanya sat next to me in yoga Saturday morning, and she had poison ivy all over her feet. It looked to me as if she'd just caught it, too. Dana and I saw tons of it at the spot where Morton went over the edge."

Dana was wide-eyed. "You didn't tell me that."

"I just remembered," Lucy replied.

"That's significant. I think you should tell the police all this stuff, Lucy," Suzanne said.

Maggie sipped her coffee and set down the cup. "I do, too. It might be nothing, but you never know."

"It could help Rob," Amy cut in. "It could help him a lot."

Lucy had been on the fence about getting involved, but the look on Amy's face touched her heart and melted her reservations. "Don't worry. I'll call and see if I can give the info over the phone to someone covering the case. I suppose Detective Dunbar might want to see me at some point, too."

"Thank you, Lucy. Thank you so much," Amy said sincerely.

Lucy wasn't sure her bits of gossip about Sam Briggs's

late-night rendezvous and Tanya's poison ivy would help Rob that quickly. But it was good to see Amy a bit more hopeful.

Lucy went into the living room and dialed the police station. She was quickly connected with Officer Hobart. He took down her information without comment, asking one or two questions to get her story straight.

"I'll pass this on to Detective Dunbar. She may want to speak to you. She's conducting an interview right now."

Lucy was tempted to say "Yeah, I know," but she put a lid on it. "That would be fine. Thanks."

When she returned to her friends, Amy was checking her phone for a message from Rob. "They left about an hour ago. Don't you think they must be done by now?"

Maggie, who had once been questioned by the police in connection with a murder, replied, "Everything happens very slowly at a police station, Amy. Sometimes they make a person wait in the interview room an hour or more, just to wear down their defenses and get them off guard."

Amy nodded, her expression tight. "I understand. At least he has Walter Addison with him. I've seen those crime shows on TV. The police can get you to say anything if you're not careful. But Rob has nothing to hide. Yes, he and Morton had some bad blood twenty years ago, but Rob hasn't been in contact with him since. Even while living here."

At least that Amy knew of, Lucy silently amended.

Lucy and her friends helped Amy clear the table and clean the kitchen. They didn't want to leave her with a mess on top of everything else she had to worry about.

"We're headed for the beach, Amy," Maggie said. "Why don't you join us? It will be a good distraction while you're waiting to hear from Rob."

"Thanks, but I'd rather stick around here. I want to be able to jump in the car if he needs me."

Rob had already suggested his attorney would give him a lift home, but Lucy admired Amy's loyalty and concern. She loved her husband very much, and they seemed to have a close, caring relationship.

Suzanne gave Amy a bear-sized, all-enveloping hug. "I'm sure he'll get in touch soon, and everything will work out fine. Just remember, we're a text message away. We want to help you and Rob in any way we can."

Amy smiled, her eyes a little glassy as she stepped back. "Thanks, Suzanne. I hope I don't have to take you up on that."

Chapter 6

After a few more farewells, compliments on the brunch, and good luck wishes, Lucy and her friends left the Cutler's cottage and headed to the beach.

They had brought their beach gear and wore suits under their shorts and sundresses. They headed for the cliff walk, and the long staircase that led to the beach, speculating more about Rob's visit to the police station on the way. As they approached the spot where Julian Morton had encountered his murderer, Lucy noticed the bench nearest the crime scene was occupied.

"There's Betty Rutledge," she murmured to her friends. Lucy had easily recognized Betty, despite her huge sun hat and big glasses. Or maybe, because of them. She sat knitting as she serenely took in the view, chatting with a man who sat with her, his back turned to Lucy and her friends.

"We should stop and say hello," Maggie said.

"Sure. A quick hello," Dana said. "It's hot out here. I'm dying to take a swim."

Betty could ramble, once you got here talking, Lucy knew Dana meant.

"Of course, a quick hello," Maggie agreed.

Betty had spotted them and waved gaily. "Headed for the beach, ladies? Perfect day for it."

"It is." Maggie led the way off the path to the bench, which was nestled between huge blue hydrangea bushes in full bloom.

"I'm happy up here, with a bird's-eye view." Betty turned to her companion, a man in late middle age, dressed in a blue polo shirt and khaki shorts. He also wore a large sun hat and protective sunglasses, matching Betty's gear. "This is my brother, Ted. He came by for a visit and took me out to lunch."

A celebratory lunch? Lucy wondered. Though she didn't dare say.

"This is Maggie, the wonderful knitting teacher I told you about, Ted. And her friends," Betty added. "They're visiting for the weekend."

"Nice to meet you." Ted took in Lucy and her group with a pleasant smile.

After hearing the horrid story about Ted's injuries, it was hard not to look for evidence of the accident. Despite his hat and large sunglasses, Lucy noticed a patch of red scarring on the left side of his face that trailed down his jaw and neck. She saw the same angry red scars on his left arm, all the way down to his fingers. She felt rude staring and quickly looked back at Betty. He had learned to live with his disfigurement, but it couldn't have been easy.

She wondered if her friends were thinking the same thing.

"Nice meet you, too, Ted." Dana shifted her tote bag to her other shoulder. "Betty told us that you live in Moody Beach. Is that a resort town, too? Don't think I've ever heard of it, but I don't know Maine very well."

"It's not far, less than an hour's drive. Depending on tourist traffic," he added. "It's a quiet spot. But we're right near Kennebunkport."

"Kennebunkport's fun." Suzanne smiled, then fanned

her face with her hand. "I don't know about everyone else, but I'd better get down the beach and under an umbrella, before I melt. Enjoy your day."

Lucy watched Suzanne head back towards the walk, obviously hoping everyone else would take the hint and follow.

Maggie smiled at Betty. "We'd better go. I hear that staircase takes time to navigate."

"Oh, it does," Betty agreed. "Watch your step," she warned.

A good slogan for Osprey Shores T-shirts, Lucy thought.

"We will," Lucy promised. "See you." She picked up her knapsack and left with the rest of her friends.

The beach access was only a short distance further down the path and Lucy found Suzanne waiting for them. "I thought we should tackle this together," Suzanne said.

Lucy thought she was exaggerating. She peered over the edge. "Wow, how many steps down do you think there are?"

"One hundred and fifty-seven," Phoebe replied. "I asked someone when I walked down on Friday."

"That's a lot of steps, but it's a beautiful day. A little exercise after that brunch won't hurt us," Dana said.

"Not one bit. I'd like to take a long walk on the beach, too, if we get a chance. It's such a great day, and what a spectacular view." Lucy set down her tote bag and put on a pair of sunglasses.

"Beautiful view, slippery footing. That's the story of this place." Phoebe peered down the long staircase again. "I suggest we tie ourselves together the way mountain climbers do. Just in case someone slips, and the law of gravity takes over."

"Don't be silly, Phoebe. We'll be fine. All those people on the beach made it down safe and sound. See?" Maggie had set down her beach bag a moment, but picked it up again. Lucy couldn't argue with her. Quite a few residents had come out to enjoy the sun and water today. But maybe they had arrived via helicopter . . . or parachute?

"We'll be very careful," Dana promised. "Why don't you go last? This way you won't feel rushed."

"I'd rather go second to last, so someone can grab my shirttail if I look like I'm going over." Phoebe had not suggested who that sympathetic someone might be, but she glanced at Lucy with wide, beseeching eyes.

"I'll walk behind you. I'll watch every step." Lucy shifted her striped canvas tote onto to her left side, to free up her right hand for shirttail grabbing. Though she doubted it would come to that. She hoped not, anyway.

The stairs were steep, narrow, and extremely long, with many switchbacks. With Phoebe's fear of heights and all the talk about Morton's deadly fall, Lucy could understand why she was nervous.

Suzanne led the way, at an uncharacteristically slow and careful pace. "You get dizzy if you stare down. Then again, I don't want to miss a step. Maybe we should have taken the car and gone the long way around."

"We're almost halfway, just keep going," Dana said.

"It was clever of Morton's murderer to lay in wait while he jogged on the cliff," Maggie said. "But these steps would make for an easy fatal fall as well."

"I was thinking the same," Lucy said from the back of the line. "But the cliff walk has more hiding places, with all the shrubbery."

"True, but a killer could wait on one of the switchbacks, and sort of duck down until the victim arrived."

"I get the point, Mag," Phoebe called out from her spot. She'd taken off her heeled slides and was going it barefoot, taking each step with great care. "It's hard enough to get down these steps without having to worry that someone might jump out and push me over. And I think it would be more constructive if you talk about the murder that actually happened."

"Very true," Lucy said. "What do you think of Betty's brother? I found their viewing point an interesting choice."

"Practically the spot where Morton went over. I thought of that, too." Dana seemed the least disturbed by the staircase and followed Suzanne with a light, agile step.

Maggie walked steadily. But looked a bit off balance from her bags. "I know it's awful to say, but they must feel vindicated by Morton's murder."

"To put it lightly," Suzanne called over her shoulder. "I bet her brother came to celebrate. They were probably doing a jig. Ding-dong, the witch is dead."

Similar thoughts had crossed Lucy's mind, though she wouldn't have put it so bluntly.

"Celebrating Morton's death? Or pulling off his murder?" Dana's voice was so quiet, Lucy hardly heard her. "Betty and her brother have plenty of motive and Ted looks fit enough to have subdued Morton, and pushed him over."

Lucy had noticed that, too. Ted wasn't young, but younger than Betty and in fairly good shape.

Lucy was relieved to see the beach come closer. "I wonder if the police are exploring that angle. Betty said she told them the story. Maybe she and Ted have solid alibis."

Dana looked back at her. "I'd still be curious to hear what their alibis are. Especially his. Something about the sight of the two of them, sitting in that particular spot, looking so cheerful and at peace . . . it gave me the creeps."

When she put it that way, it gave Lucy the creeps, too.

Suzanne paused to fix her sandal, so Dana paused, too. Causing a standstill all the way back to Phoebe. And so close to the bottom. Lucy felt annoyed but took a calming a breath.

When she stood up again, she said, "We're all assuming that Betty *did* tell the police about her dark history with Morton. Maybe she didn't."

Lucy hadn't thought of that. "Good point. I guess we could check somehow."

"We could," Dana agreed. "But it might be easier for Rob's attorney to make sure the police know about Betty and her brother, and their dark episode with Morton."

"I was just thinking the same thing." Suzanne had finished with her sandal and started down the last few steps. "I'll text Amy as soon as we get settled down here."

Lucy felt relieved to hear that. She had quickly crossed Betty and her brother off her list, but now, she was not so sure.

They had finally reached the beach. She had lost count of the steps at one hundred and thirty-three and already dreaded climbing back up. Maybe she didn't need that beach walk, after all.

They quickly picked a spot at the water's edge, where they found beach chairs and lounge chairs set up around umbrellas. The canvas fabric was classic Osprey Shores blue, with plenty of mermaid emblems. Just in case you forgot where you were.

A short distance away, two teenage lifeguards—a girl and a boy—sat in a high chair, staring out at the beautiful blue waves through dark glasses. A snack stand and shower house were also close by, not far from the staircase.

"I feel so bad for Amy, leaving her to wait all alone," Phoebe said.

"I know what you mean. But some people need to be alone at a time like this. They don't want any company."

Maggie had spread a towel over her chair and removed her cover-up.

"Amy was always like that in college. When she got a bad grade or was stressed by something, she hibernated," Suzanne recalled. "I sent her a note about Betty and I'll check in with her again soon. Maybe I'll drop by the cottage on our way home later."

"Good idea." Lucy glanced at her watch. It had been over two hours since Rob had left with the police. She wondered what was going on, and why Detective Dunbar was so intent on questioning him in a formal interview at the station. Was he a person of interest in the case? That would be serious.

Lucy and her friends decided not to talk about Rob's situation or Morton's murder for the rest of the afternoon. It seemed to Lucy they all needed a break from that topic. The breaking waves, shining sun, and soft cool breeze reminded her of why they had come to Osprey Island. Not to solve a murder case.

Lucy stretched on her lounge chair, and slowly opened her eyes. She'd been reading a book and had drifted off.

"Welcome back, Sleeping Beauty," Suzanne greeted her. "Did you have a nice nap?"

"It was lovely. This lounge is supercomfortable. I still have a few aches from our dance-a-thon." She sat up and rubbed a calf muscle.

"While the cute little bride-to-be was resting, I had an inspiration. Why don't we hit the spa today for some pampering? You could get a massage and a pedicure. I could really use a facial. Everyone should try something. It's our time to indulge ourselves."

Lucy found her water bottle and took a sip. "Great

idea. Do you think we can get appointments? It's after three."

"We can try." Suzanne took her cell phone from her tote bag.

"No messages from Amy yet?"

Suzanne shook her head. "Unfortunately. I'll call the spa first, then check in with her."

The tide was coming in, and the lacy white edge of the waves washed up closer and closer to their chairs. Suzanne walked away from the blanket, one hand pressing the phone to her head, the other hand pressing against her ear to block the sound of the breakers.

Maggie had moved her chair even closer to the water and was busily knitting. Dana and Phoebe had also left their shady, double-umbrella shelter while Lucy had been napping. But Phoebe soon appeared, her sun hat and glasses shading her face. The rest of her body was scantily covered by a colorful, knitted bikini, one of Phoebe's own creations.

She carried a paper dish of thin-cut French fries and a plastic cup of soda with a straw poking out the top. She sat down next to Lucy and dipped the tip of a fry into a mound of ketchup. Then she popped it into her mouth and smiled with satisfaction.

"Want some?" she asked, offering the snack.

"I'm fine, thanks," Lucy said. She still felt full from the brunch, and if she did have a snack it would be a lot healthier than fries and a soda. She wondered where, on Phoebe's broomstick figure, she had room for more food today. Her friend had a faster metabolism than a hummingbird. Lucky girl.

Phoebe ate another fry then sipped her drink. "Why does salty food always taste good at the beach?"

"I'm not sure but I know what you mean." Lucy had

experienced that strange effect herself. "Where's Dana? If she catches you eating fries and drinking soda, you'll get a nutrition lecture. Even if we are at the beach."

"She's taking a walk, but she should be back soon. I'd better scarf this up. You have a good point." Phoebe dipped another fry and gazed out at the water, looking perfectly content. "It's so pretty here today. I wish I had my camera."

Lucy felt bad for her. All last week, Phoebe had been talking about taking a lot of photos out here. A cell phone was convenient, but the photo quality was not the same.

"You should call Detective Dunbar and find out if they've finished with it. And if not, how much longer it will be," Lucy replied.

Phoebe looked over from under her big hat. "Good idea. She scares me a little, but if I don't nudge them they might keep it forever."

"She is a little intimidating," Lucy agreed.

Suzanne returned to her chair, shaded by an umbrella. "Sorry, Lucy. I struck out with the spa. They're fully booked today, but said we should stop by and check for cancellations later."

"At least you tried. We can stop on the way back to the cottage. If they don't have any openings for today, we can make appointments for tomorrow." Lucy was a little disappointed but it was only Saturday. They weren't leaving until Monday afternoon. They'd surely find an appointment by then.

"Good plan. I also called Amy. She just got a text. The interview is over, and Rob is on his way home."

"That's a relief," Lucy said. "I guess we'll hear soon what the police asked him."

"Personally, I'm dying to hear all the gritty details. But I don't want to be too pushy. Amy said she'd call me tonight or tomorrow. I guess we'll have to wait."

"I hope this is the end of it for him."

"I hear you, pal. Problem is, you just never know," Suzanne said quietly.

Lucy knew that was true, but hoped it was not the case for Rob and Amy.

Dana returned from her walk, looking a little sweaty, but happy with her journey. She said she felt hot and was eager for a swim. Lucy decided to jump in the waves with her, and once they got in, Maggie joined them, too.

After the swimmers dried off, the group decided to head back to their cottage. Lucy heard many complaints and groans as they climbed back up the steps. Phoebe led the way, but Lucy still stayed at the back of the line.

"Next time, we take the lazy way out and drive," Maggie said.

"Agreed." Suzanne paused and took a breath. "If the cell service wasn't so bad down here, I'd call an Uber car."

"We're almost at the top," Lucy called out from the back of the line. "And I thought we were going to check out the spa on our way to the cottage? We can get some iced tea at the café there."

"Iced tea . . . something to live for," Suzanne replied dramatically as she started climbing again.

They soon made it to the top, and Lucy glanced over her shoulder as she headed for the cliff walk. The view was dizzying. This time she had counted the steps. More than enough for one day.

Everyone was so tired from their climb and sitting in the sun all afternoon, there was little conversation as they walked to Mermaid Manor. They entered on the terrace level, breathing grateful sighs as they stepped into the air-conditioned lobby.

"Spa appointments." Suzanne pointed to the spa entrance, which was next to the fitness center. "Or iced tea?"

She pointed to the open café across the lobby that ad-joined a sunroom sitting area. "A show of hands, please."

"Iced tea!" everyone answered unanimously.

Suzanne led the way to the café, and they ordered at the counter. Lucy read the chalkboard carefully. Even a simple glass of iced tea wasn't so simple at Osprey Shores. There were too many to choose from—HEAVENLY HIBISCUS, POME-GRANATE-PEACH PUNCH, DOUBLE-MINT INFUSION, and GREEN TEA-HALF ORGANIC LEMONADE. The ungarnished, tradi-tional flavor was at the bottom of the list, aptly named ICY & NAKED PEKOE.

Lucy settled on Heavenly Hibiscus and was about to order, when someone called her name. She turned to see Dr. Fielding.

He smiled. "Are you ladies coming to the support cir-cle? We start in five minutes, out in the lounge."

Lucy suddenly recalled he had mentioned organizing a grief support event for the community. She thought it was a nice gesture, but hadn't given a thought to attending.

"Actually, we're just about to check out the spa," Mag-gie replied.

Dr. Fielding looked disappointed. "I see. Well . . . we'll be there a while. I know you're strangers here and only saw Dr. Morton in that meltdown at the poker game. But a sudden, suspicious death like this, happening in such close proximity, is still an emotional shock. I'm sure you all feel unsettled about it and may even have some ques-tions about him. Sitting in on the circle might give you all some insights and closure."

It sounded to Lucy as if Dr. Fielding was trying to drum up some business. She wasn't surprised, all things consid-ered.

Lucy glanced out at the lounge, which was filled with comfortable love seats and sitting chairs. A large circle had been set up, but there were few people to be seen. She had to admit that she did feel unsettled by the murder, and she did have questions about Dr. Morton. Was he really as awful as everyone said?

"Thanks for including us, Dr. Fielding. We're going to have our iced tea and think about it," Lucy replied, answering for all them.

"Of course. Whatever feels most comfortable. I didn't mean to put you on the spot. And please, call me Lewis."

"I think it's a great idea and will help a lot of the residents sort out their feelings about this event," Dana said.

Dr. Fielding seemed to appreciate her compliment. But he was definitely a shy, modest man. "I try to help where I can," he said with a small smile.

Dr. Fielding left them and headed to the lounge, but changed direction when Meredith Quinn entered the lobby. He quickly walked over to greet her. Another sales pitch for the grief circle? But Dr. Morton's ex-wife had good reason to be here. Though Meredith looked anything but grief-stricken, or in need of this sort of support.

Meredith smiled widely, her eyes shining, as she greeted Dr. Fielding. He seemed happy to see her, too. They stood very close, talking quietly. Intimately, Lucy thought. She also thought she saw Dr. Fielding reach over and very quickly squeeze Meredith's hand.

An innocent gesture. A friendly, or even comforting one.

It wasn't as if he leaned down and planted a big, soulful kiss on her lips. But still . . . there seemed a certain energy crackling between them.

Meredith headed to the chairs, and Dr. Fielding stayed to greet Betty Rutledge. Betty barely paused to talk to him. She didn't need a sales pitch to participate, Lucy noticed. She headed straight for the circle, her knitting tote tucked under one arm. Lucy guessed that her brother was headed back to Moody Beach by now. She wondered if Betty had asked him to come here. Lucy could think of several reasons why he wouldn't want to participate.

Had Rob's attorney brought Betty and her brother to the attention of Detective Dunbar today? Or did the police already know the story but didn't consider the two suspects? The police sometimes moved slowly on such tips. But word would get around quickly if Betty was called in for questioning.

Would Betty tell the story about Julian Morton and Ted, and the campfire? She would have a captive audience. It was interesting how certain events shaped and defined a person's life. That event had surely shaped Betty.

Lucy wondered what events had shaped her own life. A good question, but hard to answer about yourself. It was probably best answered by someone who knew you well and could see the big picture, like any one of her dear friends. She'd have to ask them sometime—after a few glasses of wine.

Lucy's curiosity about the support circle increased with each new resident she spotted claiming a chair. Her friends had been ordering their cold drinks. Phoebe skipped the tea and ordered an ice cream soda.

There was only one counter and a few small tables in the café. Most were occupied. Dana suggested that they sit in the lounge, which was large and mostly empty except for the support group.

"We don't need to sit near the circle. There's plenty of space," Dana said.

"But not too far away. I do want to eavesdrop. It could be enlightening." Lucy ignored Dana's look and took another sip of Heavenly Hibiscus tea. It was very good. Definitely in the celestial category on such a hot day.

"I'm curious, too," Maggie admitted. "There are quite a few people there now. The seats are almost full."

"Don't worry. I'm sure Dr. Fielding will find a few more chairs if we want to sit in," Lucy said.

"Do you really?" Dana asked them.

"I think it would be interesting. We might learn if Dr. Morton was the awful, self-centered person some people make him out to be. Surely he had a better side."

"Sociopathic psychos usually don't. Unless they're trying to charm and lure you to some awful fate." Phoebe fished around her drink for lumps of ice cream using a long plastic spoon. "He probably ate deep-fried kittens for breakfast."

"Phoebe . . . honestly." Maggie rolled her eyes and sighed.

Lucy couldn't help laughing. "An awful image, Phoebe. But effective. With all this talk about his death and the people he'd crossed, I'm curious to know more. I don't know about you guys, but I'm going to sit in on the circle. If I feel uncomfortable or bored, I'll just slip away."

"I'm curious, too. I think I'll join you. I do have my knitting." Maggie patted her tote bag.

"If you're both going, I guess I will, too," Dana said. "It's good to see how other therapists conduct grief therapy for a large group."

While Dana claimed only professional interest, Lucy knew she was itching to hear more about Morton, too.

"That leaves me and Phoebe. Just us chickens." Suzanne gave a little cluck. "We can either take very long showers, maybe even bubble baths, or stick around to hear some good dirt. Come to think of it, maybe I should stay for Amy and Rob's sake. I might hear something that would be helpful to them," Suzanne decided.

"If you guys are all going, I'll go too. All for one, one for all." Phoebe tossed back the rest of her ice cream soda and dumped the cup in a recycle can.

"Exactly. The Black Sheep always stick together." Lucy picked up her tote and headed for the circle.

It was hard to find five seats together, but Suzanne quickly dragged over two chairs from another part of the room and persuaded a few people to move their seats to accommodate the group. Lewis was happy to see them there and helped with the furniture rearrangement.

They were not seated far from Betty, who had already taken out her knitting. She gave them a little wave but didn't get up to chat. Lucy was thankful for that.

Lucy noticed Meredith sitting a few chairs away, directly opposite of Dr. Fielding. Considering their warm greeting, she thought they'd be seated closer to each other. She also noticed that Meredith had saved the seat next to her with her folded sweater and purse. Lucy wondered who she was expecting. A friend, maybe, who had promised to pay their respects to Dr. Morton? This was a bit like a memorial service. So far, there had been no mention of Dr. Morton's family holding one.

Aside from Betty, she recognized a few other members of Amy's knitting group, though, of course, Amy wasn't present. Derek Pullman wasn't present, either—no surprise there—but Lucy thought she recognized one or two of the other card players.

Tanya Morton was also noticeably absent. Lucy wasn't sure what to make of that. She had a feeling Dr. Fielding had encouraged her to come, but Tanya seemed the type who didn't like to mingle with "the little people." Maybe she preferred to keep her feelings about her husband's passing to herself. Or maybe she knew there would be plenty of people, like Betty Rutledge, relating Dr. Morton's less than stellar moments. She might feel put in a position to defend him. These days, anything she said or did would supply more grist for the Hearsay Shores gossip mill.

There was already plenty of talk about her angling for a divorce and trying to break the prenup agreement with Dr. Morton. Lucy could understand why she might skip this hour of sharing memories and feelings. She probably had few fond memories or feelings about her husband to draw upon.

Thoughts of Tanya reminded Lucy of her call to the police department and the information she'd volunteered about seeing Sam Briggs at the Morton cottage late Friday night. Lucy felt guilty, as if she'd singled out Tanya as a suspect. But the spouse was always a suspect, especially one trying to divorce a rich man who wanted his wife to walk away from the marriage empty-handed.

Compound that scenario with a muscle-bound paramour. A friendly, accommodating guy with plenty of brawn and motive to toss the cranky, tightwad husband over the edge. It was definitely a theory worth pursuing.

If Tanya was innocent and had no involvement in her husband's death, whatever Lucy had told the police wouldn't matter, she decided. Tanya can't go to jail for having an affair with a handyman. If there was such a law, an astounding number of women all over New England would be wearing orange jumpsuits.

Dr. Fielding appeared and took his seat. "Welcome, everyone. I'm glad you all found time to come to this support circle. Dr. Morton's tragic death was a shock to the whole community. No matter what your relationship or feelings about him, it's a help to recognize and express those feelings in a safe space. A space where there's no judgement, only acceptance and validation.

"So I ask you all now to simply listen to one another and honor each other's experiences and feelings. And to express your own feelings with honesty and trust." Dr. Fielding paused. "Who would like to go first?"

An older man with a fringe of grey hair and large thick glasses raised his hand. "I'm Oscar Newland, for those of you who don't know me. I didn't really come to talk about Morton. I know plenty of people have stories about him. I came because I'm honestly rattled. Part of the reason my wife and I chose Osprey Shores was that it looked like the safest place in the world to live. Then some guy gets pushed off a cliff. I know the police are investigating, and Morton's killer is probably someone he knew. That's what they say on the police shows. But taking a stroll on the cliff walk will never seem the same to me. Right now, I avoid it completely." Oscar paused, and his glance swept the circle of faces. "What if it was some random psycho who wants to push people off of cliffs? Whoever killed Morton is still out there. I don't know about the rest of you, but I've been double-checking our locks and windows, and our security system. I sure didn't sleep much last night and I don't expect to sleep very well tonight either."

Several people in the group nodded. "I feel the same. It was an awful shock, and I'm scared silly it could happen again. I won't dare take a walk at night," another woman said.

Dr. Fielding nodded. "I understand. The event was shocking and fractured our sense of this community as a safe and beautiful place to live. When an event like this happens, we go into our fight or flight mode, we self-protect, without much objective thought. Dr. Morton's death was frightening. But there's no reason to think a serial killer is on the loose. That's our lower brain creating some frightful disaster scenario." He leaned forward and folded his hands together. "In time, our rational thoughts will take over because the police will find Dr. Morton's murderer, and his death will prove to be an isolated incident.

"Bad things happen in life. Unexpected events. But I can almost guarantee this horrible crime is an anomaly. The norm of our community is serenity, beauty, and yes, safety. Have patience with yourself if you don't feel that way. It will take time to get our bearings and see it that way again."

Dana leaned over toward Lucy and whispered, "He's good. Who knew?"

Lucy kept her eyes straight ahead and stifled a smile since the atmosphere seemed so somber.

"Who'd like to go next?" Dr. Fielding asked the group.

"I will." A woman with dark red hair raised her hand. She was also a member of Amy's knitting group, though Lucy couldn't recall her name. She was well turned out in a silk tank top, gold bangles, and a short linen skirt. Her legs were smooth and tan, and her high-heeled sandals were stylish and uncomfortable looking. Lucy thought she was well preserved for her age, which Lucy guessed to be early fifties.

Dr. Fielding nodded. "Please. Share with us."

"Thank you, Dr. Fielding. And thank you for bringing us together this way. I think it's very helpful. My name is Helen Shelburn," she said, gazing around at the group. "I live on Hurricane Hill, next door to the Mortons. We moved into the community when it was first built and were very happy here. But when the Mortons moved in, we considered selling our place and moving to the opposite side of the development, or moving away altogether.

"Tanya is all right," she continued. "I'm friends with her, in a way. But I can honestly say that Dr. Morton was the nastiest neighbor and the most awful person you could imagine. A total nightmare."

"In what way?" Dr. Fielding leaned forward in his chair. "That is, if you feel inclined to tell us. If not, that's okay too."

"It's all right. I can tell you. He complained that we put our trash bins out too early. He said they were unsightly and should only go out after dark. When he found them out before sunset, he'd tip them over. Of course, that left a huge mess for us to clean, and raccoons sniffing around at night. But that was nothing compared to Harvey, our Cairn

Terrier. Morton poisoned our dog. He claimed it was an accident, but it definitely was not. He hated Harvey."

Helen paused and looked down a moment, clasping her hands in her lap. Lucy could tell this part of the story was hard for her tell. "We have a fence around the whole yard, but Harvey loved to dig and often dug his way out. We called him Harvey Houdini." She smiled at the recollection, but her eyes still looked sad. "He'd usually end up in Morton's yard, but never did any real harm. Scared their cat. Dug up a flower bed, maybe. But Morton was livid. He said, 'The next time I find that dog here, he's not going to make it home.' Later, he claimed that he'd only meant he'd bring Harvey to a shelter to teach us lesson."

Helen shook her head and brushed her hair back with her hand. Her voice sounded a little shaky as she continued. "The next time Harvey got out, he didn't come home. The vet said he ate rat bait. Morton claimed he'd put the bait down because mice were getting into his house. But the vet did an autopsy and said the bait had been mixed with bacon. We never gave Harvey bacon. Morton wrapped the poison in meat so Harvey would eat it. He did that purposely. But we could never prove it." She paused and dabbed her eyes with a tissue. "What kind of man would do that to a poor, sweet, innocent dog?"

No one answered. Not even Dr. Fielding.

Helen continued. "I've come here because . . . well, after everything Dr. Morton did to us, I feel guilty. Ironic, right? I told everyone I know about what he did to Harvey and said some awful things about him. I wished him ill, and now he's met such a horrible death. I know it's irrational, but I'm afraid all those bad wishes will turn back on me."

"I see," Dr. Fielding said. "You feel guilty about wishing him ill, as if you somehow caused his death?"

Helen shrugged. "I wouldn't go that far . . . but in a

way, I guess I'm afraid those bad feelings will boomerang back."

"Like bad karma? That concept?"

"I suppose so. I was taught to never speak badly about people, even if they deserved it. Partly out of the idea that no one is perfect, and it's not our place to judge. But also, because all that negativity could bounce back to you. I mean, look at how Dr. Morton lived . . . and how he died."

Helen made a good point. One that gave Lucy a chill. She wondered what Dr. Fielding would say to Helen, but another woman raised her hand and seemed eager to speak. She wore a pink polo shirt and white capris. Her shoulder-length brown hair was touched with blond highlights, and styled with a swoop of bangs above her bright blue eyes. When Dr. Fielding called on her, she introduced herself as Regina Thorne. She seemed nervous but also eager to speak.

"I've had a few run-ins with Dr. Morton, too, and I feel the same as Helen. One day, I bumped into his car in the parking lot outside the fitness center. There was a very minor dent to his bumper, more of scratch if you ask me. I offered to pay for the damage, but he got so incensed, I thought he was having a stroke. He called me some awful names. I was afraid of him, so I called security." She sighed and sat back. "Of course, I told the story to everyone I knew. Now I feel guilty for speaking badly about him, like Helen does."

"I see. Perhaps that's the reason many of you came today. Conflicted and unresolved feelings. Thank you for sharing your stories, Helen and Regina, and for sharing your feelings and fears so honestly," Dr. Fielding said.

"I didn't plan on speaking much," he added. "This is your time. But I will say that you shouldn't blame yourself for your honest reaction to losing your dog, or bumping a car, or anything else that went on between you and Dr. Morton. You had, and still have, a right to your feelings, and you should not feel guilty for them. Personally, I don't believe our lives are governed by karmic laws of actions and punishments or rewards. Just look around. Many who treat others in a disrespectful and totally insensitive way are doing just fine . . ."

He seemed about to say more, when a young man staggered into the circle, an open beer bottle in one hand. Lucy had noticed him enter the building, but thought he was headed for the café.

He was not very tall, but handsome in a raffish way, with bright blue eyes and thick blond hair that looked as if it hadn't been combed in a while. A shade of beard covered his chin and cheeks.

He squeezed past a chair and took center stage, right in front of Dr. Fielding, pointing his bottle as he spoke. "How true, Doctor. Some awful people do just fine. My father, case in point. Until someone pushed him off a cliff," the young man added. "There's a karmic punch line for you."

He spun around, nearly losing his balance. He wore a rumpled suit and tie, loosened around his neck. "Excuse me for crashing the party. But I'd like to share my feelings now. . . . I think you're a bunch of phonies and hypocrites. No one here liked my father. No one is sorry to see him go. For all I know, one of you may have even pushed him over the edge."

"Cory . . ." Meredith stood up from her chair and walked toward him. She tried to touch him, but he shook his head. "Please . . . that's enough."

"That's her son. She was Morton's first wife," Lucy whispered to Dana.

Dana nodded, her gaze fixed on the scene in the center of the support circle.

"I'm not done sharing yet, Mom," he said in slurred words. He gazed around at the group. "You're probably the only one grieving here, Dr. Fielding. But my guess is that's over losing the hefty fee my father paid you for therapy. You had him hooked. But then again, dear old Dad always loved to talk about himself. His favorite topic."

Dr. Fielding was Julian Morton's therapist? That was an interesting twist, Lucy thought.

Cory faced Dr. Fielding.

"That's not true. Though he was my patient. I won't deny that," Dr. Fielding replied evenly.

Cory laughed, a bitter edge to the sound. "Not your most successful case, I hope. No offense. But he was still a nasty bastard even after all those sessions. What did you talk about? All his little grievances? How he laughed at me when I asked him for a loan to start a business? How he treated my mother so despicably?"

"You've said enough. Let's go home now." Meredith stood between Cory and Dr. Fielding. She tried to take her son's arm, but he shook it off.

Dr. Fielding stood up now, too. "I'd be happy to talk to you privately about your father, Cory. But this is not the time or place."

Cory answered with an angry stare. He dropped his head and took a swig of beer. He wiped the back of his hand across his mouth, looking suddenly deflated.

"Not the time and place? Geez, man, I thought this was a grief circle. Guess I got it wrong again. Story of my life, if you ever heard my father talk about me." He turned to his mother, this time allowing her to take his arm. "Let's get out of here."

Meredith nodded and then glanced back at Dr. Fielding. Her gaze met his for a long moment. She seemed distressed, but his answering look was one of sympathy and comfort. Lucy had a feeling that Dr. Fielding would visit

Meredith after the circle broke up. In fact, she was sure of it.

Several more residents spoke, most either expressing fear about a possible killer in their midst or telling stories that further illustrated Julian Morton's toxic personality.

One person did relate a kind moment when Morton helped him carry a heavy cooler from the beach up the steps. Of course, this was because Morton pushed past the man and made him fall to his knees on the steps. Morton helped him up, grabbed the other end of the cooler, and openly admitted he didn't want the man to sue him.

It was *almost* kind, Lucy decided.

After a few more comforting words from Dr. Fielding, the circle dispersed. Many people had seemed eager to express their feelings about Morton, but Lucy wondered if the circle had helped them.

She did think about what Oscar Newland had said, and even what Cory had shouted accusingly to the group. Was the killer among them, hiding behind the beautiful, serene, and safe surroundings of Osprey Shores?

Chapter 7

"Time to crank up the barbie and break out the margarita ingredients, gang," Suzanne said, heading straight into the kitchen when they returned from the grief circle. "I don't know about you, but something about that support group made me very nervous."

When Suzanne was nervous, she liked to cook . . . and eat. And it was time for dinner. Or at least, appetizers and cocktails. They'd decided to barbeque and enjoy a leisurely dinner at the cottage. Lucy was happy about that. Any suggestion to repeat last night's festivities would have sent her straight to her room.

Everyone pitched it to do their share—making a salad, setting the table, and chopping onions and other ingredients for Suzanne, whom they all recognized as the master chef and kitchen boss.

"Phoebe, whip up those cocktails, will you? The blender is ready to launch." Suzanne handed Phoebe a bowl of ice. "Just add a few cubes."

Phoebe did as instructed, whirring up Suzanne's tasty blend.

"What's for dinner, chef?" Lucy sliced red and green peppers into the exact dimensions Suzanne had requested.

"Shish kebabs. Lamb and chicken, and shrimp for our non-carnivores. A Greek salad and rice pilaf."

"Sounds yummy." Phoebe began to pour out the cocktails but stopped when Suzanne gasped.

"Phoebe, honey . . . you forgot to dip the rims in the sea salt. Use those glasses in the fridge. I've been chilling them." Suzanne pushed a dish with the salt mixture toward their newbie barista.

Phoebe stared at the glass, then at the salt. "I always wondered how you got that stuff on there."

Suzanne dipped the first glass, showing her how to do it. "Easy, right? But a nice presentation."

Phoebe coated the rims and filled the chilled glasses, handing them out around the kitchen. Lucy took a refreshing sip. "Yum. Best margarita in town, I'll bet."

"Thank you. No applause necessary. Wait till you taste the kebabs. My secret marinade is to die for," she promised.

"Speaking of secrets, there was a lot of confession going on at the support circle," Dana said. "I was surprised at the openness and honesty. It's not as if all of the residents are friends. But I wasn't surprised about the stories concerning Morton."

Phoebe had finished serving the drinks and Suzanne set down a mezze platter on the kitchen island where they had gathered. The tray of Middle Eastern appetizers she'd prepared to complement her menu looked good enough to star in a cooking show: a bowl of homemade hummus, another of yogurt dill dip, *tzatziki* sauce, a bowl of Gaeta olives and a basket of toasted pita chips.

"The worst was poor Harvey. I felt so bad, I started to cry. That story would give me good motive to hurt somebody. Hurt them bad." Phoebe sounded angry and like she might cry again.

"I'm not surprised the Shelburns wanted to move," Dana said.

"I'm sure Betty Rutledge felt validated, even though she didn't tell her story," Maggie said. "I felt sure she would. I wonder why she held back."

"Maybe, after all the other dark tales, she decided she didn't need to," Lucy said.

Suzanne turned from the counter where she was seasoning skewers of meat and vegetables. "Maybe, after what Oscar said, she thought people might suspect her or her brother of giving Morton his fatal, final push."

"We've always thought she could have done it with some help. Maybe not even her brother. Maybe a neighbor." Lucy popped an olive into her mouth. "There were plenty of candidates airing serious grievances this afternoon."

Dana dipped a celery stick into the hummus. "I'm more interested in people who had grievances and didn't show up."

"Tanya Morton, you mean?" Maggie replied. "I wondered about that."

"I did, too," Lucy said. "But I can understand why she stayed home. I'm sure she knew there would be few—if any—pleasant remembrances about her husband. Maybe she didn't want to be embarrassed, or put on the spot, feeling like she had to defend him. Maybe she didn't want to share her feelings about his passing."

"You mean his pushing," Suzanne said. "Maybe because she teamed up with that hunky handyman, who did the heavy lifting?"

Maggie picked up a pita chip but seemed undecided about where to dip it. "From what Lucy saw last night, it seems those two have a relationship. But it's a big jump to say they conspired to murder her husband."

Suzanne was whisking together olive oil and two kinds of vinegar for the salad dressing. "Not so big a jump in my book. And by relationship, I think you mean affair. Unless he was making a late-night call to unclog her garbage disposal."

"Not likely." Lucy had to laugh. "But from what I saw, even at a distance, they didn't look happy. He was pounding on the door, and she greeted him with a real scowl."

Suzanne seasoned the dressing and set it aside. "A lover's quarrel. These deadly duos always turn on each other sooner or later. Didn't you ever see *Double Indemnity*? When illicit lovers team up to do in a spouse they always go for each other's neck right after the crime. Remember when Barbara Stanwyck says, 'We're both rotten'? And Fred MacMurray says, 'Yeah. But you're a little more rotten.' "

Dana tried the yogurt dill dip with a carrot stick. "I don't remember that part, but I remember everyone smokes a lot of cigarettes, and he shoots her at the end." She shaped her hand like a pistol and pointed it at her stomach. "She says something like, 'But I love you,' and he says, 'I love you, too, baby.' Then bam. It was very film noir."

"As much as I love film noir, I still think it's a big leap to say Tanya and Sam are another dark-hearted duo," Lucy said. "There could be an innocent explanation for Sam going to her house that night."

"Right, Lucy. You're so naïve sometimes. I love you for that, honestly." Suzanne made a kissy face as she lifted a lid and checked what was cooking underneath.

"I'm just trying to be objective. To keep an open mind. There are a boatload of people who had motive to kill Morton."

"It's like a line at the deli counter. Take a number, please." Phoebe pulled a ticket from an imaginary machine.

"And we've totally forgotten Derek Pullman," Lucy added. " A man with a lot of motive, and one who physically threatened Morton. Didn't he say, 'Watch your back, old man'?"

"He did. And painted CHEATER on Morton's car," Suzanne added.

"I still think that would be an illogical thing to do if you were about to kill somebody." Lucy took a sip from her margarita to wash down the dips, which were delicious.

"I agree." Dana nodded, munching a mini carrot. "But, as Lucy and I have already discussed, I still think it's possible that Pullman started off just wanting to damage the car, and then saw Morton on the cliff walk later. Or followed him out there and lost control. Maybe he confronted Morton again about the card game and his debt, and it got physical."

"He does have a good alibi. But alibis can have holes in them once you look closely," Lucy pointed out. "I guess the police are also figuring out these scenarios. And even if there aren't any security cameras on the cliff walk, the police can probably search tapes to figure out who was headed in that direction Friday morning."

"But it was so foggy. That will make it harder to identify people conclusively," Dana pointed out.

Right, the pea soup fog. Lucy had forgotten about that. "Tanya was going to the yoga class, so she would have some logical reason for leaving her cottage in the time frame of the murder. But she got to the class late. That would have given her an opportunity to go out onto the walk and push her husband over the edge. Or sneak out there and wait for him while he was fussing over his car with the security guards, and then rush back to the fitness center for Meredith's class."

"That would have worked out perfectly for her," Phoebe said. "Maybe Sam was already on the walk, waiting, and she went out there just to distract Morton."

"And Sam Briggs is all over the development from early in the morning, riding around in his pickup truck," Maggie said. "No one who saw him driving or walking around the grounds that morning would have thought it odd or suspicious."

"It all seems to fall together, if they are having an affair," Lucy said. "But maybe a little too easily?"

"How do you mean?" Dana asked.

"Well, if we can come up with this scenario so quickly, why aren't the police taking Tanya and Sam in for questioning?"

"Maybe they are, and we just haven't heard about it," Phoebe said.

"I doubt it. News like that would travel fast around here," Maggie said. "Maybe they both have good alibis for the time of Morton's murder and were eliminated from the suspect list. But now that Lucy told the police she saw them together in a compromising situation, it might change things."

"She does have the most motive. She wanted a divorce and a good chunk of his money." Suzanne swept in, carrying the platter of perfectly grilled kebabs. She'd obviously been tuned into the conversation while outside, cooking.

"Pullman has motive too," Dana pointed out. "With Morton gone, he's free of a hefty debt. Amy said he was an investment banker but lost his job. Even if he has a good cushion of savings, this isn't exactly a budget-wise place to live," Dana added.

Phoebe wandered over to the stove, where Suzanne had left the kebabs. She hung over the platter, inhaled deeply, and practically swooned. "Speaking of ups and downs, I could down some of this delicious food. It smells amazing, and the grilled vegetables are so beautiful. Wait . . . let me take a picture. It will look good, even on my cell phone."

Lucy smiled. Why did people Phoebe's age feel compelled to take photos of everything they ate, then post it on Facebook and Instagram? Although, Lucy had to admit, Suzanne's cooking was worthy of going viral.

"This meal does looks like the cover of a gourmet cooking magazine," Maggie said.

"Gee, thanks, guys. Just a little something I whipped up. We can keep the hummus and yogurt sauce on the table. I grilled some pita bread, too," Suzanne said, showing them another platter. "And there's Greek salad in the fridge."

"What a feast. I won't eat for a week after this." Dana rose and carried her glass to the sink. "Let me help you," she said to Suzanne. "Tell me what to do."

"Before we all faint from hunger, the first thing we need to do is clean up from our first course and set the table outside." Maggie picked up her glass, and Phoebe's.

Lucy got up from her comfy seat and set to work, too. A few minutes later they were seated on the patio behind the cottage, enjoying their Mediterranean banquet along with a light white wine.

"I couldn't find Greek wine. It's Italian, close enough. A crisp little *Frascati*," Suzanne explained.

"It goes perfectly with the meal." Lucy took a sip of the wine and then a taste of her salad. Everything was delicious.

"I know you paid a small fortune to take us out to dinner last night, Suzanne. But this meal is even better," Maggie confessed.

"Aww. Come on. Of course it's not. It's just some shish kebabs. I make them all the time at home."

"Then your family is very lucky. This is even better than a restaurant. And the company helps, too," Dana added. "A toast to the chef." She raised her glass to Suzanne and everyone did the same, clinking glasses with each other.

"Definitely . . . here's to Suzanne. Long may she cook, and very often, for us," Phoebe said, making everyone laugh.

They enjoyed the rest of dinner without talking about Dr. Morton's murder or the possible suspects. Instead, talk turned to Lucy's wedding. Lucy actually found talking about the murder less stressful, but she had to indulge her friends.

They worked together clearing the table and cleaning the kitchen. Suzanne's phone rang just as she was serving dessert.

Lucy could tell Amy was on the line. The conversation was brief, with Suzanne saying, "Really?" and "I'm not at all surprised" several times. The group sat silently, waiting for Suzanne to finish the call.

"Breaking news. The police took both Tanya and Sam in for questioning. Amy just heard it from Helen Shelburn, who saw Tanya escorted into a police cruiser. She asked around and found out Sam was taken in, too."

"I'm not surprised, either," Maggie said. "Maybe the police finally have the same idea that we do, and this case will be solved before the night is through."

"Maybe even before we finish playing Scrabble?" Phoebe added, a hopeful and questioning note in her tone.

Some of her friends were not as keen as Phoebe on playing Scrabble. Who could be? Phoebe was a bona fide Scrabble fiend, employing great strategy and possessing a rich Scrabble vocabulary.

Scrabble champions knew a lot of words with Q and Z,

the highest scoring letters. *X* was up there, too. Obscure words like quixotic and xenophobic came to Scrabble champs easily. Lucy didn't doubt that if there was such a thing as Scrabble Olympics, Phoebe would definitely bring home the gold.

"I know I'm a lamb hopping off to slaughter, but I'm in," Lucy said. "Maybe we will hear more about Tanya Morton and Sam Briggs while we're playing."

"Like an eight-letter word that begins with *A*?" Phoebe said. "Arrested. Or maybe apprehended, pinched, collared, nabbed, nailed?"

Suzanne grinned, spooning out a mixture of fresh berries over scoops of creamy vanilla and strawberry ice creams, piled onto a shortcake. "We get the gist, Phoebe. How many points would you rack up for one of those?"

Phoebe shrugged. "Depends if you hit any double letter or double word boxes. Or a triple letter or triple word box. That's sweet, too. Sometimes a short word can score bigger than a longer one. You have to look carefully. Get the big picture."

"You already beat me. I think I'll watch a movie on Netflix. Anyone want to join me?" Suzanne added a spoonful of berry sauce to Phoebe's dessert and passed it over.

"That sounds relaxing," Dana said.

"I'll try my hand at Scrabble. I have to give Lucy some support," Maggie said.

Lucy appreciated the gesture, though she knew Maggie wasn't very serious about the game and would probably knit while they played.

"What's on the agenda for tomorrow? I have an appointment for a Reiki massage and a facial." Suzanne had served everyone and now spooned up a taste of her own dessert. "You're coming with me, right, Lucy?"

"I'm all in on the pampering session. But I just have a facial scheduled so far."

"I think I'll skip the spa. I might just sit on the beach again and read," Dana said. "That's relaxing enough for me."

"I was thinking of a mani-pedi," Maggie said. "But I'm scheduled to do that second knitting class in the afternoon, to see how everyone is doing with the pattern. I wanted to get further along on it myself."

"Do you think people have been knitting with a murderer on the loose?" Suzanne asked in her blunt style.

"Actually . . . I do. Maybe even more than usual. It's a real stress buster. You know that," Maggie said, taking out her own knitting.

"I agree with Maggie. I think Dr. Morton's murder has inspired some busy needles this weekend. It's the perfect distraction from all this stressful news," Dana said.

Suzanne added an extra spoonful of berries to her dish. "When you put it that way, I have to agree. But all things considered, Maggie, you really don't have to give another workshop. I'm sure everyone will understand."

"I know, but I did promise Amy. It will be a good distraction for her, too," Maggie said. "And a few in her group have approached me with questions. I hate to leave them all dangling, having to sort things out by themselves."

"That's very responsible of you," Lucy said.

"I made a promise. And frankly, I'd rather be helping knitters than be pummeled and prodded on a massage table."

Suzanne quickly came to the defense of the massage therapists. "They don't pummel unless you ask them to. I think it's delightful. I just zone out."

Phoebe had taken out her Scrabble deluxe edition box, and began setting up for the game. "I'm in Maggie's camp.

I'm not into spas, either. I feel weird, having everyone wait on me, and walking around in a bathrobe and flip-flops all day. I'm going out for a hike on the beach. Maybe take more photos . . . with my phone."

Lucy heard her give a little plaintive sigh. "When will you get your camera back? Have you called the police station?"

Phoebe glanced at her and then shook the bag of tiles. "I thought about it. But Dunbar scares me."

Lucy couldn't help smiling, though she didn't mean to make light of Phoebe's feelings. "Do you want me to call for you?" She glanced at her watch. "I can call right now. She might not be on duty, but I'll leave a message."

"Okay. If you want to. That would be great, Lucy. Thanks."

Phoebe took her place at the table, opposite Lucy across the Scrabble board. Lucy took out her phone and dialed the police station. Then she was transferred to Detective Dunbar's line. Another officer picked up and quickly checked on Lucy's question.

When Lucy ended the call, she was happy to relay good news. "They said they're done, and you can pick it up tomorrow."

"Great! At least I have one more day to take pictures before we leave on Monday."

"I guess that means we won't see much of you tomorrow, Phoebe," Dana said. "Just be careful out near the cliff," she added. "It's easy to get distracted, focused on the view or a bird in flight, and forget how close you are to the edge."

"Never mind some creepy killer sneaking up behind me. I'm done taking pictures from the cliff top, thank you. I'll be down on the beach, on solid ground. I don't even like looking over the edge," Phoebe admitted,

"Acrophobia?" Dana asked.

"Exactly. And thanks for the word," Phoebe replied. "Definitely high scoring, with proper placement."

Lucy and Maggie had already taken their places at the board and picked out their tiles from the bag.

Lucy glanced at Maggie. "We're going to get crushed." She sighed. "But it will be fun."

"How about vanquished? A few more tiles and I can put that one down."

"I picked some good tiles, too," Maggie murmured as she arranged hers on a little wooden tray. She sounded more into the game than Lucy expected. Focus, Lucy. You could come in low scorer tonight if you're not careful.

Suzanne and Dana sat side by side on the couch, negotiating over which movie to choose. Suzanne's phone rang, and she quickly answered it. Once again, Lucy could tell it was Amy and, once again, the room went silent waiting to hear what she said.

The call was brief. Suzanne put her phone down and turned to her friends. "That was Amy. She just heard from Helen Shelburn. Sam Briggs was released by the police, but they're still questioning Tanya."

"They didn't keep him very long," Maggie said. "I wonder why they're keeping her longer."

"They must suspect her more, or have more on her," Suzanne said.

"Not necessarily," Dana replied. "Maybe Sam has a better lawyer."

"I doubt that," Suzanne said.

"Maybe they're just being thorough. It doesn't mean anything. Maybe she's just a wife who wanted a divorce, and her husband died before they could hash it out," Maggie replied. "I guess you could say she just got lucky . . . in a way."

Lucy fiddled with her Scrabble tiles. She had a good word to put down: enigma. Not bad right out of the gate.

"A lucky coincidence? Maybe," Lucy speculated. "But I have a feeling there's something more going on with Tanya. More than her nasty divorce or even a thing with Sam. Something the police haven't figured out yet."

Chapter 8

Lucy woke slowly from a deep sleep, as if she were underwater and pushing her way up to the surface. Images of the cliff walk and frolicking mermaids lingered in her mind's eye as the bedroom came into focus.

Her room was dark. Rain spattered the window. She heard a cell phone ring in the next room where Suzanne and Dana were sleeping. Finally, it stopped. Lucy was sure it was the middle of the night, and she took her phone from the night table to check the time. It was a few minutes before six. She heard Suzanne talking to Dana, though she couldn't make out what they were saying.

She slipped out of bed and knocked on their door. "Come in," Dana called out quietly.

"Hey guys. What's up?" Lucy felt groggy. She blinked and rubbed her eyes, then sat on the edge of Suzanne's bed. Suzanne and Dana were sitting up and looked wide awake. Suzanne still held her phone in her hand.

"Is everything okay at home, Suzanne?"

"The home front is hunky-dory. But the Cutler front is a Dumpster fire. The police just came back to their cottage. They asked Rob a lot of questions, then took him to the station for another interview."

"Another interview? But why?" Lucy was shocked.

Dana sat up and hugged her knees. "Amy said it has to do with Tanya Morton and something she told the police last night. Now they suspect some connection between Rob and Tanya."

Lucy felt another shock wave ripple through her. "It's Rob and Tanya now? Not Sam and Tanya?"

Suzanne shrugged. "Who knows what Tanya would say to save her own glorious skin. I really doubt Rob would be unfaithful to Amy. Though that Tanya is a knockout."

Dana leaned back on her pillows. "Tanya could be involved with both men. That's not beyond the range of possibilities. One has brains, and the other, brawn. The total package if you put them together."

"Did she need a total package to kill her husband? If she did conspire to kill him, I mean," Lucy said.

Suzanne checked her text messages and put her phone aside. "It's all very muddled. All I know is that Amy is practically hysterical. I'm going over there right away."

"That's good of you, Suzanne." Dana got of bed and slipped on her robe. "But why don't you ask Amy to come here? Having all of us around will be more of a distraction. I'll make breakfast. You can just focus on her."

Suzanne stared at Dana a moment. "Deal . . . as long as we're not eating scrambled tofu and sipping green smoothies."

Dana laughed. "Don't worry. I'll make something fun. I think I saw a waffle iron in the cupboard."

"You did. I brought it from home." Suzanne got up, too, and put on her slippers.

"You brought a waffle iron? Seriously?" This was hard to believe, even for Suzanne.

"Why not? It comes in handy on a long weekend. I rarely travel without a hair dryer or a waffle iron."

"How about a Cuisinart?" Dana asked. "Do you have one of those stashed somewhere in your car?"

Suzanne pulled on a kimono, purple silk covered with pink and lavender blossoms. "Don't be silly. I just bring the mini chopper."

As Suzanne sashayed out of the bedroom, Dana and Lucy stared at each other a moment, then laughed. Lucy followed Dana to the kitchen, careful not to wake Maggie and Phoebe.

"So how long did the Scrabble tournament last? You three were going strong when Suzanne called it a night," Dana asked.

"We were up a while after you turned in. Four rounds. Phoebe won all the games by a wide margin, of course. Maggie and I each made second place twice." Lucy gratefully accepted a mug of coffee that Dana handed over to her.

"Good thing you weren't playing for money."

"Real good thing. I'd be wiped out. I still have some strange words floating in my head. Ubiquitous. Mimesis . . . Phoebe knows them all."

"Are you sure she didn't make a few up?" Dana was kidding of course.

"She was prepared for fact-checking with a *Webster's Pocket Dictionary.* I have to work on my vocabulary."

"That little Phoebe, she's full of surprises."

"You guys talking about me?" Phoebe walked into the kitchen in her pajamas—polka-dot cotton shorts and a black Hello Kitty T-shirt. Her long hair was in a high ponytail, her eyes still half-closed.

"Only in a good way, honey," Dana said. "Coffee?" She held out a mug, and Phoebe took it gratefully.

"Sorry if we woke you. Amy just called. The police came to the Cutlers' early this morning and took Rob back to the station for more questioning."

Phoebe was curled in an armchair. She put down her coffee and gasped. "OMG! That's awful. Why would Rob want to murder Dr. Morton? He hardly knew him. That makes no sense."

"Tanya told the police something that's turned their focus back on Rob. We don't know what she said yet," Lucy explained.

"Rob and Tanya . . . an item?" Phoebe looked shocked again. "No offense, but he's sort of a science nerd and she's . . . well, like a supermodel."

"Catalogs, I heard," Lucy clarified. "But still. I get your point."

Dana had already taken out the waffle iron and was measuring ingredients. "Opposites attract?"

"I agree with Suzanne. I doubt it's an affair. But if it's not . . . what is their connection?" Lucy was stumped.

"Maybe we'll learn more when Amy comes," Dana said.

"Amy is coming? Now? It's barely seven AM." Maggie walked in, tying the belt on her dark blue bathrobe.

Dana quickly caught her up on the morning's events.

"My goodness . . . it sounds like Rob is a person of interest in this case."

"We know what happens after that. From person of interest to suspect number one," Phoebe said. "I don't know why they've singled him out. There are so many other people, a lot closer to Dr. Morton, who hated him and had more reason than Rob to do him in."

"Let's hope so." Maggie nodded and sipped her coffee.

Suzanne came into the kitchen, freshly showered. She wore dark blue shorts and a blue and white long-sleeved top that had a little gold anchor sewed near the shoulder. A nautical look, though it was hardly sailing weather. A bit cool this morning, and still raining.

"Amy will be over in a few minutes. She liked the idea of hanging out with us this morning. And the waffles nailed it."

"We're having a waffle-fest? Yum." Phoebe sat up, looking as interested as Lucy's dog Tink did every time she heard her kibble bag rattle.

"I'm going to make a batch and put them in the oven. We can put the leftover berries from last night's dessert on top."

"Maybe some of the leftover whipped cream would be nice, too," Suzanne suggested. "I didn't realize you were such a good cook, Dana."

"I'm just the understudy today, stepping in for the star," Dana said modestly. Lucy thought that they all gave Suzanne so much attention for her culinary artistry, it was hard for Dana's kitchen flair to be noticed.

By the time Amy's knock sounded on the door, the table was set for six and everything needed for the waffle-fest—berries, cinnamon, and syrup—was set out along with coffee and juice.

"Thank you so much for having me over." Amy pushed back the hood on her yellow rain slicker. "I'm sorry I called so early, Suzanne. But I was going a little stir-crazy, alone in the house and worrying about Rob."

"Of course you were. We're glad you came." Maggie took Amy's wet jacket and put an arm around her shoulder. "How annoying is it to be woken up by the police at your front door? Couldn't they wait until a decent hour?"

"They try to catch you unaware," Amy said. "That's what our lawyer told us. I think they had just brought Tanya Morton back to her cottage after her questioning. And came straight to our house to take poor Rob in for another interrogation. He was hardly awake, or coherent. They tripped him up with some questions about Tanya Morton when they walked in. Before I knew it, they put him in the police car again."

Suzanne shook cinnamon onto her waffle. "What sort of questions?"

Lucy was glad Suzanne asked. She was just about to.

"Mainly, about their relationship. Which they don't even have," Amy insisted. "But for some reason, the police think they do. They say a witness saw Rob and Tanya on the beach, the morning of Dr. Morton's death. But Rob went out surf casting that morning, and she was at the yoga class. A secret rendezvous would have been impossible."

Lucy could see that Amy was upset and wanted to think only the best of her husband and her marriage. While it was true Tanya was at the yoga studio, she did arrive late. There would have been time to meet Rob on the beach, even time to push her husband off the cliff with Rob's help, before she arrived at the studio. And she did have that poison ivy on her feet.

Lucy guessed that her friends were considering the same timeline but didn't want to upset Amy even more.

"What did Tanya say about Rob last night? Did the police let on this morning?" Maggie asked.

"Not much. She claims Sam Briggs saw her and Rob together, and that Sam was blackmailing her . . . but she never said she was having an affair with my husband," Amy quickly added.

But why else would someone be blackmailed, Lucy wondered?

"I'm sure Rob wasn't fooling around with Tanya," Suzanne said. "But Tanya is a perfect target for a slime like Sam Briggs. A rich trophy wife, desperate for a divorce, and in a battle over the prenup. Low-hanging fruit. If Morton suspected Tanya was having an affair, she wouldn't have a chance of getting a decent settlement."

"Yes, that's it. Sam Briggs was trying to make something out of nothing," Amy said. "Maybe Rob and Tanya did speak to each other once or twice. Maybe she was running on the beach and stopped to talk to him. It doesn't mean anything. Sam was trying to exploit Tanya, and her sensitive situation."

Lucy noticed Amy's words ended on a quiet note, as if she wasn't entirely sure. Everything in Amy's world was upside down this morning. Upside down and inside out.

Dana pushed back her plate and looked up at Amy. "Rob will tell his side of it. It's his word against hers. There's no law against talking to your neighbor on the beach, or anywhere else for that matter. If Tanya said something incriminating about Rob to turn the focus away from herself, I'm sure his attorney can handle it."

"Walter is a good attorney. I'm sure he won't let the police confuse Rob, or let him say more than he has to." Amy nodded and took a sip of coffee. She sat back, her glance sweeping around the table.

Amy was overwrought, all stirred up defending her husband. Lucy's heart went out to her. But had Rob let the past get the best of him? Had he teamed up with Tanya to murder Morton? Or had he simply met up with Morton on the way to the beach and confronted him? Maybe intending to talk things out, once and for all, but somehow finding himself in a physical confrontation. Had Morton's death been an unintended accident?

That was another possibility. One that police were very likely to consider, too.

Soon after they'd cleared up breakfast, it was time for Lucy's and Suzanne's spa appointments. It was still raining, and Lucy was glad they had scheduled something fun to do. Everyone gathered at the door to put on rain slickers and find their umbrellas.

"I feel so bad leaving you, Amy. I won't go. I'll stay here and keep you company," Suzanne said to her old friend.

"That's very sweet of you. But I'll be fine. It was a great

break to join you for breakfast. You have some pampering. I'm going back to the cottage to wait for Rob to call."

Suzanne pulled on a shiny rain jacket, cherry red, and
pulled up the hood. "All right . . . but you could come,
too. I'm sure they could fit you in somewhere. You can
have one of my appointments."

"Thank you, but I wouldn't feel right indulging myself
while my poor husband is being badgered by the police.
You guys have fun. That's what you're here for. Not to
babysit me."

"We don't feel like that at all, Amy. We want to help you
in any way we can," Maggie assured her.

"I'm afraid the only way you could help us is to figure
out who really pushed Julian Morton off the cliff. I know
my husband didn't do it."

Maggie exchanged glances with her friends. Lucy knew
what she was thinking. Could they help Amy and Rob?
Perhaps, she thought. They had certainly talked about the
crime and the various players enough.

Lucy and Suzanne quickly parted ways at the spa.
Phoebe was unable to take a hike in the rain but happy to
stay back at the cottage, knitting with Maggie and Dana.
It was a perfect day for that.

After she checked in, Lucy was handed a blue spa robe
and soft slippers. She changed in a little wood-paneled
booth with a locker. Phoebe was right. This was the part
of going to a spa that she didn't like, either; walking
around in a bathrobe and slippers all afternoon. It reminded her of having a cold.

Pitchers of green tea with slices of citrus and floating
bits of mint were everywhere. Lucy poured herself a glass
and waited in the treatment room for her facial.

Another woman, also dressed in a blue robe, walked in. Lucy recognized her right away—Helen Shelburn, from Amy's knitting group. She had spoken at the support circle. The woman who was neighbors with the Mortons.

"I'm sorry. Do I have the wrong room?" she asked Lucy.

"I was told that the spa is short on staff today, and I'd be sharing a room with another client."

"That must be me. They forgot to give me the same warning. I'm Helen Shelburn," she said, holding out her hand.

"Lucy Binger." Lucy shook her hand and sat back down again.

"I saw you in the support circle run by Dr. Fielding, and at Amy Cutler's knitting group the other night."

"Oh right . . . I remember. You and your friends are visiting Amy for the weekend." Helen sat back in her chair and chose a magazine from an overflowing basket. She held it in her lap but didn't open it. *Vogue*, Lucy noticed. That figured.

"Quite the weekend for visitors. You must think our community is some sort of soap opera set."

Lucy smiled. "Not at all. But it was a shock to hear how Dr. Morton died, and that there was foul play. Even though we didn't know him."

"Yes, it was a shock. But who really knew the man? He was just a bundle of grudges and pathology, if you ask me."

From what she'd heard, Lucy could understand that. Julian Morton had killed Helen's dog. Of course she had a harsh opinion of the man. But hadn't Meredith said how charming Julian Morton was when she'd first met him, before they married? Everyone has several sides to their personality and an inner life that no one else ever sees.

"Now the police are trying to pin Tanya with his murder. They came to her house Saturday night and took her down to the police station. I know because she texted me and asked if I'd look in on her dog if she wasn't back by midnight. Goodness knows, she had plenty of cause to want to do her husband in. He was a penny-pincher and didn't want to give her a cent more than their prenup specified, which was peanuts. He got away with murder when he divorced Meredith," Helen added. "Did she ever get a raw deal."

Lucy nearly smiled at Helen's choice of words. "That's too bad. I did hear she was left with nothing when she divorced Morton. She told me herself," Lucy said.

"Then you know the whole story. The poor thing can hardly make ends meet, working two jobs. She's always coming down with something—a cold, a skin rash. She's worn out."

Meredith may have been worn out from making ends meet, but she had a strong spirit. Lucy could see that just from talking to her once or twice. But Lucy wanted to talk more about Tanya, and she wondered if Helen knew what Tanya had told the police. "So, what time did Tanya get back? Did you have to walk her dog?"

"She got back just before midnight. She called me, and we talked a little. The police thought she was having an affair with Sam Briggs. If that was the case, half the women in this development should be called in for questioning. It wasn't like that at all. Sam isn't Tanya's type, despite the muscles and beach-boy looks. The idea that they were lovers and conspired to kill her husband is preposterous. And I really don't think she did it alone, either. Tanya can be self-centered and even manipulative, but she's no killer."

Lucy was interested in Helen's assessment of Tanya. Helen was smart, and she knew Tanya. Lucy wondered if she should tell Helen that Sam had tried to blackmail

Tanya because he'd spotted her and Rob together. But, if Tanya hadn't told her neighbor, Lucy didn't feel she should disclose the information. Maybe Helen knew and didn't want to disclose the information, either.

Instead Lucy said, "I heard Tanya told the police something about Rob Cutler."

Would Helen bite? Did she even know the lowdown?

Helen didn't answer right away. She opened her magazine, and flipped a few pages. She spoke without looking up. "Well, there was something going on between Tanya and Rob, but it wasn't romantic. More like a business deal."

"Business deal?"

Helen shrugged, her gaze fixed on a glossy page, where models posed in high fashion swimwear were surrounded by penguins. "That's all Tanya would say about it."

Lucy wished Helen knew more. What sort of business deal could Tanya have with Rob? That didn't make sense. Had Helen misunderstood Tanya's explanation, or was Tanya trying to cover up something?

Lucy wanted to ask more, but the door opened and two women walked in, dressed in pale blue cotton uniforms that looked vaguely medical. They also wore the same hairstyle, a tight bun.

The older of the two wore a white coat with a mermaid emblem on the pocket. She smiled and introduced herself.

"Good morning, ladies. I am your facial therapist, Monique." She had slight accent, Lucy noticed. Russian maybe? "This is my assistant, Jacqueline. Your skin is in for a wonderful experience."

Jacqueline, the assistant, tucked Lucy's hair into a terry cloth turban and released a lever on her chair that made the back drop. Lucy had no choice but to lie flat. Then she did the same to Helen, who seemed more accustomed to the routine.

Monique snapped on gloves. Then she rolled over a large magnifying glass on a metal stand and positioned it over Lucy's face. Lucy looked up into Monique's distorted eyes.

"Just relax, dear. Your skin is in good hands," Monique said in a soothing voice. Then her expression grew serious as she slipped on glasses that hung from a chain around her neck. She peered at Lucy's skin through the thick magnifying lense, her expression intense.

Lucy couldn't imagine what she was seeing. Something like the craters on the Moon?

"Do you hydrate, dear?" Monique asked.

"Drink water, you mean?"

Monique nodded. "How many ounces a day?"

Lucy wasn't sure. "A lot. Especially if I'm exercising."

"You should drink ten glasses. Or more. And exfoliate? How many times a week?"

Exfoliate? A great word for Scrabble. Even Phoebe hadn't hit on that one yet. Lucy knew what Monique meant by exfoliate—to scrub her skin with lotion that had sandy grains that scrape off the dead cells. She'd tried it once or twice, and ended up looking like she had a blotchy sunburn.

"I'm not sure . . . I scrub well with a washcloth, and I never sleep with makeup. I hardly even wear makeup."

"Hmm." Monique did not look impressed.

I floss twice a day. Does that count?

Monique pushed the magnifying glass aside. She reached over and picked up a slim blue binder from the counter, then flipped through the pages.

"Here is our treatment menu. It's very extensive. For you, I would recommend the Pomegranate Clay Mask, a magnesium-rich clay that will absorb impurities, detoxify, and exfoliate. It's infused with Tasmanian pepper berry, lilly pilly, and muntrie berry for deeper hydration."

Great. I was wondering if any lilly pilly or Tasmanian pepper berry would be involved, Lucy wanted to say.

Instead she just nodded. "Sounds good. Can I take a look at the other choices?"

"Of course, dear. Here you are. While you're browsing, I'll examine Mrs. Shelburn."

"Take your time," Lucy replied. She sat up and flipped through the binder. Menu was the right word. Reading the ingredients started to make her hungry. Especially the Egg Cream Facial and the Avocado, Ginseng, and Honey Mask. The prices were shocking. Charging a lot made customers feel they were getting something special. But you're not here to save money. You're here to fling, she reminded herself.

In the nearby recliner, Helen was undergoing the magnifying glass routine, but she was the one asking Monique questions.

"How do my pores look today, Monique? Do you see that awful sun spot over my left eyebrow? Can you do anything to fade it?"

"Of course we can, Mrs. Shelburn. A dab of seaweed and volcanic ash should do the trick. No worries."

"Great. Thanks." Helen settled back in her chair with a sigh.

Helen chose the Lingzhi-Rose Mask, with the volcanic ash extra. Lucy went with the Pomegranate Clay suggested by Monique.

Lying back in the chair again, Lucy's skin was cleansed with scented wipes, and then a purple-colored goop was smeared all over her face and under her chin.

Let the exfoliation begin! Lucy's inner cheerleader shouted.

Lucy had hoped that once Monique and Jacqueline left to see other clients, she could wheedle more information out of Helen. But her face immediately seized into a Kabuki mask as the clay solution quickly hardened.

"I'll be back soon. I know it's hard, but no chatting, ladies. It will ruin your treatment," Monique advised as she lowered the lights and lit several scented candles before she slipped out the door.

And you're paying an arm and a leg for this silliness, Lucy reminded herself.

She turned her head slightly and tried to catch Helen's eye. But her treatment mate lay with her eyes shut, looking as if she was drifting off to the sounds of the soothing, Asian lute tunes that drifted through the sound system.

Lucy sighed and lay back, too. At least my pores will be clean for the wedding. Check that one off my to-do list.

Lucy didn't think she would fall asleep, but soon did. Awakened by the sound of Monique returning, she felt disoriented and couldn't remember for a moment where she was.

Monique's smiling face loomed over her. "Did you have a nice rest, dear? That helps the treatment penetrate."

Lucy tried to smile back, but her facial muscles met heavy resistance.

Removing the mask was a bit more complicated than slathering it on, and after the clay chunks were removed, a seemingly endless series of face wipes and creams were applied by both Monique and her assistant.

When Jacqueline finally cranked up the chair, Lucy felt dizzy. The many scents of the lotions and candles filled her head.

Jacqueline removed her turban. Lucy generously tipped the attendants and said goodbye to Helen, who was examining her sun spot with a handheld mirror and did not look pleased.

"Nice to chat with you, Helen. Maybe I'll see you again before we leave. Maggie is giving another class this afternoon on the project she introduced Thursday night. In case you didn't know," Lucy added.

"Really? I didn't hear about that. Amy usually calls around. I guess she's had her hands full."

Waiting to see if her husband was going to end up arrested for murder, Lucy knew Helen meant.

"Yes, she's been busy," Lucy said. "I'll remind her to make sure the group knows about it."

Lucy left the treatment room and soon found Suzanne, who sat reading a magazine in the reception area, where they had planned to meet up.

"Lucy, you're practically glowing. What did they do to you in there?"

Lucy felt alarmed. She checked her image in a mirror. "Do I look bad?"

"I meant glowing in a good way. Your skin looks really . . . fresh!" Suzanne reached over and stroked Lucy's cheek then gave it a little pat. "Smooth as a baby's bottom."

"Thanks. I think. Must be the Tasmanian pepper berry."

"The what?"

"Don't ask. The goop they put on my face had a lot of exotic ingredients. But even more interesting, was the chat I just had with Helen Shelburn. We were sharing the treatment room. Helen is in Amy's knitting group. Dark red hair, wealthy, and well-preserved looking?"

"The Mortons' neighbor. She told the story about poor Harvey?"

"That's right. She had a few more stories to share. About

Tanya. She said Tanya wasn't having an affair with Rob. She said Tanya told her it was a business deal."

Suzanne looked puzzled. "A business deal? What sort of deal could bring Tanya and Rob together? And force them to meet in secret, no less."

"I wondered about that, too. I wonder if Rob is back yet. I'm sure he had to tell the police what was really going on. At least, his side of the story. Maybe he's told Amy, too."

Suzanne closed her magazine. "Let's get out of these robes and find out. I'm starting to feel like a patient in a fancy mental health facility."

"What about your Reiki massage?"

"Reiki-schmeki. This is more important. I felt so bad when Amy said the only way we could help was to find out who murdered Morton. It wasn't Rob. I feel sure of that. Despite his past bad blood with the not-so-good doctor, Rob is just not that sort of person."

Lucy had trouble picturing Rob pushing Julian Morton over the edge, too. "I doubt Rob did it. But it seems he was up to something with Tanya that's made him a prime suspect. I'd also like to get out of this robe, and this music is making me crazy," she added in a quieter voice.

"It's making me hungry for sushi. But that's another problem altogether."

The friends agreed to dress and meet back at the same spot. Suzanne was going to text Amy and find out if Rob had returned and if they wanted visitors.

Lucy was the first one dressed, but soon saw Suzanne come through the doors of the treatment area to meet her. "What did Amy say?"

"She said Rob is back. They had a long talk, and now he's taking a nap. She wants to see us and tell us what happened. She's coming over to our cottage."

The rain had stopped, but it was still misty. Lucy pulled

on her khaki-green jacket. "That's a good plan. She can be more open without Rob around," Lucy said.

Suzanne zipped up her slicker and pushed through the glass doors to the terrace outside. "Yes, she can talk more freely. I can hardly wait to hear what she has to say."

Chapter 9

Lucy felt as if she was in a footrace, trying to keep up with Suzanne as they did a speed walk back to the cottage.

They found Maggie, Dana, and Phoebe gathered in the living room. Maggie and Dana were knitting, and Phoebe was checking photos on her digital camera.

"You got your camera back," Lucy greeted her.

"The police called a little while after you left. Dana drove me into town in Suzanne's car."

Dana looked up from her knitting. "I hope you don't mind that I borrowed the SUV without asking, Suzanne. I tried to call, but you must have been in the midst of your spa experience."

"I did shut my phone off. At those prices, you don't want to be interrupted by some whining adolescent, asking when you're coming home."

Suzanne had twin boys and an older daughter. She handled them well, considering how much time she had to spend out of the house for her job. It was quite a juggling act. Lucy didn't envy her and could totally understand why she'd shut off her phone.

"It's no problem at all. I'm glad you got your camera back, Phoebe. Any interesting photos?"

"I got some great shots of the birds making their nests. I'm going to edit a few and show you later."

"I'd love to see them, too, Phoebe," Lucy said. "Let me know when you're done. How about the mysterious shadow in the shrubbery? Did the police say anything about that shot?"

"No, they didn't. I've been looking at it again. I think it's just fog."

"Another dead end in the investigation. But I'm not surprised," Maggie said.

"Never mind shadows in shrubbery. We have some real news to pick over," Lucy said. "I was chatting with a woman at the spa. She was having a facial in the same treatment room as me. She spoke at the support circle. Helen Shelburn."

"The Mortons' next door neighbor?" Dana said.

"Harvey's mom?" Phoebe added on a sadder note.

"One and the same. She told me that Tanya was definitely not having an affair with Sam Briggs, which we already knew. And she said Tanya was involved with Rob, but not romantically. Tanya told her it was more of business deal."

"That sounds highly unlikely to me. What sort of business could they have together?" Maggie asked.

"Yes, it's sort of fishy," Phoebe agreed. "But maybe he was catching fish when he was out surf casting and gave them all to Tanya to sell at a farmers' market or something. That's why he never brought any home to Amy."

Lucy wanted to laugh at the idea of Tanya as a fish monger at a farmers' market, but she didn't want to hurt Phoebe's feelings. "I don't think selling fish is exactly Tanya's style. But you might be on to something, Phoebe. Maybe the surf casting was just a cover for meeting with Tanya on the beach to talk about whatever they were working on," Lucy said.

"I was thinking the same thing," Dana added. "It's very secluded down there. No one would notice if a woman jogging stopped to talk to one of the fishermen. And Rob could easily park far from the other surf casters."

"Or they could talk in his car. Or behind his car. He has a large SUV, a Volvo, I think," Maggie said. "It would be much safer than texting or sending emails. No trail of their conversations. I've heard that, even if you delete emails, investigators can still find them."

"That makes sense to me. Face-to-face conversations leave no trail. Rob is smart with technology," Dana said.

"Okay, so we have Rob and Tanya holding secret business meetings on the beach, while Rob is pretending to be this devoted fisherman," Lucy proposed. "We still don't know what they were talking about."

Suzanne flopped on the couch next to Maggie. "That question might be answered very soon. Rob got back from the police station a little while ago. Amy said they had a long talk, and now he's taking a nap, so she's coming over here to fill us in."

Maggie looked up from knitting. "Good work, Suzanne. I'm interested to hear what she has to say. I'm curious, of course, but I do hope there's some way we can help them. Just because Rob and Tanya had some secret business scheme, it still doesn't mean he killed Dr. Morton."

"I agree. We have to help them, if we can." Lucy rose from her chair. "I'm going to make some tea. Would anyone like some?"

"I think we'd all like some. Make a big pot, and we'll have some of those burnt butter sugar cookies Suzanne brought along," Maggie suggested.

Lucy was in the kitchen, preparing the tea when she heard a knock on the door, and then, Suzanne greeting Amy as she came into the cottage. The tea kettle screeched a moment, but Lucy quickly shut off the burner, to better hear the conversation in the next room.

"How are you? How is Rob?" Suzanne asked.

"To be totally honest, I'm worn to a frazzle. And Rob is . . . well, he's scared to death. We both are. The police have named him as a person of interest in the case. Rob's lawyer barely got him out of there without charges. Luckily, there's no physical evidence or witnesses that place Rob at the scene of Morton's death. The police even checked his shoe size."

"Lucy and I were at the crime scene," Lucy heard Dana say. "The police took imprints of footprints on the path and in the brush. We saw the leftover plaster that they used."

Then Maggie added, "Not anywhere as conclusive as fingerprints. But it does give them something to go on."

"Just remember, if you kill someone, throw out the shoes you were wearing," Phoebe said.

"Luckily, the size didn't match." Amy sounded relieved.

"That is lucky. Was the impression bigger or smaller?" Suzanne asked her.

"I don't know. Rob didn't say. I don't think they told him."

Lucy walked in with their tea tray, which held several cups, a plate of cookies, a brimming teapot, and all the other necessary fixings. She placed it in the middle of the coffee table.

Suzanne leaned forward and poured a cup of tea. Then she handed it to Amy. "So why did they bring him in again? You thought it was something Tanya said, in her interview last night."

Amy nodded, her teacup clasped with both hands. "Rob swore to me that there's no affair. And I believe him. But he told me Tanya had come to him, knowing how her husband had cheated Rob in the past. She told Rob that once Morton realized that Rob lived here, he bragged about how he'd stolen Rob's idea. She told Rob her husband was just about to finish the plans on a new invention."

"Betty Rutledge told us that. She said Morton was bragging about his new idea and claimed it would make him a fortune."

"For obvious reasons, Tanya wasn't going to be cut out of that payday. She told Rob she wanted to steal the plans and sell the invention herself, since she wouldn't get anything out of the divorce. But she didn't know how or where to market it. She asked Rob to help her, to claim it was his invention and sell it somewhere. And they'd split the profits."

"Wow, that's a devious proposition," Suzanne said.

"Rob said she seemed desperate. Desperate to get away from Morton, but she didn't want to leave without a nice chunk of his money. Tanya felt she'd earned it, being married to Morton for almost ten years."

"She has a point there. From what we've heard, being Morton's significant other must have been tortuous," Lucy said.

"How was Rob supposed to pull this off? Was she going to give him the plans?" Maggie kept knitting but Lucy could tell by her slower pace that she was more interested in the conversation.

"That's what she said. The final plans, along with some of the preliminary drawings and notes. She thought Rob should recopy and change them a bit, so he'd have some proof he'd been working on the same idea."

"The little minx." Suzanne shook her head and bit into a cookie.

Dana put her knitting aside and poured a cup of tea. "What was Rob's response?" Dana asked. "Did he agree to do it?"

"Not at first. He claims he didn't want to get involved,

as much as he despised Morton. Two wrongs don't make a right and all that . . ." Amy's voice trailed off, and she sighed.

"But?" Suzanne prodded her. "Tanya got him to agree, eventually?"

Amy nodded. It was clearly hard for her to admit that her husband had entered into such a nefarious scheme. "She worked on him, he said. She wouldn't stop bugging him and pushed a lot of old buttons. He admitted that deep down, he liked the idea of taking revenge on Morton in this way, which was just what Morton had done to him."

"That makes sense. Anyone in Rob's position would have been tempted," Maggie said.

"Also, Rob finally told me he's been feeling some financial pressure. He made a pile of money in California. That's why we were able to retire so early. But he confessed that we've been overspending since we moved here, and that he'd made some bad investments that have cut into our savings. He felt embarrassed about that and didn't want me to worry."

"So the opportunity to plump up the nest egg was tempting," Suzanne said.

"Very. Especially at Dr. Morton's expense," Amy added. "I'm not condoning what he did, but I can understand how she persuaded him."

"I can see how it happened," Dana said. "And Tanya has all the makings of a real siren."

"And this is just the place to find one," Lucy added.

"Well, my husband was tempted, I must admit. But he didn't jump overboard. There was one major glitch to Tanya's scheme. She found notes and drawings, but she couldn't find the final plans for the invention. She kept promising Rob that she would find them and pass them along. But Rob was getting cold feet. And not just from standing in the icy surf in rubber boots every morning."

Interesting twist, Lucy thought. "So, he backed out?"

"That's what he told me, and I believe him. But I suppose we'll never know," Amy answered with surprising honesty. "We do know that Tanya gave the police a different story. One that paints Rob in a much more incriminating light."

Lucy was unhappy to hear that. The version Amy had just told them was certainly bad enough, and provided plenty of motivation for murder.

Suzanne crunched down on another butter cookie. "What did she say? It was all Rob's idea?"

"More or less. Tanya said that Rob had heard her husband boasting about his latest breakthrough invention and came to her, proposing the scheme. She said he asked her to find the notes and sketches, and the final plans, and promised he would market the project discreetly, claiming it was his idea. Tanya told the police she wouldn't go along with the scheme at first. But when Morton stonewalled her about a divorce settlement, she felt angry, agreed to Rob's offer. She said Rob saw her as an easy target and took advantage of her."

"That size-zero witch." Suzanne dipped the edge of another cookie into her tea. "Of course she'd turn it all around, to make herself look like the innocent victim."

"Exactly." Amy took a sip of her tea and sighed. "Tanya also claimed she could never find the final plans and told Rob she couldn't go through with it. The complete opposite of what he says. There are no witnesses to their conversations and no way to prove who instigated the plan. But they've both confessed to being involved in this venture, no matter whose idea it was. And the police see it as a strong motive to murder Morton. A conspiracy, they called it."

Amy placed her cup on the table with a shaky hand; the

china rattled. She was crying and dabbed her eyes with a wad of tissues she pulled from her purse.

"I feel so . . . awful. So betrayed. How could Rob get involved in something like that, even if it wasn't his idea? How can I believe anything he says now? It's almost as bad as if they did have an affair."

Suzanne patted Amy's shoulder. "Nobody's perfect. We all have our weak moments. Morton stung Rob badly. It was only human to want revenge when it was offered so easily. And remember, Rob said that in the end, he couldn't go through with it."

Amy was still crying, but stopped a moment to dry her eyes again. "If you want to believe that version of the story, and it was only because Tanya couldn't find the plans."

"It gave him time to think. To let his better self step up and take control," Dana contributed.

Maggie nodded. She had put her tea aside and was knitting again. "Like Suzanne said, he was tempted, but he did the right thing and told Tanya he wouldn't go through with it. I think you should believe him and give him the benefit of the doubt."

Amy sat with her head bowed, twisting her wedding rings. "I do give him the benefit of the doubt. Most of the time. I'm trying hard to support him. We'll never get through this if we don't stick together."

Suzanne put her arm around Amy's shoulder. "That's the spirit. It's a nightmare, but Rob is innocent. The police can't arrest him, or Tanya, just because they were seen on the beach together. Or even because they had a plan to steal Julian Morton's invention. They have to see that and start looking in some other direction."

Amy lifted her head and pushed her hair back from her face. "I hope so." She sat back and picked up her purse.

"Thanks for the tea and sympathy, everyone. I don't know what I'd do if I didn't have all of you to talk to this weekend. I'd better get back to Rob. I think it's best if he's not alone too much right now."

"Sure. Let me walk you to the door." Suzanne rose from the couch and walked with Amy toward the front door.

"Let's talk later. I just want to know how you're doing and if you need anything," Lucy heard Suzanne say as she and Amy said good-bye.

When Suzanne returned, her friends were silent for a few moments. Then Lucy said, "Bad break for Amy and Rob. I didn't want to say it in front of Amy, but that scheme with Tanya casts a very dark, deep shadow. Especially considering Rob's history with Morton, threatening him, and the order of protection. I'm sure the investigators are factoring all that into his story now."

"I'm sure they are." Maggie set her knitting down in her lap. She peered at Lucy over the edge of her reading glasses. "I also believe he didn't kill Morton. What would be the point? Part of the joy of stealing the invention would be seeing Morton's reaction when he was duped."

"That's true, Maggie." Dana poured herself another cup of tea. "That moment of victory may have even tempted Rob more than the money."

Suzanne took a seat on the armchair again. "I know how I feel when Marcy Devereaux steals a listing from me," Suzanne said, mentioning her office rival. "I get mad and do everything I can to do the same to her."

" 'Revenge is sweet and not fattening,' " Phoebe said, still fiddling with her camera.

Suzanne laughed. "That's exactly the way I feel. Did you just make that up, Phoebe?"

Phoebe shook her head. "Alfred Hitchcock. I took a film studies class last semester."

"The question of who pushed Dr. Julian Morton over the edge is worthy of a Hitchcock plot. Or an Agatha Christie novel," Lucy said. "Now his invention is in the mix. Rob and Tanya may not have been the only ones looking for it. I wonder if the police have thought of that."

"Good point, Lucy." Maggie looked up briefly from her work. "Tanya wanted it because she wasn't getting a divorce settlement. But Morton had cheated plenty of people in his life. Derek Pullman, Meredith, and Cory Morton, to name a few."

"A very bitter young man, isn't he?" Dana shook her head. "He clearly felt shortchanged on approval and love from his father. Not to mention financial support. It sounds like there wasn't much child support or alimony."

"Meredith told me Cory asked for a loan to start a business and Dr. Morton turned him down. Cory did sound terribly angry. But angry enough to kill his own father?" Lucy finally gave in to the tempting butter cookies and took a small bite. "That would be a stretch for me. But not a stretch to think he might steal the invention plans, deciding his father had shortchanged him and his mother all his life, and here was a chance to make up for it."

"Cory may have had a chance to steal the plans if he visited his father and Tanya. And had the time to find them," Dana said. "But it didn't sound as if they had much of a relationship or saw each other much, either."

"Meredith mentioned that to me Saturday night, when she was tending bar. She talked a lot about Cory and seemed to believe he wanted a closer relationship with his father. Maybe he had come around and tried to visit, uninvited."

"Maybe Tanya couldn't find the final plans because Cory already stole them," Suzanne suggested.

"But what about Morton's murder? Do you think Cory

did that, too?" Maggie had finished knitting and begun packing her bag.

"Meredith told me that Cory lives in Boston and made the trip up Saturday night, after he heard that his father had died," Lucy said.

Suzanne shook her head, crunching on another cookie. "Boston isn't far. He could have snuck into town, waited in the shrubs for his father to pass on his morning jog, and done the nasty deed. Then hoofed it back to the city to wait for his mother's call. He looks strong enough to over-come his father, especially if he stunned him with a blow to the head."

"That sounds plausible to me," Lucy said. "I wonder if the police are even considering him a suspect."

"Yes, I wonder. They seem so focused on Rob," Dana noted.

"And Tanya. Let's not forget the lovely siren." Maggie carefully placed her knitting in her bag and rose from the couch. "I'd love to sit and unravel these questions with you, but I have to lead that second knitting workshop. I'd better be on my way."

Lucy jumped up from her seat. "I planned on com-ing, too."

Suzanne and Dana echoed her reply. Lucy never thought for one moment they'd let Maggie go to the group on her own, though Maggie seemed to think so. Unless she was just pretending she didn't expect them to join her because she didn't want anyone to feel pressured. That might have been it, too, Lucy reflected.

"I think I'm just going to hang out here and work on my photos some more." Phoebe stood up, still holding her camera. "I got some great shots of the plover and terns building nests. Want to see?"

Phoebe held out the camera and Lucy stared down at

the screen. "This is a wonderful photo, Phoebe. Straight out of a nature magazine. I love the way the fog is swirling around the bird, and the water is glistening on the rocks near the nests. What's the bird holding in its beak? A bit of beach grass?"

Phoebe took the camera back, looking pleased at Lucy's compliments. "I think so. I didn't enlarge this one yet, so it's hard to tell. The birds find the oddest things and weave them into their nests. I saw one carrying a popsicle stick. That's in another shot."

"I want to see them all, but I'd better get going or I'll be late for Maggie's workshop. Can you show them to me when I get back?"

"Sure. I'll be done editing them by then, too."

Phoebe seemed pleased to have time alone to work on her photos. She was truly a creative soul. A real artist, Lucy thought as she hurried to gather her knitting and set off for Mermaid Manor with her friends.

The rain had finally stopped, and a late-day sun struggled to break through the clouds. "We might have a dry sunset at least," Suzanne said. "Cocktail hour on the covered porch tonight?"

"I second the motion." Lucy fell into step beside her friends. "I don't mean to complain, but it's been annoying to lose a whole day of our weekend to the rain."

"I feel the same. I would have liked another afternoon on the beach. That was so much fun," Dana said. "I heard it will be perfect weather tomorrow. That always happens, right?"

"I have no reason to rush back to Plum Harbor. Maybe we should stay and enjoy the sunshine. Does anyone else need to be home early in the day?" Maggie glanced at Suzanne, who had the most home front responsibilities and the strictest office hours.

"I'm down with that plan. Kevin can handle the kids a few more hours than he expected. I usually take Mondays off anyway, so work isn't a problem."

"Great. It's decided then." Maggie pulled open the heavy wooden door at Mermaid Manor's main entrance. "No sense in cutting short Lucy's weekend. As far as I can see, she's hardly flung."

"I'm flinging plenty. Honestly," Lucy protested. "Let's stop worrying about that and enjoy the rest of our time here."

Her friends nodded, though Lucy could see Dana and Suzanne exchange glances, about to burst out laughing at her little tirade.

Lucy was glad when they reached the library, where everyone in Amy's knitting group waited for Maggie. Lewis Fielding was there, sitting next to Meredith Quinn. Betty Rutledge, Helen Shelburn, and Regina Thorne were there as well. They greeted Lucy and her friends as they walked in and found seats.

Maggie stood at the head of the long library table and took out the shawl she had been working on. "How are you all doing with the pattern? Coming along?" she asked, her tone encouraging. "I know I said this pattern could be completed in a weekend, but I've been having so much fun with my friends, I'm only halfway done myself."

"I'm almost finished. It was easy, once I got into it." Regina Thorne held up her work. The peachy shade of yarn was soft and feminine looking.

"I love that color, Regina. It will look great on you." Meredith held up her own project, which was not that far along, but the summery, lime-green shawl would be beautiful when completed. The color would bring out her green eyes, Lucy thought. "I always get chilly in the yoga studio, and this shawl is just the right weight to wear there."

"I was working on another project, but I'm enjoying this one." Betty Rutledge showed her progress, too. She had chosen a sunny, yellow yarn.

Lucy was not surprised to see Betty, though she did wonder if Betty had been contacted by the police again. Lucy watched her pick up her needles and begin to knit, looking placid and unruffled, as she usually did. Perhaps she had told told the police about her brother's dark history with Morton early in the investigation, as she'd claimed and maybe Betty and Ted had solid alibis for the time of Morton's death. Still, Lucy wondered if Betty and Ted could be struck off their list of suspects so easily.

Seated on the far side of the table, Helen called out to Maggie. "I guess I'm the only one having problems. I don't know what I'm doing wrong." Helen held up her work; only a few rows were completed. The lace work looked gnarled, even from a distance.

"Let me take a look. We'll figure it out." Maggie spoke in a reassuring tone as she made her way to Helen's spot at the table.

Lewis Fielding was still working on his granddaughter's scarf, in her college colors, but for some reason, he had come to the workshop anyway. Maybe he just enjoyed the company. He and Meredith had been chatting quietly as he snipped lengths of gold yarn for the scarf's fringe.

Meredith began coughing. She covered her mouth with her hand and tried to get a breath, but the coughing wouldn't stop. Lewis looked concerned. He touched her arm. "Are you all right, Merri? Let me get you some water."

Meredith nodded, overtaken by another wave of coughs. "I just need some air," she gasped. She rose from her seat, but seemed weak, shaky. Lewis grabbed her around the waist, catching her before she fell.

"Merri? What's wrong? Maybe you should lie down . . ." He was trying to lead her to one of the couches in the room when Meredith gripped her chest, her face contorted in pain. "I can't breathe, Lewis. I can't get a breath . . ."

"Someone call 911! Please!" Lewis shouted. He scooped Meredith up in his arms and carried her to a long leather couch.

Betty was the first with her phone out. Lucy heard her tell the emergency operator where they were and what was going on. "She might be having a heart attack. It's hard to tell," Lucy heard Betty say.

Most of the group sat in stunned silence. Amy and Helen tried to try help Lewis and Meredith. Lucy didn't know what to do. Meredith had stopped breathing, and Lewis was giving her mouth-to-mouth resuscitation, and practically crying between breaths. Whispering, "Hang on, Merri. Stay with me. Please . . ."

"Give me a turn, Lewis. I used to be a nurse," Regina said.

Lewis stepped back, and let Regina take over. He looked bereft, his eyes glassy with unshed tears. He stood close to Meredith and held her hand while Regina worked on her.

"I'll go watch for the ambulance." Helen headed toward the mansion's entrance.

"My goodness. I hope she's all right," Maggie murmured as Lucy and her friends clustered together.

"She was coughing in our yoga class, but nothing like this. She said it was allergies," Lucy recalled.

"This seems like more than hay fever," Suzanne replied. "Poor thing. This seems serious."

"She's breathing again." Regina stood up and took Meredith's pulse.

"Thank God," Lewis said.

"Her pulse is very fast. She needs to get to a hospital."

Lucy silently agreed. She didn't have to be a nurse to see that Meredith was in dire need of medical attention.

Lucy heard the ambulance siren outside and moments later, emergency medical workers rushed into the room. It may have been only minutes since Betty called, but it felt much longer. One of them gently peeled Lewis away from Meredith. Another quickly strapped an oxygen mask on Meredith's face. She had roused somewhat, and was still coughing but not as violently.

Lucy heard the emergency team ask Lewis questions about what happened and what Meredith's symptoms were. Another was trying to question Meredith, but she was too weak to answer.

They soon wheeled Meredith away on a stretcher. Lewis ran alongside, still holding her hand. It seemed more than friendly support to Lucy. She'd already had a hunch that Lewis and Meredith were romantically involved, and this scene supported that theory.

Once they were gone, the room seemed strangely silent. The knitters stood in small groups around the room, whispering to each other.

Helen stood with Lucy and her friends. "I wonder what's wrong with her, poor thing. My son had a serious asthma attack, and he couldn't breathe. Just like that. They gave him a shot of adrenalin, and he was fine. Maybe she has the same thing."

"Maybe." Lucy nodded. She had heard that asthma attacks could be life threatening. Though Meredith's illness seemed more than asthma.

"The hospital is nearby, thank goodness. That's one of the reasons I chose this place," Betty said. "They'll find out what's going on with her quickly. Poor thing."

Regina had offered the most hands-on help and looked

a little shaken. "At least she has Lewis. She must be terrified. I wonder if Cory is still in town."

Maggie turned to her. "Good question. I'm sure he'd want to know that his mother is ill. Was he staying with Meredith, do you know?"

Meredith didn't live in the Osprey Shores condos, Lucy recalled. The development was too expensive for her. She had an apartment in Eaton's Landing.

"I'm not sure if he's still in town, or if he went back to Boston. He may have just come up to see if his father left him anything in his will," Helen replied. Lucy knew the answer to that. Meredith had already told her, that as far as she knew, Cory was not named in the will.

"I guess Lewis will get in touch with Cory," Betty said.

"Yes, Lewis will let him know. I wonder if Meredith has any other close family who would want to be informed about her emergency," Helen replied.

Maggie nodded. "I'm sure Lewis will handle all that. I think I'll call the hospital later and check on her condition." She looked around at the women who were gathering their handbags and knitting totes. "I'm sorry our meeting was cut short. I'll be here until tomorrow evening. If you have any questions, please get in touch," she said politely.

A few of the knitters stopped to thank her for the workshops as they headed out of the library. Maggie packed up, and Lucy and her friends put the room back in order. Then they left, too.

Meredith's emergency had been unsettling. A strange note to end the day. It was fortunate that Lewis Fielding was there to help her. Once again, Lucy had the sense that their relationship was much closer than they let on in public. But why the secrecy? They were both single. It seemed an interesting question. Another interesting question, Lucy noted.

Chapter 10

Back at the cottage, Lucy and her friends sat on the porch and sipped a batch of Suzanne's cocktails. They should have been figuring out where to have dinner. The drinks were strong and the appetizers—chips and salsa and some goat cheese dip—on the light side. But instead they were talking about Meredith Quinn's health episode.

"Here's what I don't understand. It seems obvious to me that Lewis and Meredith are more than knitting-group friends. Did you see his reaction when she lost her breath? And the way he took care of her until the ambulance came? He also called her Merri. Nobody else calls her that," Lucy noted. "That night we were at The Warehouse he was eating dinner alone at the bar. I thought that he looked sort of sad, and he must have been out, trying to meet someone. But Meredith was working. I think he was there to spend time with her on a Friday night, even though she was tending bar. I think they have a romantic relationship. But act as if they hardly know each other."

Maggie scooped up a bit of salsa on a chip. "I noticed that, too. I wondered if Meredith was a patient of his. So they would act a bit distant in social situations. A therapist isn't supposed to get involved with a patient. Isn't that so, Dana?"

"It is difficult to have a social relationship with a patient. There are limits. And you're absolutely not allowed to get romantically involved. I suppose it's possible that she's his patient, or was. Her ex-husband, Dr. Morton, was also in therapy with Lewis Fielding. Cory told everyone that at the support circle. Maybe Dr. Fielding felt that dating a patient's ex-wife was a conflict of interest. Some would see it that way."

"Maybe Lewis didn't want Dr. Morton to know. Maybe Lewis thought Morton would get angry and leave therapy if he knew that he and Meredith were an item," Maggie said. "Morton sounds like someone whose feathers would have been ruffled by something like that. He wasn't exactly a 'live and let live' sort of guy."

"Excellent point, Maggie. But Morton is dead. Why not come out of the therapy closet?" Lucy sipped a blue concoction Suzanne had mixed. She called it a Mischievous Mermaid. *Or a Malicious Mermaid, depending on how you feel about those deep sea sirens,* Suzanne had said as she served them each a glass.

Lucy wasn't sure how she felt about mermaids, or how Suzanne had made the drink blue. Was it food dye or a special tequila? She didn't want to know. The best part was the garnish, strung on a long toothpick—a raspberry head, a slice of mango carved with mermaid curves, and a triangular slice of pineapple for a tail fin. A clever touch. Lucy wasn't sure what was in the mix, but it was very tasty and went down in easy sips.

Maggie shrugged and spread a bit of goat cheese on a cracker. "Maybe they're not ready to be an item. This community is a beehive of gossip. Maybe they don't want people talking about them."

"Or maybe Cory objects to Dr. Fielding having a relationship with his mother for some reason?" Phoebe suggested. She was still fiddling with her camera. "I mean, who would object to Dr. Fielding? He's a total teddy bear. But Cory seems like a real piece of work."

Dana sipped her cocktail and made a face. Lucy had guessed she wouldn't like the drink, which was a bit sweet. "As I mentioned yesterday, Cory definitely has issues. Phoebe might be right. When Lewis tried to calm Cory down at the support circle, Cory shook him off. Then Cory made that crack about Lewis mourning the loss of the fee from Morton's therapy."

Suzanne had finished her Mermaid and poured herself another. "That was cold. Maybe Phoebe is right. Cory doesn't seem to like, or even respect, Lewis."

"Come to think of it, since Lewis was Morton's therapist, maybe we should add him to the list of people who knew about the invention. Morton must have bragged about his brilliant creation, and maybe even how cleverly he hid the final plans." Lucy sat up and looked around at her friends, to see what they thought of this revelation.

Dana took another small sip of her drink. "Morton was clearly a narcissist. He would brag a lot to his therapist. But those conversations are largely privileged information, and the client's privacy is protected by strict laws. There are exceptions that differ from state to state, especially if the information is relevant to a criminal investigation. But so far, the police aren't looking at anyone but Rob and Tanya in connection to the hidden plans."

Lucy considered Dana's words. "Unfortunately for Rob. I still have a niggling feeling that if Dr. Fielding knew where the plans were hidden, it would connect him to this whole tangled mess."

Maggie set down her cocktail and picked up her phone. "I'm going to call the hospital and see how Meredith is doing. If it was something simple, like an asthma attack, she might be on her way home by now."

"I hope so," Lucy said. Meredith did not have it easy.

Lucy wondered if she even had insurance to cover a hospital visit and stay. The poor woman didn't need a health crisis on top of everything else.

They waited as Maggie was connected to various operators. Finally, she reached patient information. "I'm calling to check on a patient, Meredith Quinn. She came into the emergency room a few hours ago," Maggie explained.

Lucy and her friends were silent as Maggie waited for a reply.

"Oh, dear. That's not good news. Thanks for your help."

Maggie hung up the phone, her expression bleak. "She's in the ICU. She must be in very serious condition."

"For goodness' sake. That's awful." Suzanne looked shocked. "Did she have a heart attack or something? Did they say what's wrong with her?"

"I'm sure the hospital staff isn't allowed to say, even if they know. Her condition is clearly more serious than we thought."

"I feel so bad for her. She seems so alone in the world, struggling to get by," Lucy said. "At least, that's the idea I got talking to her in the bar Saturday night. I think we should call Lewis and see what's going on."

Dana picked up her phone and began typing. "He might still be at the hospital with her, but I'll look him up online. He must have a listing for his practice. Maybe he's listed his cell number, too. Let's see . . ." Dana scrolled the screen on her cell phone. "Here it is. There are two numbers. I'll try both."

Dana called the first number and Lucy could hear Lewis's voice on a recording. Dana left a quick message and then tried the other number.

It rang a few times. Then Dana said, "Lewis? This is Dana, one of Amy Cutler's friends, visiting for the weekend. We're concerned about Meredith and wanted to know how she's doing. We called the hospital and they said she was in the ICU."

Dana had put the call on speaker so they could all hear his response.

"That's right," Lewis said. "I'm here with her now. And Cory is here, too. She's hanging in there. I'm praying she can weather this episode."

"That's too bad. What's the problem? It looked as if she was having an asthma attack, or something like that."

Lewis didn't answer right away. "I suppose it's all right to tell you, though Meredith never wanted this widely known, afraid it would scare off her employers." He paused again. "She has a rare blood disorder. She's been in remission for a while, but it's flared up again. There's no cure. The treatments to control it are . . . limited, you'd have to say. The condition seems to have advanced." His voice sounded sad, his words choked.

"Oh, dear . . . I'm so sorry to hear that. We're all sorry," Dana added. "Please let her know we're rooting for her recovery. We'll all say a prayer for her, too."

"Thanks. I'll tell her. And thanks for your concern."

There didn't seem to be any more to say. Dana said good-bye and ended the call.

Suzanne was the first to react. "What awful news. Just goes to show, you never know. Meredith looks like the picture of health, leading yoga and fitness classes. Meanwhile, she's carrying around this awful diagnosis."

"She definitely hid it well," Maggie said. "The poor woman, having that sword hanging over her head. It sounds as if her condition is . . . well, terminal."

"He said there was no cure. And not many treatment options." Lucy put her drink down. She'd lost her appetite. "That sounds like a dire situation to me."

"She's gravely ill," Maggie agreed. "Though Lewis did seem to hold out hope she could get through this crisis."

"Yes, he did. But, of course, he would cling to any hope. I think he loves her," Lucy said. Once she said it aloud, she knew it was true.

Dana seemed suddenly restless. She stood up and poured herself a glass of water from a pitcher that was on the table. "I was thinking the same thing. Just from the tone of his voice, talking about her, you could tell. Both of them seem somewhat isolated and lonely. But now that they've found each other, it looks as if they won't have any time together. That seems so unfair."

"A tragic love story." Suzanne wasn't being sarcastic. For once, Lucy noticed. Her eyes actually looked glassy. "Like a movie you'd see on the Lifetime channel. Only thing, this is for real. I feel so bad for both of them."

Lucy felt the same. Meredith and Lewis were both nice people. It seemed so sad and unfair that Lewis might lose her.

Lucy and her friends decided on take-out from a Mexican restaurant Amy had recommended. After dinner, they gathered together in the living room to knit, chat, and watch a movie. As they scrolled through the choices on Netflix and Amazon, many films seemed tempting. But when they hit on *Bridesmaids,* the vote was unanimous.

"We have to watch this. The perfect, prewedding primer," Suzanne insisted, hitting the select button. The wacky comedy lifted their spirits a bit, but the bad news about Meredith still cast a shadow on their last night at Osprey Shores.

When the movie was over, they all stretched and yawned. "I wish I had given out puppies at my bridal shower," Lucy said, recalling one of her favorite scenes.

"It's not too late to give them out as wedding favors," Suzanne cheerfully suggested.

"Birds would be easier. Pairs of lovebirds in little cages with a ribbon on top," Phoebe said.

"Nice idea," Lucy replied, though she had no intention of following through on either suggestion. "I do think you're a little obsessed with feathered creatures right now, Phoebe. How did those photos turn out?"

Phoebe had been fiddling with her camera most of the evening. Lucy was curious to see her photos.

"I guess you can take a quick look. I'm not done editing yet. I got a few great shots and enlarged them, and worked the exposure and color saturation. I might even try some in black and white. More dramatic."

Lucy knew how Phoebe was about her creative projects. She hated to show any works in progress. "You don't have to show me yet if they're not ready. I understand."

Phoebe considered Lucy's words a moment. "I guess I'd rather wait until they're all done. If you don't mind."

"I don't mind," Lucy said sincerely. "Honestly."

"Thanks, Lucy. The editing is actually the fun part for me. Sometimes a really messy shot comes out great once you crop out all the noise."

Lucy considered Phoebe's words. "That's a good metaphor for many things in life, Phoebe." Trying to figure out who killed Dr. Morton, for instance. It was a messy picture, with so many possibilities. But Lucy was sure the killer was hiding in plain sight, if they could only crop out all noise.

No late-night knitting fests or Scrabble tournaments were proposed after the movie. Lucy and the others cleaned up the empty popcorn bowl and tea mugs from the sitting room. Then they turned in on the early side, looking forward to sitting on the beach under sunny skies for their last few hours on the island.

Lucy had forgotten to draw her shades down all the way before she went to bed. In the morning, a blade of sunlight slipped under the curtains and wouldn't let her rest. She thought she was the first one up, until she heard Suzanne's voice in the kitchen. It sounded as if she was talking on the phone, and Lucy assumed she was settling some situation at home. After all, it was Monday morning, just about the time Suzanne's brood would be heading off to school.

Lucy went into the kitchen and poured herself a mug of coffee. She quickly realized Suzanne was not talking to one of her children. It was Amy on the line. Again.

"That's terrible. How could they do that? That's no proof at all. Did you call his lawyer yet?"

Lucy felt her stomach drop. It sounded like the police were moving in on Rob and had found another link to tie him to Morton's murder.

"I can wait with you. I'll meet you at the station in a little while." Suzanne paused, listening. "All right. I understand. But please call me if you change your mind, and let us know what's going on. This isn't right."

Suzanne ended the call and looked up at Lucy, her expression bleak. "The police took Rob back to the station for another interview. They've been in touch with a few biotech firms in the area and learned that someone was shopping around a new device—just the type Morton would design—and conducting business in a suspicious way. For one thing, the seller claimed to be representing an inventor with a list of inventions to his credit, but wouldn't give his name. The companies couldn't find any history of this sales rep in the field, either."

"Now the police think that Tanya did find Morton's final plans, and Rob was trying to sell it to a biotech firm?" Lucy took a sip of coffee. "But I thought his plan with Tanya was to sell it under his own name. He has an impressive track record and selling a new device wouldn't seem suspicious at all. Rob had no reason to act under a false identity."

"That's what I thought, too. It doesn't make sense. The police are also questioning Tanya. Probably trying to get her to admit that she did find the plans and gave them to Rob. Who knows, maybe once Rob got cold feet, she worked her wiles on some other sucker and persuaded him to sell the invention."

Lucy nodded. "Did Amy hear the name the police think Rob used? I can do a search on the Internet."

"Let me think. I know Amy mentioned it. . . . I thought it was a strange choice for a fake name. Maybe it is real." Suzanne tore open two packs of diet sweetener and stirred them into her coffee. She suddenly looked up. "I remember now. Fred Sigmund. That's the name the police mentioned."

"Fred Sigmund? That is a strange choice. A far cry from Joe Smith."

"I guess whoever got their hands on Morton's invention was trying to be convincing."

"Unless that's the guy's real name."

"Here, try to find out if this Fred Sigmund exists. You're good at that stuff." Suzanne's notebook computer was on the kitchen counter, and she slid it toward Lucy.

"I'm sure the police did the same thing and came up with zero. That's why they think it's an alias Rob made up. I'll give it a try anyway."

"That's the spirit. Work your magic, Lucy," Suzanne said.

Lucy took her coffee and the computer into the living room and began her search. She didn't know if she had any magic in her fingertips, but she was good at searching the Internet for personal information. There were a number of paths into that maze.

She soon heard Dana come into the kitchen, but Maggie and Phoebe were still sleeping. A rare indulgence for a Monday. Lucy didn't blame them.

Suzanne quickly filled Dana in on the latest news from Amy. Then added, "If Rob wanted to sell Morton's invention, why use a fake name? It's his reputation and track record that would convince a company he'd actually created the device. It doesn't make any sense."

"No sense at all." Dana sipped her coffee. "Maybe there's another player in this picture. Maybe Tanya had more than one accomplice on the line."

"That's what Lucy thought. Right now she's searching the name this mystery salesman used."

Lucy had quickly located a few Fred Sigmunds but none seemed a likely partner in crime for Tanya. She headed back to the kitchen to give her report.

"I found a few Fred Sigmunds. There's one in Madison, Wisconsin. He's eighty-three, a children's book illustrator. There's another in Lubbock, Texas. But he's in high school and an Eagle Scout. There are two in California, one in Florida, and five in New York and New Jersey. But for various reasons that I won't bore you with, none seem likely to be Tanya's second choice."

"Great job, Lucy. There are a lot more Fred Sigmunds running around than I expected," Suzanne said.

"Me, too. But none running around New England, trying to sell Morton's stolen invention, as far as I can see. I guess it is an alias."

"Are the police sure it was a man trying to sell the device? Maybe Tanya decided to go it alone and just impersonated a man's voice on the phone," Suzanne suggested.

"She does have a deep voice." Dana had fixed a bowl of yogurt and fruit and sprinkled some granola on top.

"That's a possibility. Though the police seem fairly certain a man was trying to sell the invention. Enough to reel Rob back into the interview room."

"Poor Rob. Poor Amy." Suzanne shook her head. "I think

I should skip the beach and go to the police station to keep her company. Even though she said she didn't want me to."

"That's sweet of you, Suzanne. Maybe you could meet us there later. Certain members of our beach party are still in dreamland," Dana noted.

"We're the early birds today. It's so nice to see the sun after all that rain. I think I'll take a quick bike ride since Maggie and Phoebe are still sleeping." Lucy had poured herself a small bowl of granola and spooned it up quickly. "Want to ride with me, Dana?"

"I thought you'd never ask." Dana rinsed her yogurt bowl and set it in the dishwasher. "Meet you on the porch in ten minutes?"

"I'll be there," Lucy said, finishing up the last bite of her breakfast.

A short time later, Lucy and Dana headed over to Mermaid Manor where Dana needed to pick up a bicycle. As Dana examined her choices, Lucy saw Lewis Fielding coming out of the glass doors that led to the fitness center. His clothes looked rumpled, his hair was uncombed, and he definitely needed a shave on the small patches of skin above his beard. He must have slept at Meredith's bedside and had just returned.

"Lewis . . . how's Meredith doing?" Lucy greeted him.

"She's hanging in there. She's a fighter. It's hard to tell if the medication is helping, but she seemed a bit brighter this morning. A bit more awake and aware. The doctors might move her out of the ICU to a subacute area tomorrow."

"That's good news. Glad to hear it," Lucy said.

He seemed tired and totally drained, though a spark of optimism shone in his eyes. "Thanks for your call last night. She appreciated it."

"We're all thinking of her. I'm glad to hear she seems better today."

"Me too," Dana said. "I hope the treatment continues to help, and she pulls through quickly."

"That's my hope. As sick as she is, she's still concerned about her classes and students. She sent me over here to talk to her boss and put a note on the door, apologizing for having to cancel today."

"She's a very dedicated teacher. You can see that right away," Dana said.

"And a very good one," Lewis added. He paused and glanced over his shoulder at the main road. "I noticed some police cars at the Cutler's cottage when I got back. Is everything all right?"

Dana glanced at Lucy a moment. "The police have some strange idea that Rob Cutler is involved in Dr. Morton's murder. But it just isn't so," Dana insisted. "They keep questioning him."

"But they haven't found one shred of evidence yet that connects him to Morton's murder. It's all circumstantial," Lucy added.

Lewis looked concerned. "That's too bad. I had no idea. I heard that the police questioned him, Tanya Morton, and Sam Briggs. But I didn't think it had come to much."

"So far, it hasn't. Thank goodness," Lucy replied quickly.

He nodded, looking concerned about Rob. "I'd better get home. I'm just going to clean up and head back to the hospital. Thanks again for your good wishes."

Lucy and Dana said good-bye. They watched Dr. Fielding get into his car and drive out of the parking lot.

"He was trying to put a positive spin on Meredith's condition," Dana said. "But I don't think she's out of the woods yet."

"It's still very serious," Lucy agreed. "I didn't know how much to disclose about Rob's situation. But I thought it was best to be discrete. I'm sure Amy and Rob don't want all their neighbors to know Rob was involved in a scheme to sell Morton's invention. Even though he backed out."

"I thought the same thing. Gossip gets around here. Dr. Fielding knew about Rob being questioned. And, as we've already determined, he's also a person who may have known about the invention and where it's hidden. If it's still hidden."

Lucy didn't answer. As they walked their bikes up to the main road, thoughts and theories about Morton's murder swirled in her head.

"I hate to say this, because he's such a nice guy, but Lewis's knowledge from treating Morton could have made it possible for him to be Tanya's accomplice once Rob backed out. Or even act on his own, if he was able to get his hands on the invention plans." Lucy glanced at Dana. "He told me he visited Tanya after Dr. Morton died, to offer his condolences and find out if she was planning a memorial service. Maybe he took the plans then. They probably weren't on Morton's computer, or Tanya would have found them. But there could have been a little stick drive or a CD hidden in a place Tanya couldn't figure out."

Dana turned to her. "Definitely possible. But what would his motivation be? Sheer greed? Feeling cheated by Morton in some way? Or just a deep hatred for the man?"

"Any one of the above?" Lucy thought a moment. "And there's Meredith, connected to both men. Lewis obviously loves her, and it's common knowledge that Morton treated her badly when they were married, and when they divorced. Lewis must have been very angry at Morton for that. Being denied an adequate divorce settlement was tough on her, especially after she got sick. Her medical costs must be astronomical. I think we would have heard if her ex-husband had helped with those bills. Maybe Lewis was angry about that."

"I think you're on to something. Something worth

bringing to the police. You know what I just realized? Fred Sigmund is the perfect alias for a psychiatrist. Sigmund Freud, the father of modern psychiatry? Duh . . . why didn't I get it sooner?"

Lucy stood dumbfounded a moment. Then had to laugh. "Of course. That makes perfect sense. Even if Dr. Fielding isn't connected to the murder, I think there's a good chance he can tell the police something about Fred Sigmund."

"And get Rob off the hook." Dana got on her bike, ready to ride. "I'll return the bike later. Let's head back to the cottage. Maybe Suzanne didn't leave yet. We can go to the police station together."

Lucy got on her bike, too. "Good plan. We'll tell Rob's lawyer what we've figured out, and hopefully Detective Dunbar will listen to this new theory," Lucy added.

When Lucy and Dana arrived at the cottage a few minutes later, Maggie and Phoebe were having coffee in the kitchen. Suzanne was dressed, about to leave for town.

"Can you wait for us? We need to go with you," Dana said to Suzanne. She glanced at Lucy. "Lucy came up with a great theory that might get Rob off the hook."

"And Dana figured out who Fred Sigmund is . . . I mean, where the name probably came from," Lucy added.

They quickly filled their friends in on their speculations about Lewis Fielding, how he had either located the invention plans or was Tanya's second-choice accomplice, after Rob backed out.

"Interesting. And logical," Maggie said. "But are you saying Dr. Fielding killed Morton in order to get the plans and sell them? Or he just took advantage of the fact that Morton was dead, and he knew where the plans were, so he managed to get his hands on them?"

"I'm not sure. I don't see him as a killer. But I also didn't see him as the type of person who would steal intellectual property and try to sell it under the table. Not before this morning." Lucy shrugged. "He seems so stable and re-sponsible. He seems so . . . kind. He'd mentioned that he was at the hospital Thursday night into Friday morning, dealing with a patient emergency, and didn't get back to Osprey Shores until the police cars were whizzing past his cottage."

"The time of Morton's murder has to be a very small window," Dana pointed out. "He was killed sometime be-tween setting off for his run, maybe about seven-thirty, after he reported the car vandalism, and a quarter past eight, when the fishermen on the beach saw his body fly-ing off the cliff."

"So the police must have ruled out Dr. Fielding quickly," Suzanne said. "But suppose he got back from the hospital earlier and hid his car somewhere? He could have killed Morton, hoofed it back to his car, and sailed through the gate just ahead of the police cruisers, giving him a solid alibi."

"He could have worked it that way," Dana agreed. "I guess the police will have to take a closer look at the time he left the hospital and the time he drove through the gate, and see if there was enough slack for him to track down Morton. They probably didn't bother to check his alibi that closely since they had no reason to suspect him."

"But they will check the timing closer now, we hope. Once we lead them on the scent." Suzanne looked fired up, eager to go.

"Enough said. You ought to set off right away," Maggie urged them. "Phoebe and I will head to the beach. You can meet us there when you get back."

"Good plan. I'm going to text Amy and let her know that we're coming and have some news. She said they just started questioning Rob."

"I hope they hear us out and don't think we're a bunch

of silly, gossiping women. Strangers to the area, to boot," Dana said.

"They might think that at first. But we'll convince them otherwise." Suzanne had on her game face, her tone tough and confident.

Lucy didn't want to cause a scene at the police station, but she knew Suzanne wouldn't mind doing so. If that would produce the results she was seeking.

A short time later, they arrived at the Eaton's Landing police station. Amy was nowhere to be seen in the outer lobby, and Suzanne sent her a text to let her know they'd arrived. Amy texted back quickly. She was in a waiting room upstairs and would be down to meet them soon. Detective Dunbar had called a break in the interview, and Amy was talking to Rob's attorney.

"Well, no time like the present," Suzanne said, glancing at a glass window behind which a police officer presided. He was looking through some paperwork and didn't seem to notice them. "Let's try this guy and see how far we get."

Lucy and her friends followed Suzanne to the window. The officer stared back at them with a grim expression. "Can I help you?"

"We have some important information for Detective Dunbar, regarding the Morton murder case," Suzanne announced.

"Important information?"

"That's right. Very important," Suzanne echoed with confidence. "This could break the case wide open."

The officer looked doubtful that anything Suzanne had to say could help the police. "Detective Dunbar is conducting an interview. I'll see if I can find someone to take your information. Name please?" Suzanne quickly replied, and he jotted it on a slip of paper. "You can wait by those chairs near the exit."

"Thank you, officer." Suzanne graced the dour man with a huge smile.

She turned to Lucy and Dana. "That wasn't too bad," she said in a hushed voice.

Dana led the way to a row of plastic chairs. "Well done, Suzanne. I could tell he wanted to brush you off, but you sounded too determined."

"I am determined. To help Amy and Rob. And get Detective Dunbar to start looking in a different direction for Morton's murderer."

They waited in the drab lobby for someone to come out and speak to them. Suzanne and Dana checked their phone messages. Lucy read the yellowed safety posters that warned about drunk driving and home security.

"I wish I'd brought my knitting. I didn't think we'd have to wait this long," Dana said.

Suzanne looked up from her phone. "I wish I was on the beach with Maggie and Phoebe. But this is more important."

A few minutes later, Officer Hobart walked out a door near the glass window. "Suzanne Cavanaugh?"

Suzanne waved her hand and stood up, though they were the only ones in the lobby. "Right here, Officer. Remember me? You interviewed us Friday morning at Osprey Shores."

"Yes, I remember." The police officer walked over to them. "You have some information for us about the Morton case?"

"My friends figured out something you need to hear," Suzanne replied.

Officer Hobart looked over at Lucy and Dana. "Is there something you didn't tell me when I interviewed you?"

"No, nothing like that," Lucy replied. "But we do have a good idea who found the plans for Dr. Morton's invention and used the alias Fred Sigmund to try to sell them. And it's not Rob Cutler. Or Tanya Morton."

"So you already know about that? News travels quickly." Officer Hobart was clearly surprised that they knew so much about the investigation. "I guess you ought to come back to my desk and tell me your . . . theory."

He sounded smug and patronizing, as if he was obliged to hear them out but didn't believe they had anything worth saying. Lucy couldn't do anything about that. She hoped he would at least pass their ideas on to Detective Dunbar, who must be frustrated by making so little progress in finding Morton's killer. She might be ready for a fresh point of view.

It didn't take long for Lucy and her friends to explain that they suspected Dr. Fielding and why they suspected him. To his credit, Officer Hobart took notes. His expression was hard to read. Lucy couldn't tell if he was interested and thought the lead was worth pursuing, or if he would toss his notes into the trash as soon as they left.

"I'll pass this information to Detective Dunbar," he said. "If she has any questions, she'll call you."

"Thank you, officer. We hope you figure out the case soon," Suzanne said.

"So do we," Officer Hobart replied.

When they returned to the lobby, Amy was waiting for them. "Where were you? The desk sergeant said you were speaking to Officer Hobart."

"We were. Lucy and Dana figured out that Fred Sigmund is probably Dr. Fielding's alias," Suzanne replied quickly. "Morton was his patient and probably told Dr. Fielding all about the invention and even where it was hidden. We have a strong suspicion Dr. Fielding found the plans and was the one trying to sell them."

Amy looked surprised at this theory. "Dr. Fielding? But he's such a nice man. Do you really think he'd do something like that?"

"We think he's nice, too. But he certainly has motive," Dana said.

"He loves Meredith, and must have felt great distress seeing her treated so badly by her ex-husband. Especially now that she's sick," Lucy added.

"Do you think Dr. Fielding killed Julian Morton?" Amy looked surprised again, coming to this conclusion.

"We're not sure," Dana replied. "He has a good alibi for the time of the murder. He told us that he was at the hospital all night, caring for a patient and returned to the development right after the police arrived. But he could have parked his car outside of the development, gone on the cliff path and killed Morton. Then walked back to his car and driven through the main gate as if he was just getting home."

"We'll leave that part to the police to figure out," Suzanne said.

Amy's expression was thoughtful as she seemed to consider the theory. "I guess anything is possible. I hope they take your theory seriously and look into it. It would certainly draw Detective Dunbar's attention away from Rob."

"That's what we hope, too," Lucy said.

Suzanne wanted to stay with Amy, so she gave Lucy the keys to her SUV. She would get a ride back to the development with Amy and Rob, once Rob was released. Lucy and Dana left the police station and drove back to Osprey Shores without much conversation.

"That went better than I expected." Dana had been looking out her window but now turned to Lucy, who was driving. "Amy seemed pleased that we told the police our ideas. At least Officer Hobart was polite and professional."

"I think it did boost Amy's spirits. But I felt like Hobart didn't take us seriously, despite being so polite."

They were driving along the main road, which was lined with houses and a few B&Bs and small hotels. The water was visible in the distance, and Lucy realized that any one of the crossroads she passed would eventually lead to the cliff path. The killer could have easily parked on a road a short distance from the development and come down the path, then waited to kill Morton without driving through the Osprey Shores gate, as they now suspected Dr. Fielding had done.

Dana's words interrupted Lucy's thoughts. "As long as Officer Hobart passes our information to Detective Dunbar, we've got a shot at helping. I wonder if he would interrupt Rob's interview to give it to her?"

"That seems doubtful. He'll probably wait until Rob's interview is done," Lucy replied.

"Either way, Detective Dunbar looks sharp. I think she'll look into it," Dana replied.

Lucy wasn't so sure of that. But she did think the detective would at least consider their theory. "Hard to say what will happen now. We'll be leaving in a few hours. We probably won't be here to see how this puzzler turns out."

"I guess not," Dana agreed. "Though now I'm itching to know."

"You're sure that's not poison ivy?" Lucy teased her.

Dana laughed. "I'm sure. Though I think we all feel the same. Curiosity can be just as contagious."

Chapter 11

Lucy and Dana met Maggie and Phoebe on the beach a short time later. Lucy set herself up on a lounge chair under an umbrella, facing the waves. She slapped on sunscreen and took out a book and her knitting. She was determined to enjoy their last few hours on Osprey Island, though she felt distracted and unsettled by the morning's events.

Dana's phone rang. She quickly scooped it out of her tote bag. Lucy could tell Suzanne was on the line. Dana sighed, then replied in a bright tone.

"I'm so relieved. I hope the police leave Rob alone now. They have a whole new trail to follow with Dr. Fielding. Or should I say Fred Sigmund?"

Dana laughed at something Suzanne said. Then replied, "Really? Fast work. I guess they took our information seriously. Let me know if Rob's attorney has any more inside news." She paused, listening. "Oh, interesting. I guess that nails it. Okay. We'll see you down on the beach soon. We're in the same spot we had the other day."

Dana ended the call and put her phone away. "Good news! The police released Rob. They couldn't find any link between him and the mysterious Fred Sigmund so they had to let him go. Amy's attorney doesn't think they're going to pursue the scheme with Tanya to sell the device either, since it didn't come to much. So that's another bullet dodged.

"Meanwhile, Detective Dunbar did follow through on our information, and Rob's attorney said Dr. Fielding was just brought in for questioning. They found him at the hospital, visiting Meredith."

Lucy put her knitting down and sighed. "I know I helped bring that about, but now I feel bad. How embarrassing for Dr. Fielding and how upsetting for poor Meredith. I hope this doesn't affect her recovery."

"That is a concern." Maggie was also knitting and paused to glance over at Lucy. "But I think you did the right thing. These situations are rarely black and white."

"It is complicated," Dana agreed. "I do believe Dr. Fielding found the invention plans and was trying to sell them. But he does seem like such a solid, genuinely good person. It's hard to process."

Process was a good word; as in food processor. Lucy felt like she was in an emotional blender. She couldn't get her mind around all this information and come to a satisfying conclusion.

"Dr. Fielding probably tried to sell the plans for the invention. But now I'm not really sure he killed Morton, too. I hope the police don't jump to that conclusion," she said finally.

"I don't see him as a cold-blooded cliff pusher either," Maggie said. "But now that we've opened Pandora's box and handed it to Detective Dunbar, who knows what will pop out."

True enough, Lucy thought. She didn't know what else to say.

"I feel badly, too . . . and I barely had anything to do with pointing a finger at Dr. Fielding," Maggie added. "Maybe we should stop by the hospital on our way out of town and bring Meredith some flowers or something. Dr. Fielding seems to be her main support. I'm sure she's upset and could use some company."

"Good idea. We don't know her well, but friendly faces are always welcome when you're alone in a hospital room. And with the police questioning your romantic partner, no less," Dana said.

Lucy and the rest of her friends agreed on the plan. Lucy felt a bit better. She felt responsible for Dr. Fielding's absence from Meredith's bedside today, while the poor woman was still critically ill. The least they could do was bring her some flowers and show her some concern and kindness.

Suzanne soon arrived. She seemed happy to relax and enjoy the beach after such a long visit to the police station. "I told Amy we would swing by before we leave later, to thank her and say good-bye."

Everyone agreed that was a good idea, though no one was in a hurry to leave the beach. It had turned out to be a perfect day, and when the sun slipped toward the horizon and the shadows grew long, it was very hard to pack up and head back to the cottage. Lucy and her friends still lingered.

"Listen, I'm fine with getting back late tonight. I don't need to be at work until eleven," Suzanne said.

"I have late patients, too," Dana replied. "It's Maggie and Phoebe who are the early birds and need to open the shop."

"Oh, we'll manage. A late opening won't matter one way or the other. I don't have any classes scheduled." Maggie turned to her knitting and began a new row. She didn't look eager to leave the beach today either. "Let's take our time. No sense driving right into rush hour on the thruway. There won't be any traffic later. We'll fly home."

"With Suzanne at the wheel, we will," Lucy agreed. She worked from home, and everyone knew she made her own hours. The worst delay she'd face starting her day late would be complaints from her dogs, who were used to an early walk.

Phoebe had taken a stroll with her camera and returned looking pleased. "I got some good shots of an egret. The light is perfect now." She dropped into a chair with the camera in her lap.

"I'd love to see your photos, Phoebe. Are any ready for prime time yet?" Lucy teased.

"You can't see the egret shots yet. But here are the photos I took the first morning. I finally finished working on them."

Phoebe handed Lucy the camera and helped her scroll through the photos. Beautiful beach scenes, all featuring the nesting birds and rocky shoreline, with the early morning fog drifting in smoky clouds.

"These are beautiful, Phoebe. Very artistic," she added.

"Here's a good one. The bird is carrying something to build her nest. Isn't that sweet?"

Lucy looked over the photo. Phoebe had enlarged the photo a lot to get a close-up of the bird. She'd also brightened it and enhanced the color. It was a very beautiful picture with high contrast. The drops of sea spray clinging to the mossy, black rocks and the plover's fine feathers looked distinct enough to reach out and touch.

"I thought she was carrying beach grass in her beak at first. But once I enlarged the photo, I could tell it was a piece of yarn," Phoebe explained.

Lucy took a closer look. A bit of lime green yarn was clamped in the bird's beak, about six inches long. It made for a charming picture. Though Lucy wondered where the bird had found this precious bit of nest-building material.

Maybe from residents who sat on the cliff walk benches and knitted. Lucy hadn't seen any knitters out there, but it was possible.

"It's a lovely photo, Phoebe. Really. And that bird is a very clever, resourceful builder. I bet she'll be a great mother."

Phoebe looked back at the photo. "I think so, too."

They lingered on the beach a while longer, until their cold drinks and snacks gave out. Finally, everyone was ready to go, albeit reluctantly.

Back at the cottage, they showered, dressed, and packed up. Lucy hadn't brought much, and she packed quickly. Why was it always so easy to pack up after a trip, but impossible to pack when you were going away? She'd left her bedroom at home filled with discarded outfits and shoes. Too many choices.

She searched the cottage for forgotten belongings, books, her bicycle helmet, and extra sandals. Once the car was packed with their luggage, Lucy and her friends quickly cleaned up, determined to leave the cottage in the same pristine condition they had found it.

Suzanne stood at the fridge with her coolers. "Luckily, not much food to bring home. Or wine and tequila, for that matter."

"We can't help it if you're such a great cook and mixologist," Lucy teased. "Among your other talents."

Suzanne looked pleased by the compliment. "What can I say? You guys inspire me."

They were soon all out on the porch, watching Suzanne lock the front door. "Let's walk over to Amy's and drop off the key," she suggested.

"Of course. We need to send her a thank-you gift when we get home," Maggie noted.

They followed Suzanne up the path to Amy and Rob's

cottage. The door flew open before Suzanne had time to knock or ring the bell.

Amy greeted them, holding open the door so they could all come in, her cell phone in her other hand. "I was just going to call you. Rob's attorney called. He said Rob's off the hook. Dr. Fielding confessed to everything—stealing the invention plans from the Morton's cottage, shopping it around to biotech firms as Fred Sigmund, and . . ." She paused and took a deep breath. "He confessed to killing Dr. Morton. Can you believe it?"

Lucy was stunned. Stealing the invention was one thing. But she found it hard to believe Lewis Fielding was a murderer. "I hardly know the man. Maybe he has a deeply hidden dark side. But that last part is hard for me to accept. He just doesn't seem like a killer. Do the police have other evidence, besides his confession?"

Amy nodded. "They say the shoe imprints they found at the scene match a pair of rubber boots they found in his cottage. That seems conclusive to me."

Lucy didn't answer. It didn't seem that conclusive to her, but she didn't want to argue with Amy. Amy was surely pleased that Rob was finally in the clear and relieved to hear that Dr. Fielding had confessed.

"It is solid, physical evidence," Dana agreed. "But I'm still surprised. Did Dr. Fielding say why he did it?"

"It seems he's in a serious relationship with Meredith Quinn. He said he did it for her. She wanted to try an experimental treatment for her illness, but the cost was very high, and her insurance didn't cover it. She appealed to Morton for a loan, but he wouldn't help her. Morton told Dr. Fielding about that conversation in his therapy, and Dr. Fielding said he even laughed about it. Dr. Fielding said he was overwhelmed with rage and a desire to get back at Morton for treating Meredith in such a cold, heartless way. As Meredith got sicker, he felt even angrier and planned to sell the invention to fund her treatment. He said he had to kill Morton to cover up the theft."

Lucy understood Lewis Fielding's deep motive for revenge. Yet, it was still a stretch to see him as a killer.

"Where were the plans hidden? Did the attorney say?" Dana asked.

"A little stick drive, in the battery compartment of Morton's beard trimmer," Amy replied. "Dr. Fielding was lucky Tanya let him visit so soon after her husband's death. She hadn't cleared away any of his personal items yet. I guess Dr. Fielding asked to use the bathroom. He knew where the device was hidden and found it easily."

"Tanya will probably be kicking herself when she finds out the plans were under her nose the whole time," Suzanne said.

Lucy thought that was true, but before she could comment, Suzanne was thanking Amy again for the loan of the cottage, and saying their farewells.

Amy hugged each one of them. "I feel badly that your weekend has been ruined with this police investigation. But thank you ever so much for your help getting Rob off the hook. I hope you'll come back sometime, when it's peaceful around here. As it usually is," she added.

"We had a great time," Suzanne replied.

"It was wonderful. Honestly," Lucy said. "We can't thank you enough for loaning us the cottage."

"It was great to meet all of you. I'll have to come down to Plum Harbor sometime and take another knitting class with Maggie."

"Please do. On the house, any time," Maggie added.

"I'm just happy that we're able to leave knowing Rob is in the clear. I hope you two are going to celebrate tonight," Suzanne said.

"We will. Then we'll have a long-overdue talk. I know Rob feels he needs to protect me, but he kept too many secrets. It's going to take us a while to sort this all out. But I do love him," she added. "And I know he loves me. We'll be all right, in time."

"I know you will," Suzanne assured her. "Every marriage hits a speed bump or two . . ." She glanced at Lucy. "Remember that, Lucy."

Lucy had been married once and already knew this to be true. Although she didn't expect many speed bumps with Matt, that was for sure.

"Where's Rob? We want to thank him, too," Maggie added.

"Where do you think? Out surf casting," Amy laughed. "But this time, I know he's really fishing," she added. "Maybe he'll even bring home a catch or two."

Lucy and her friends laughed. It was a comfort to see Amy in good spirits again and to leave knowing the cloud that had hung over her and Rob the last few days had passed.

After a few more good-byes, they walked back to Suzanne's SUV and took their usual places. "It's great to see Amy smiling again," Lucy said as they drove toward the gatehouse. "And it's good to know all of Rob's police business is resolved. It sounds as if the police are going to overlook his plans with Tanya to steal the invention and sell it. They have bigger fish to fry, I guess. No pun intended," Lucy added.

"Lucky for him," Maggie agreed. "I guess they're just satisfied to have found Morton's killer."

"Everyone's happy about that. Except Meredith, I'd say. That is, if she even knows that Lewis has confessed." Phoebe sat in the middle of the back seat, as usual, and took out her knitting. Lucy squeezed closer to the door to give her some elbow room. She also didn't want to get jabbed with the end of a knitting needle.

"We're still going to visit her, aren't we?" Maggie asked.

"I think we should. She needs some support and friendly faces now more than ever," Dana said.

"Yes. Let's. Dr. Fielding's confession will be a blow. Especially in her condition. It's a sad situation." Suzanne sighed and shook her head.

Dana pulled up the location of the local hospital on her phone's GPS and guided Suzanne. They didn't pass any flower shops on the way, but found a large bouquet in the hotel gift shop.

Fortunately, Meredith had been moved to a room where she was allowed to have visitors. Lucy and her pals were unusually quiet as the elevator carried them up to Meredith's floor.

"This is isn't going to be easy. But we're doing a good deed," Suzanne reminded them.

"It's hard to say what we'll find. She might feel so upset about Lewis, she won't want to see us," Dana replied.

"That's true. We'll respect her wishes, whatever they may be." Maggie moved the bouquet to her other arm, then switched it back again. Lucy could tell she was nervous. Lucy felt a little nervous, too, and took a few deep breaths.

They found the room quickly. Suzanne led the way and softly knocked on the door, which was open. "Meredith?" she called.

"I'm awake. You can come in," a weak voice replied.

Suzanne walked in first and everyone followed. A petite woman, Meredith looked even smaller in the hospital bed, propped up by a pile of pillows. Her skin was sallow with dark circles shadowing her eyes. An IV tube was attached to one arm. The line led to a bag of fluids hanging from a pole. She was also connected to a monitor with several wires, to monitor her vital signs, Lucy guessed. She looked weak, barely able to sit up and smile as they walked in.

"We don't want to disturb you. We just wanted to see how you were doing before we headed home," Suzanne explained.

"We brought you some flowers." Lucy handed over the bouquet.

"How lovely. Tiger lilies and yellow roses, my favorite. How did you know?" She leaned closer and smelled the flowers, but seemed too weak to hold the bouquet.

Lucy held them out to her, so she could see the arrangement, then took them back. "I'll try to find a vase and set these up for you."

"Don't worry. Cory will do that. Just leave them on the table. He'll be back any minute. He just went to get some coffee. It's so nice of you to think of me. I wish this was over with. I hate being stuck in bed," she added.

She was a very active person, and Lucy didn't doubt it was frustrating to her to be immobilized this way.

"Lewis told us that you were coming along. He seemed very hopeful you'd be home soon," Dana said.

"Lewis, always so optimistic. I don't know what I'd do without him," Meredith replied. "I'm worried about him. The police are questioning him about Julian's murder, of all things. He has no connection to that. I don't know what they can be thinking. He said he would let me know when he was done, but he hasn't called yet. I must have left about ten messages." She checked her cell phone on the nightstand. "Have you heard anything over at Osprey Shores?"

Lucy and her friends glanced at each other. What should they say? Was it their place to tell Meredith that Lewis had confessed to killing Dr. Morton?

Before anyone replied, Cory came into the room.

"I have some lovely visitors, Cory, and some beautiful flowers," Meredith said. "Maybe you can ask the nurse for a vase when you get a chance."

Cory didn't seem to hear her and barely seemed to notice Lucy and her friends. He walked straight to Meredith's bedside and took her hand.

"I have some bad news, Mom. I'm really sorry to have tell you this." His voice was hoarse and strained, as if he might burst into tears at any minute. "Lewis has been arrested for killing Dad. I heard that he confessed."

Meredith sat up, her mouth hung open in shock, her eyes wide. "Lewis confessed? He didn't kill Julian. Why did he say that? He didn't kill Julian. . . . I know he didn't."

Cory squeezed her hand and put his arm around her shoulder. "It's true. I'm so sorry to be the one to tell you. His attorney just called me."

"Oh, my God . . . this can't be." Meredith sunk back against the pillows, her hands over her face as she began to cry. Lucy and her friends stood silently, not knowing what to do or say.

"Lewis . . . Lewis. Why did you do such a foolish, reckless thing?" Meredith murmured. "Why did you do it?"

Lucy wasn't sure if Meredith was asking why Lewis confessed, or why he killed Dr. Morton.

Meredith suddenly looked up at everyone, a bit calmer, though her eyes were still wet with tears. "He did it for me. Foolish, wonderful man. But it won't help. He can't save me." She sat back and sighed.

"What do you mean, Mom? He confessed to a crime he didn't commit?" Cory stood back from the bed, but still held his mother's hand.

Meredith squeezed her son's hand. "Yes, dear. That's what I mean."

"But why?" Lucy didn't mean to break into their conversation, but the words just popped out.

"To protect me. I killed Julian. I did it all on my own. Lewis didn't have anything do with it. Julian was a despicable human being and didn't deserve to live. He not only refused to help me pay for the treatments I needed, but he told me that he'd cut Cory out of his will. His only child. He said it was for Cory's own good. He said real money would ruin him entirely, which isn't at all true. He was just being vindictive, trying to get back at me for divorcing him. I'd had enough," she added bitterly. "That was the last straw. I'm so sorry, but it's true." She looked up at Cory, her eyes begging him to understand.

"You did it, Mom? Really? But how? Dad was so much bigger than you. I don't believe it," Cory insisted.

"He was bigger, but I surprised him. I'd been waiting for a foggy morning, and Friday was perfect. I struck him on the head with a stone and stunned him. A few kickboxing moves and he was over the fence and on the ground. He was barely conscious. It wasn't hard after that," she added quietly.

Lucy could suddenly see it: A small but strong Meredith crouched in the shrubs in the fog, waiting for her ex-husband to pass. She may have even been the ghostly image that Phoebe had captured on her camera.

Dana stood at the foot of Meredith's bed. "So when you opened the door for the yoga class and told us you'd been meditating, you had really been out on the cliff walk."

"Yes, that's how I managed my alibi. I arrived at the fitness center early and went into the studio and locked the door. I set up some incense just in case anyone walked by. Then I left and reentered through the glass slider on the terrace. It was surprisingly easy."

"But the police have physical evidence that ties Lewis to

the scene. Footprints found at the scene match a pair of his rubber boots," Suzanne said. "That's what Amy told me."

"That was my one mistake. I stayed over at Lewis's cottage Thursday night. Luckily, he was called out on an emergency and stayed at the hospital all night. I had time alone to plan and get an early start Friday morning. But I borrowed a pair of his boots so I wouldn't get poison ivy. The shrubs around the cliff walk are full of it."

"We noticed," Lucy said. "Did you tell Lewis what you did? Is that why he was trying to protect you?"

Meredith shook her head. "I never told him. I didn't want to get him involved. But I had a feeling he'd figured it out. We were very close. Most of the time, we knew each other's thoughts without needing to speak." She sighed and picked up her cell phone. "I've got to call the police right away and tell them the truth. I can't stand the idea of Lewis alone in a jail cell, because of me."

Cory placed his hand on her shoulder. "All right, Mom. If that's what you want to do."

She looked up at him. "Do you hate me for what I've done?"

He stared down at his mother a long moment, tears filling his eyes. "I could never hate you. You're all I've ever had."

She squeezed his hand again, a peaceful look washing over her face. "That means the world to me. Now I have the courage to do this."

Meredith picked up her phone and searched for the number of the police station. But just before she was connected, she began to cough uncontrollably. She covered her mouth with a wad of tissues as Cory rubbed her back. Lucy spotted a few drops of bright red blood on the tissues as Cory tossed them in a bedside wastepaper basket.

"I'll call the nurse. Hang on. You need some medication," Cory said.

Meredith nodded, unable to speak.

"My mother is very tired. She needs to rest," Cory told them.

"Of course. We'll go." Suzanne turned and glanced at Lucy and their friends a moment, uncharacteristically at a loss for words. She looked back at Meredith. "We're all . . . very sorry. About everything."

Meredith nodded and raised her hand, saying good-bye as they walked out. Cory had run out into the hall, and was returning to the room with a nurse.

A short time later, they were in Suzanne's SUV, stunned to silence by the scene that had unfolded in Meredith's hospital room.

"What will happen now?" Phoebe said quietly. "Meredith will confess to the police, but she's much too sick to go to jail."

"What if they don't believe her?" Maggie replied. "It's occurred to me she might be confessing to get Dr. Fielding off the hook. Knowing how sick she is, and that she might not have much time left."

Dana had been staring out her window and turned to look at her friends in the backseat. "It's a bittersweet puzzle, isn't it? It's like an O'Henry short story, two lovers making sacrifices for each other. The boots place Lewis at the scene, but maybe she did borrow them."

"I tend to believe her story over Dr. Fielding's," Lucy said. "He was at the hospital all night with a patient, and if that alibi and the timing of his return holds up, it would have been impossible for him to have killed Morton in the time frame of the murder." She paused. "One more thing comes to mind. A bit of physical evidence that may place Meredith at the crime scene. On Thursday night, when we chose yarn to make our shawl projects, she was the only one who picked lime green. And a bit of lime-green yarn showed up in one of Phoebe's photos. A bird is carrying a strand of that same-colored yarn. Maybe it caught on Meredith's clothes and rubbed off on a bush or fell to the ground while she was dealing with Morton."

"Brilliant, Lucy," Maggie noted. "That could very well be. You'll have to tell the police. Call Detective Dunbar or send an email. They might not get it at first, but once Meredith confesses, I bet they'll be happy to have that bit of evidence backing up her story."

"And the police can confirm it by checking the dye lot and fiber and matching it to the ball of yarn she took. There's so much they can do in a forensic laboratory," Dana added.

"Very true. I guess I should send an email. I'll do it later, while we're driving." Lucy turned to Phoebe. "So there was an important photo on your camera after all, Phoebe. But the police missed it. Too concerned about the shadowy figure in the fog."

"Now they'll want the camera again," Phoebe said with a long sigh.

"We can attach a file with the email I'm going to send. Maybe that will satisfy them," Lucy suggested. "I wonder if that shadowy form in the fog behind the shrubs was Meredith?"

"Or a creepy mermaid who came ashore, cheering Meredith on?" Phoebe replied.

"The creepy mermaid didn't get her fins on Morton. He landed on the rocks, not in the sea," Dana pointed out.

"The mermaids wouldn't want Morton even if they could get their fins on him." Suzanne shook her head, her eyes on the road. "It's almost unfathomable to imagine how much grief, distress, and hatred he inspired. I think the mermaids would have tossed him back onto dry land."

Lucy had to agree. Though she would never condone Meredith's actions, she did have sympathy for all the players in this drama—Meredith and Lewis, Rob, Tanya, and Cory. And she couldn't forget Betty and her brother, Ted. Each of them deeply wronged by Julian Morton and all with a viable motive for murder. While there was no excuse for taking a life in such a premeditated way, the way Dr. Morton had treated everyone in his life certainly tested that rule.

Chapter 12

It was after ten o'clock when Suzanne dropped Lucy off at home. She rolled her bike up to the porch, opened the door, and dropped her bags on the floor. The dogs, Tink and Wally, ran to greet her, panting and wagging their tails.

Tink carried her furry chew toy, which Lucy called Road-kill, because that's what it looked like. The golden retriever offered it happily, though Lucy gently declined. The dogs had both been snoozing in the TV room at the back of the house, lying at Matt's feet. Lucy heard the Red Sox game, and Matt looked a little snoozy, too. His thick brown hair going in all directions and his blue eyes, half closed.

He smiled and stood up as she walked into the room. "Hi, honey. I was waiting for you." Lucy walked into his open arms and they shared a tight hug and a kiss. "How was your weekend. Did you have fun?"

"We did, actually. It was a beautiful setting, right on the ocean. We did a lot of fun stuff. Though there was something going on in the community that was distracting, to say the least. I'll tell you about it later," she added. Lucy held on to him, her hands looped around his waist as she leaned back. "It was great to hang with my gal pals. But I'm happy to be home with you."

"I missed you, too. It got a little lonely around here with just my dog friends. They don't talk much and they never have dinner ready for me."

Lucy laughed. "Is that the only reason you missed me? No one to cook your dinner?"

Matt stared back at her, wide-eyed and apologetic. "You know I didn't mean that. I missed you for other reasons, too. My bride-to-be . . ."

He pulled her close and kissed her deeply. Lucy didn't have any more questions.

Lucy woke up Tuesday morning in a panic. "Only five days left. I have so much to do." She and Matt weren't even out of bed.

"I think we're in pretty good shape. What's left? I can help you."

"Mostly phone calls, confirming things, the flowers and cake and all that. My mother is coming on Thursday, remember?"

"I do. Is she staying here?" Matt was up and headed for the shower.

"I wanted her to, but she insisted on staying at The Lord Charles," Lucy said, mentioning the inn on the village green in town where the ceremony and reception would be held. "She said it will be convenient for her, and she thinks we need some privacy before the big day and doesn't want to intrude."

"That's considerate of her."

"Yes, it is." Her mother was very considerate that way. "But I'm glad she'll be around, helping the last few days. I still have to clean the house and plan a special dinner. And I have one more fitting for the gown. Suzanne says I need special, heavy-duty undergarments. Body smoothers, she calls them. Which sound more like body armor to me. She said I really should get some. But I hate to feel like tooth-paste squeezed into a tube all day."

"You'll look absolutely beautiful, no matter what you do. Don't worry so much."

Lucy was trying not to, but it was hard. She'd been the coolest, calmest bride in history for weeks. But reality and her to-do list had suddenly hit her like a meteor from outer space.

The dogs came into the bedroom, eager to be let out. Tink found one of Lucy's slippers and waved it around. Her special signal that the situation required urgent atten-tion. Lucy took the slipper from Tink's mouth and slipped it on, then located the other one. "I still don't have any-thing for Tink and Wally to wear when they walk down the aisle. Maybe some bows and flowers on their collars?"

"No worries. I got that covered. A catalog came to the office, and I ordered them each a wedding outfit. Wally has a tux and tie, and Tink has a flower garland and a pink satin dog dress."

Lucy stared at him in surprise. Tons of catalogs for pet care came to Matt's veterinary office. But she never ex-pected he'd take the initiative and complete this task for her.

"That's great, honey. Sounds adorable." She leaned over and kissed his cheek. "I'll check that off my list." She felt a bit more upbeat as she left the room, the dogs scampering ahead and racing down the stairs. "One down, a thousand and one to go."

The knitting group usually met on Thursdays, but they moved this week's meeting up to Wednesday night, since Lucy's mother was coming, and they all had things to do before the big day.

They met in Maggie's shop, and, as usual, Lucy was the last to arrive. She had made a tasty dish for their dinner—

penne pasta with fresh tomatoes, zucchini, basil, and moz-
zarella. She parked in front of the shop and carried the
large casserole of pasta on a tray, surprised to see her
friends gathered on the porch, waiting for her.

"What's up? Are we sitting outside tonight?" It was a
warm night, and they sometimes sat outside on the shop's
wrap-around porch in the summer.

"We were waiting for you. We're going to launch Maggie's new sign," Suzanne shouted back.

Lucy paused on the walkway and looked up. She hadn't
even noticed, but the shop's sign had been changed. It had
always read THE BLACK SHEEP KNITTING SHOP. But now it
said BLACK SHEEP & COMPANY in bold block letters. And
below that, in finer print: FINE YARNS, FIBER ARTS, AND
MORE.

"Black Sheep and Company! I love it," Lucy replied.
She climbed up to the porch and set the tray down. "I
guess Phoebe is the 'and company'?"

"Exactly. I'm also the fiber arts," Phoebe added proudly.

"That she is . . . and more," Maggie replied, making a
small pun. "Suzanne insisted on champagne. Though
we're not going to break the bottle over the sign, as if it
were a ship's bow."

"We're not? I thought that would be the fun part."
Suzanne sounded disappointed.

"For one thing, you'd need a ladder, and it would waste
a perfectly good bottle of champagne." Maggie shrugged,
setting out champagne glasses on a small wicker table.

"All right. If you say so. But I did bring two bottles."
Suzanne was busy unwrapping the foil covering and eas-
ing up the cork.

"We'll save one for Lucy's wedding," Dana suggested.

"Good idea!" Suzanne hopped down the steps and stood
on a patch of grass in front of the shop. "Can I at least aim
the cork at the sign, just for luck?"

"All right, if you insist. I hope you're a good shot. Duck everyone," Maggie added quietly.

"I'm a crack shot. No worries." Suzanne pushed the cork up with her fingers. "Three, two, one . . . happy new sign!"

The cork sailed out of the bottle with a loud pop, along with a spray of foam. They all heard it hit the sign, a bull's-eye as Suzanne had promised. And then, as everyone cheered, they heard a small thump.

Maggie ran out to the lawn to see what had happened. "Oh dear. It loosened a bolt or something."

Lucy and her friends followed. They stared up at the sign, which now hung at a slight angle.

Suzanne wore a sheepish expression. "Sorry, Mag. I'll call a handyman tomorrow and have it fixed for you."

Maggie looked peeved for a moment and then laughed. "That was strong champagne. I guess it's very lucky. Come on, everyone. Let's have a glass and a toast."

They were soon all lifting their glasses as Suzanne proposed a toast. "To Maggie and Phoebe, and a new era of the Black Sheep Knitting Shop. To its continued success and artistry. It just keeps getting bigger and better."

"Here, here." Lucy took a sip from her glass; the bubbles tickled her nose.

"Well said, Suzanne. And here's to the Black Sheep Knitters, the best knitting group and best friends anyone could ask for," Dana said.

"I'll drink to that," Maggie said happily. "This shop wouldn't be the same without all of you. I don't know what I'd do."

They finished their champagne and brought their meeting inside, to the back room of the shop. The food Lucy had brought was still warm, and she placed the casserole dish on the oak buffet.

"What did you make for dinner, Lucy? It's smells

yummy." Phoebe placed a basket with a crusty loaf of bread next to a bowl of green salad.

"A pasta dish with vegetables. I think we ought to eat before starting to knit, everyone. It could get messy."

Maggie had set up the dishes and silverware, and everyone helped themselves to dinner.

"Hmm, this is delicious," Maggie said after a bite or two.

"It's pretty easy to make. I got the zucchini at the farm stand on the Beach Road, and the tomatoes and basil are from our garden."

"You and Matt are so cute. I just love the idea of you two, working together out in a vegetable garden. Like two rabbits in a picture book. How cute is that?" Phoebe said.

Lucy had never felt like a rabbit in a picture book, getting down and dirty with the weeds, worms, and tangled vegetable vines. But she knew what Phoebe meant.

"A garden is a lot of work. But I read a new study that found there's some bacteria in the soil that gardeners inhale. It wards off depression and even causes sort of a gardener's high," Dana said.

"Interesting." Lucy forked up another bite. "Matt and I do feel good after we work together outside. Especially if I cook something tasty for dinner with the vegetables. You can also add shrimp or even lobster to this dish, to bump it up a notch for company."

"I like it just fine, as is." Suzanne wiped a bit of tomato from her mouth. "Speaking of lobster, you just reminded me of Maine. I heard from Amy today. There's a footnote to the Julian Morton murder case."

Maggie tore a slice of bread in half and took a bite. "I was wondering how it all spun out. I assume Meredith confessed to the police."

"Right after we left," Suzanne reported. "The police even followed through on that green yarn tip you sent, Lucy. They matched it to the yarn in Meredith's possession, from her summer shawl project, as we suspected they would. It turns out Lewis did not have any time to spare between leaving the hospital and returning to Osprey Shores. Certainly not enough time to hide his car some distance from Osprey Shores, walk up the path, and murder Dr. Morton. Security cameras at the hospital garage and the record at the Osprey Shores gate confirmed his alibi."

Dana, who loved any dish with vegetables, helped herself to more pasta. "So she wasn't taking the blame for Lewis," Dana said. "She actually did it."

"The police think so. Lewis was released, and Meredith was charged, but she's out on bail right now. Everyone says she's too sick to stand trial. I believe her attorney is pursuing that line of defense."

"Is she out of the hospital?" Lucy asked.

Suzanne sighed and put her dish aside. "Yes, they sent her home. But she's lost a lot of ground. Her disease is advancing. Amy said Lewis moved her into his cottage, so he could take care of her. Amy heard that her doctors don't give her much more time."

"How sad." Lucy also put her empty dish aside.

"It is sad," Maggie agreed. "But at least she won't live out her last days in a jail cell. She and Lewis can spend whatever time is left together. That has to be some comfort."

"Cold comfort. But something," Suzanne said. "Oh . . . and get this. Tanya has now officially inherited her husband's intellectual property, the mysterious, hidden invention. Lewis gave the police the memory stick with the final plans. Amy heard she's already sold it to a big biotech firm."

"She's a very rich woman after all. That was her main goal," Maggie observed. "At least someone's happy."

"She is. Rich and happy," Suzanne agreed. "But here's

the surprising part. Tanya is trying to make amends for Julian's misdeeds. She's given Cory a fair share of his father's estate and is also taking care of all of Meredith's medical costs."

Lucy was surprised, but pleased by that news, and the way it overturned everyone's expectations of the crafty beauty.

"She always reminded me of an evil mermaid," Phoebe admitted. "But I guess the gorgeous, scheming, ex-lingerie model has a heart after all."

"Seems so. Though Amy says Tanya has other motives besides pure largess. Tanya told Helen Shelburn she's doing it as a way to get back at her husband, who was such a miser and turned his back on Meredith and Cory. She hopes Julian is watching his money being given away and turning over in his grave."

"Whatever Tanya's twisted motives, the end result is kindness and benevolence. I'm sure Cory and Meredith never expected it," Lucy said.

Maggie nodded. "I agree. But a lot of unexpected things happen on Osprey Island. The place seems so picturesque and serene. Meanwhile, there's a lot going on below the surface," she observed. "Why don't we clear the dishes away and start our knitting? I have a new pattern to show you."

"Great. I can use a new project." Dana scooped up the salad plates and some utensils. Suzanne and Phoebe had already brought the dinner dishes to the storeroom, which doubled as a fully-equipped kitchen.

"Are you going to bring your knitting on your honeymoon, Lucy?" Phoebe said as she returned.

Lucy nearly dropped the salad bowl. "I hadn't thought about it."

Suzanne was right behind Phoebe and started laughing.

"Good one, Phoebe. Who's going to knit on their honeymoon? For goodness' sake. She and Matt have better things to do. I'd be worried if she brought her knitting."

"Good point, Suzanne." Maggie glanced at Lucy.

Lucy didn't answer, feeling her cheeks flush. She hated when she blushed, but she couldn't help it. Head down, she headed into the storeroom, hearing her friends giggling behind her.

The next day, Lucy was happy to see her mother, who drove in from North Hampton and arrived around lunchtime. A professor of anthropology at the University of Massachusetts Amherst, Isabel Binger had a way of bringing calm and order to most any situation. Lucy felt relieved just seeing her mother's battered green Volvo wagon pull up in the driveway.

Her parents had divorced when Lucy was in high school. Now her father lived in Florida with his second wife. Both her father and Lucy's stepmother enjoyed golf, very dry martinis, and watching CNN most of the evening. Her father was coming in on Friday night, right before the wedding, and also staying at the Lord Charles. Which was just as well, Lucy thought, since it was stressful for her to juggle her father, her mother, and her stepmother, even though they all seemed to get along just fine. In public, at least.

Lucy's older sister, Ellen, was the maid of honor, and Matt had asked his brother to be his best man. Lucy's two nieces were junior bridesmaids. And then there were Tink and Wally, sure to steal the show when her nieces led them down the aisle.

Lucy wished she could have asked her best friends to be in the bridal party, but that just wasn't practical, and they understood. She knew her best buddies would be walking down the aisle in spirit with her, definitely cheering her on, and probably even weeping a little in their front-row seats.

She and Matt had tried their best to keep the wedding simple and fun. But they had still invited nearly a hundred guests and booked a large reception room at the inn and a six-piece band.

A justice of the peace would perform the ceremony in the lovely garden behind the inn, if the weather held up. Lucy had always wanted to be married in a garden, under a trestle of flowers. She and Matt had written their own vows, though Lucy hadn't actually finished hers—another item on her list. She was more of a visual person, but hoped that something poetic and heartfelt would come to her once she sat down and concentrated.

"All right, let's just focus on what you have left to do, Lucy," her mother said as they finished their lunch at the bakery café in town. "Do you have a list with you?"

"I do, Mom." Lucy pulled a battered notebook from her large handbag. "It's not so bad . . . I hope. Forty-eight hours and counting."

Her mother looked over Lucy's scrawled notes, even the cross outs and extra bits jotted in the margins. "Not so bad. Don't worry. We'll get this done with time to spare."

Lucy smiled with relief. "You think so?"

Her mother laughed. "A wedding is like Christmas, honey. If you can't finish every bit of trimming, most people won't even notice. Let's focus on the most important items first. Your dress fitting. Guess we'll skip dessert."

Lucy sighed. She'd been so good, just ordering a salad. Dessert was the best part of coming here. "I guess so," she agreed, taking a last sip of iced tea.

With her mother at the helm of the to-do list, the next two days passed in a blur. Lucy soon found herself sitting beside her father in the back of a black limousine that pulled up to the front of the Lord Charles Inn. He wore a tuxedo, the stark white shirt contrasting sharply with his golfer's tan and greying dark hair. He pulled at his burgundy bow tie a bit, then patted her hand.

"You got a perfect day for a wedding. That's good luck. Are you nervous, honey?"

"A little," Lucy admitted.

"Don't worry. Nothing to it. We'll just stroll up the aisle, and everyone will be gaga about how beautiful you look. Then you'll say your vows, kiss Matt, and the rest of it will be easy as pie. Try to enjoy yourself, Lucy. It will go by too fast. That's my advice. For your wedding day and the rest of your life with Matt," he added in an unusually somber tone.

"Thanks, Dad. I'll remember," she promised.

Her father kissed her cheek, then helped her from the car and led her toward the inn, where she was immediately swarmed by her mother, sister, and nieces. The dogs, dressed in their wedding attire, looked too adorable to be believed.

Her mother smoothed Lucy's veil down over her face as they approached the back of the garden. Lucy felt like the queen of the bee keepers in her long dress and veil, but she was still glad she had chosen a traditional, but simple, gown. She saw Matt up at the top of the aisle, waiting with his best man beside the trellis of flowers.

The garden was cool, lush, and green. The wedding guests were festively dressed, looking excited and happy. A musical trio played a piece by Bach on a cello, flute, and violin. The flower arrangements—cream-colored roses, white hydrangea, and lilies—looked abundant, elegant, and just right. The whole scene was just as Lucy had pictured it, and she felt as if she had stepped into a lovely dream.

But when the opening notes of the "Wedding March" sounded, and her father tucked her arm into his, she felt a nervous flutter in her stomach. It was no dream.

"That's our cue. Showtime, honey," her fathered murmured.

She walked slowly up the aisle, smiling at friends and relations on either side, all the while gazing back up at Matt, who waited for her with a serious, but loving expression.

Matt's vows were well written, and made Lucy teary eyed as he cataloged the many reasons he loved her and looked forward to their life together.

Lucy's vows were shorter but no less emotional. Taking her mother's advice, she drew upon a poem by Elizabeth Barrett Browning—"How Do I Love Thee?"—to find the words that were so hard for her to express.

The justice of the peace soon pronounced them husband and wife. They kissed to great applause and began their walk back down the aisle. Lucy paused as she passed her knitting group friends, seated front and center as she had predicted.

"Lucy, we love you! Congratulations!" Phoebe said.

"You look awesome. So gorgeous, I could die," Suzanne called out.

"Much love and happiness," Maggie said.

"What a happy day! Joy and love to you both, always," Dana added.

Matt put his arm around Lucy's waist and hugged her close.

"Happy?"

"Blissfully," she replied. "Are you?"

"Absolutely. I can't remember when I've been happier."

"This is the happiest day of my life. Since my felted tote won second prize at last year's craft fair," she added, teasing him.

Matt laughed. "Will I have to hear everything compared to knitting projects for the rest of my life?"

Lucy gave him an innocent look. "I thought that was one of the many things you loved about me."

He nodded and grinned. "Come to think, I guess it is."

They had reached the end of the aisle. Her family waited by the exit, forming a receiving line. Matt pulled her close for a surprisingly deep kiss.

He grabbed her hand. "Come on, Lucy. Let's start our married life. The best is yet to come."

Lucy didn't answer; she didn't have to. She knew in her heart it was true. She also knew it would all go by much too quickly. It was so important to sit back and savor the ride.

From the Black Sheep & Company Bulletin Board

Dear Knitting Friends,

Sorry I haven't posted any new patterns for a while. I've been recovering from a girls-only weekend on Osprey Island. A wild weekend, in a few ways, though I won't elaborate here.

Days after our return, Lucy Binger and Matt McDougal were married. Such a joyful occasion. All the best wishes and tons of love to the most adorable couple in the universe.

The bride looked stunning, and her posse of bridesmaids-in-spirit—and BFFs—looked pretty good, too, I must say. You can see from the photos, we sat front and center, cheering on our pal, all of us wearing the same lacey, summer shawl.

The shawl is so fast and easy, most of us finished the project during our weekend away. In between getting into mischief, that is.

I've posted the link below. I think you'll find that this lovely, lightweight wrap will add a touch of elegance to your wardrobe any time of the year.

Stay calm and stitch on!

Maggie

https://www.allfreeknitting.com/Knit-Shawls/an-easy-shawl-to-knit

Hi Everyone,

We sure had fun on our pre-wedding getaway. We gave Lucy a great send-off from singlehood and even got her up on the dance floor one night. Wonders will never cease. But that's as far as I'm permitted to go. Sorry to disappoint—no incriminating photos.

We did enjoy some beautiful beach days, spa visits, and lots of knitting, of course. Not to mention delicious food. I was in charge of the cooking, as usual. What can I say? It's hard to be humble.☺

My friend Amy Cutler also treated us to a spectacular brunch. The baked French toast with berries was so delicious, I had to get the recipe. I might switch it around a bit and give it the Suzanne Cavanaugh touch. Maybe try it with peaches, or even apples in the fall?

Make it for your next brunch get-together. Or surprise your family with a special breakfast this weekend. Everyone will love it.

I can't wait to go away again with my gang. Sigh... and I won't let them wait for a special occasion next time, either.

XOXO
Suzanne

P.S. If anyone is interested in renting luxury accommodations at Osprey Shores, Osprey Island, Maine, please get in touch. It's a quiet and luxurious spot to unwind. I can almost guarantee it.

Amy's Baked Berry French Toast

2 cups of fresh berries (blueberries, raspberries,
    strawberries. A mix works well, too.)
1 to 2 tablespoons cinnamon
3 tablespoons brown sugar
3 tablespoons white sugar
½ teaspoon nutmeg
8 eggs
1½ cups whole milk
1 cup heavy cream
1 teaspoon pure vanilla extract
¼ cup maple syrup
1 loaf of quality white bread (Unsliced from the bakery is
    best. Day old is even better.)
1 to 2 tablespoons butter

Heat oven to 350 degrees. Butter a 9 x 13 inch baking pan
or glass casserole.

Rinse berries. Pick off any stems. Air dry by spreading out
on a cookie sheet lined with paper towel.

In a small bowl, mix cinnamon, brown sugar, white sugar,
and ½ teaspoon of the nutmeg and set aside.

Place berries in a medium-sized bowl. Add about half of
the cinammon/sugar/nutmeg mixture. Toss to coat and let
sit.

Beat eggs in a large mixing bowl. Add milk, cream, vanilla,
and maple syrup. Tear or slice bread into pieces about 1

inch wide and 2 inches long and add to egg mixture. Coat all sides of bread, but try not to break bread pieces.

Let the bread soak up the egg mixture for a few minutes. Fold in the berry mixture and pour everything into the baking pan. Dot with bits of butter.

Cook at 350 degrees for 40 to 45 minutes. When toast looks golden and puffy on top, sprinkle with remaining cinnamon/sugar/nutmeg mixture, and let cook for another few minutes until the sugar melts.

Serve warm with maple syrup and butter.

This dish can be made ahead and reheated before serving.